Hollywood HIGH

Ni-Ni Simone
Amir Abrams

Dafina KTeen Books
KENSINGTON PUBLISHING CORP.
http://www.kensingtonbooks.com

DAFINA KTEEN BOOKS are published by

Kensington Publishing Corp.
119 West 40th Street
New York, NY 10018

All Kensington titles, imprints, and distributed lines are available at special quantity discounts for bulk purchases for sales promotion, premiums, fund-raising, educational, or institutional use.

Special book excerpts or customized printings can also be created to fit specific needs. For details, write or phone the office of the Kensington Special Sales Manager: Attn.: Special Sales Department. Kensington Publishing Corp., 119 West 40th Street, New York, NY 10018. Phone: 1-800-221-2647.

KTeen Reg. US Pat. & TM Off.
Sunburst logo Reg. US Pat. & TM Off.

ISBN-13: 978-0-7582-6317-9
ISBN-10: 0-7582-6317-1

First Printing: October 2012

10 9 8 7 6 5 4 3 2 1

Printed in the United States of America

To the Universe,

for the gift of manifestation

ACKNOWLEDGMENTS

First and foremost, I thank my Lord and Savior Jesus Christ. Your word said we have not because we ask not. Well, I asked and here I am. I thank You, my Father, for your great and perfect gifts! I can only pray that I'm able to show at least one person that through You all things are possible!

To my husband, children, parents, aunties, uncles, cousins, and friends, thank you so much for all of your support! I love you dearly.

To Keisha and Korynn, I can never thank you enough for being my literary ride or die!

To my agent, Sara Camilli: thank you for all of your hard work. I know I say this in every book, but you are truly the best!

To Selena James and the Dafina family: thank you so much for your hard work. Your time, talent, and support means the world!

To Amir Abrams: there are no coincidences and in God's universe everything aligns and works together for the good. So seven years ago on the train, we may not have known then, but we certainly know now that this was the plan all along! So, my brotha, here's to that train ride and the twelve pages on Ni-Ni Girlz that got this party started!

To the fans, the bookstores, the blogs, schools, librarians, and anyone who has ever supported me in my career:

thank you, thank you, thank you! Be sure to e-mail me and let me know your thoughts—ninisimone@yahoo.com.

One Love,
Ni-Ni Simone
www.ninisimone.com

Welcome to Hollywood High,
where socialites rule
and popularity is more of a drug
than designer digs could ever be.

1

London

Listen up and weep. Let me tell you what sets me apart from the rest of these wannabe-fabulous broads.

I *am* fabulous.

From the beauty mole on the upper-left side of my pouty, seductive lips to my high cheekbones and big, brown sultry eyes, I'm that milk-chocolate dipped beauty with the slim waist, long sculpted legs, and triple-stacked booty that had all the cuties wishing their girl could be me. And somewhere in this world, there was a nation of gorilla-faced hood rats paying the price for all of this gorgeousness. *Boom,* thought you knew! Born in London—hint, hint. Cultured in Paris, and molded in New York, the big city of dreams. And now living here in La-La Land—the capital of fakes, flakes, and multiple plastic surgeries. Oh... and a bunch of smog!

Pampered, honey-waxed, and glowing from the UMO 24-karat gold facial I just had an hour ago, it was only right that I did what a diva does best—be diva-licious, of course.

So, I slowly pulled up to the entrance of Hollywood High, exactly three minutes and fifty-four seconds before the bell rang, in my brand-new customized chocolate brown Aston Martin Vantage Roadster with the hot pink interior. I had to have every upgrade possible to make sure I stayed two steps ahead of the rest of these West Coast hoes. By the time I was done, Daddy dropped a check for over a hundred-and-sixty grand. Please, that's how we do it. Write checks first, ask questions later. I had to bring it! Had to serve it! Especially since I heard that Rich—Hollywood High's princess of ghetto fabulousness—would be rolling up in the most expensive car on the planet.

Ghetto bird or not, I really couldn't hate on her. Three reasons: a) her father had the whole music industry on lock with his record label; b) she was West Coast royalty; and c) my daddy, Turner Phillips, Esquire, was her father's attorney. So there you have it. Oh, but don't get it twisted. From litigation to contract negotiations, with law offices in London, Beverly Hills, and New York, Daddy was the power-house go-to attorney for all the entertainment elite across the globe. So my budding friendship with Rich was not just out of a long history of business dealings between my Daddy and hers, but out of necessity.

Image was everything here. Who you knew and what you owned and where you lived all defined you. So sur-rounding myself around the Who's Who of Hollywood was the only way to do it, boo. And right now, Rich, Spencer, and Heather—like it or not—were Hollywood's "It Girls." And the minute I stepped through those glass doors, I was about to become the newest member.

Heads turned as I rolled up to valet with the world in the palm of my paraffin-smooth hands blaring Nicki Minaj's

"Moment 4 Life" out of my Bang & Olufsen BeoSound stereo. I needed to make sure that everyone saw my personalized tags: LONDON. Yep, that's me! London Phillips—fine, fly and forever fabulous. Oh, and did I mention... drop-dead gorgeous? That's right. My moment to shine happened the day I was born. And the limelight had shone on me ever since. From magazine ads and television commercials to the catwalks of Milan and Rome, I may have been new to Hollywood High, but I was *not* new to the world of glitz and glamour, or the clicking of flash bulbs in my face.

Grab a pad and pen. And take notes. I was taking the fashion world by storm and being groomed by the best in the industry long before any of these Hollywood hoes knew what Dior, Chanel, or Yves St. Laurent stood for—class, style, and sophistication. None of them could serve me, okay. Not when I had an international supermodel for a mother who kept me laced in all of the hottest wears (or as they say in France, *haute couture*) from Paris and Milan—Italy, that is.

For those who don't know. Yes, supermodel Jade Phillips was my mother. With her jet black hair and exotic features, she'd graced the covers of *Vogue, Marie Claire, L'Officiel*—a high-end fashion magazine in France and seventy other countries across the world—and she was also featured in *TIME*'s fashion magazine section for being one of the most sought-out models in the industry. And now she'd made it her life's mission to make sure I follow in her diamond-studded footsteps down the catwalk, no matter what. Hence the reason why I forced myself to drink down that god-awful seaweed smoothie, compliments of yet another one of her ridiculous diet plans to rid me of my dangerous curves so that I'd be runway ready, as she liked to call it. Translation: a protruding collarbone, flat-chest, narrow hips, and pancake-flat booty cheeks—a walking campaign ad for Feed the Hungry. *Ugh!*

I flipped down my visor to check my face and hair to make sure everything was in place, then stepped out of my car, leaving the door open and the engine running for the valet attendant. I handed him my pink canister filled with my mother's green gook. "Here. Toss this mess, then clean out my cup." He gave me a shocked look, clearly not used to being given orders. But he would learn today. "Umm, did I stutter?"

"No, ma'am."

"Good. And I want my car washed and waxed by three."

"Yes, ma'am. Welcome to Hollywood High."

"Whatever." I shook my naturally thick and wavy hair from side to side, pulled my Chanels down over my eyes to block the sparkling sun and the ungodly sight of a group of Chia Pets standing around gawking. Yeah, I knew they saw my work. Two-carat pink diamond studs bling-blinging in my ears. Twenty-thousand-dollar pink Hermès Birkin bag draped in the crook of my arm, six-inch Louis Vuitton stilettos on my feet, as I stood poised. Back straight. Hip forward. One foot in front of the other. Always ready for a photo shoot. Lights! Camera! High Fashion! Should I give you my autograph now or later? *Click, click!*

2

Rich

The scarlet-red bottoms of my six-inch Louboutins gleamed as the butterfly doors of my hot pink Bugatti inched into the air and I stepped out and into the spotlight of the California sun. The heated rays washed over me as I sashayed down the red carpet and toward the all-glass student entrance. I was minutes shy of the morning bell, of course.

Voilá, grand entrance.

An all-eyes-on-the-princess type of thing. Rewind that. Now replace princess with sixteen-year-old queen.

Yes, I was doin' it. Poppin' it in the press, rockin' it on all the blogs, and my face alone—no matter the headline—glamorized even the cheapest tabloid.

And yeah, I was an attention whore. And yeah, umm hmm, it was a dirty job. Scandalous. But somebody had to have it on lock.

Amen?

Amen.

Besides, starring in the media was an inherited jewel that came with being international royalty. Daughter of the legendary billionaire, hip-hop artist, and groundbreaking record executive, once known as M.C. Wickedness and now solely known as Richard G. Montgomery Sr., President and C.E.O. of the renowned Grand Records.

Think hotter than Jay-Z.

Signed more talent than Clive Davis.

More platinum records than Lady Gaga or her monsters could ever dream.

Think big, strong, strapping, chocolate, and handsome and you've got my daddy.

And yes, I'm a daddy's girl.

But bigger than that, I'm the exact design and manifestation of my mother's plan to get rich or die trying—hailing from the gutters of Watts, a cramped two-bedroom, concrete ranch, with black bars on the windows and a single palm tree in the front yard—to a sixty-two thousand square foot, fully staffed, and electronically gated, sixty acre piece of 90210 paradise. Needless to say my mother did the damn thing.

And yeah, once upon a time she was a groupie, but so what? We should all aspire to be upgraded. From dating the local hood rich thugs, to swooning her way into the hottest clubs, becoming a staple backstage at all the concerts, to finally clicking her Cinderella heels into the right place at the right time—my daddy's dressing room—and the rest is married-with-two-kids-and-smiling-all-the-way-to-the-bank history.

And sure, there was a prenup, but again, so what? Like my mother, the one and only Logan Montgomery, said, giving birth to my brother and me let my daddy know it was cheaper to keep her.

Cha-ching!

So, with parents like mine my life added up to this: my social status was better and bigger than the porno tape that made Kim Trick-dashian relevant and hotter than the ex-con Paris Hilton's jail scandal. I was flyer than Beyoncé and wealthier than Blue Ivy. From the moment I was born, I had fans, wannabes, and frenemies secretly praying to God that they'd wake up and be me. Because along with being royalty I was the epitome of beauty: radiant chestnut skin, sparkling marble brown eyes, lashes that extended and curled perfectly at the ends, and a 5'6", brickhouse thick body that every chick in L.A. would tango with death and sell their last breath to the plastic surgeon to get.

Yeah, it was like that. Trust. My voluptuous milkshake owned the yard.

And it's not that my shit didn't stink, it's just that my daddy had a PR team to ensure the scent faded away quickly.

Believe me, my biggest concern was my Parisian stylist making sure that I murdered the fashion scene.

I refreshed the pink gloss on my full lips and took a quick peek at my reflection in the mirrored entrance door. My blunt Chinese bob lay flush against my sharp jawline and swung with just the right bounce as I confirmed that my glowing eye shadow and blush was Barbie-doll perfect and complemented my catwalk-ready ensemble. Black diamond studded hoops, fitted red skinny leg jeans, a navy short-sleeve blazer with a Burberry crest on the right breast pocket, a blue and white striped camisole, four strands of sixty-inch pearls, and a signature Gucci tote dangled around my wrist.

A wide smile crept upon me.

Crèmedelacrème.com.

I stepped across the glass threshold and teens of all shapes and sizes lined the marble hallways and hung out in front of their mahogany lockers. There were a few new-bies—better known as new-money—who stared at me and were in straight fan mode. I blessed them with a small fan of the fingers and then I continued on my way. I had zero interest in newbies especially since I knew that by this time next year, most of them would be broke and back in public school throwing up gang signs. Okay!

Soooo, moving right along.

I swayed my hips and worked the catwalk toward my locker, and just as I was about to break into a Naomi Campbell freeze, pose, and turn, for no other reason than being fabulous, the words, "Hi, Rich!" slapped me in the face and almost caused me to stumble.

What the...

I steadied my balance and blinked, not once but four times. It was Spencer, my ex-ex-ex-years ago-ex-bff, like first grade bff—who I only spoke to and continued to claim because she was good for my image and my mother made me do it.

And, yeah, I guess I'll admit I kind of liked her—some-times—like one or two days out of the year, maybe. But every other day this chick worked my nerves. Why? Be-cause she was el stupido, dumb, and loco all rolled up into one.

I lifted my eyes to the ceiling, slowly rolled them back down and then hit her with a smile. "Hey, girlfriend."

"Hiiiiii." She gave me a tight smile and clenched her teeth.

Gag me.

I hit her with a Miss America wave and double-cheeked air-kisses.

I guess that wasn't enough for her, because instead of rolling with the moment, this chick snatched a hug from me and I almost hurled. Ev'ver'ree. Where.

Spencer released me and I stood stunned. She carried on, "It's so great to see you! I just got back from the French Alps in Spain." She paused. Tapped her temple with her manicured index finger. "Or was that San Francisco? But anyway, I couldn't wait to get back to Hollywood High! I can't believe we're back in school already!"

I couldn't speak. I couldn't. And I didn't know what shocked me more: that she put her hands on me, or that she smelled like the perfume aisle at Walgreens.

OMG, my eyes were burning...

"Are you okay, Rich?"

Did she attack me?

I blinked.

Say something...

I blinked again.

Did I die...?

Say. Something.

"Umm, girl, yeah," I said coming to and pinching myself to confirm that I was still alive. "What are you wearing? You smell—"

"Delish?" She completed my sentence. "It's La-Voom, Heather's mother's new scent. She asked me to try it and being that I'm nice like that, I did." She spun around as if she were modeling new clothes. "You like?" She batted her button eyes.

Hell no. "I think it's fantast!" I cleared my throat. "But do tell, is she still secretly selling her line out of a storage shed? Or did the courts settle that class action lawsuit against her for that terrible skin rash she caused people?"

Spencer hesitated. "Skin rash?"

"Skin to the rash. And I really hope she's seen the error of her...ways..." My voice drifted. "Oh my...wow." I looked Spencer over, and my eyes blinked rapidly. "Dam'yum!" I said tight-lipped. "Have you been wandering skid row and doing homeless boys again—?"

"Homeless boys—?" She placed her hands on her hips.

"Don't act as if you've never been on the creep-creep with a busted boo and his cardboard box."

"How dare you!" Spencer's eyes narrowed.

"What did I do?!" I pointed at the bumpy alien on her neck. "I'm trying to help you and bring that nastiness to your attention. And if you haven't been entertaining busters then Heather's mother did it to you!"

"Did it to me?" Spencer's eyes bugged and her neck swerved. "I don't go that way! And for your information I have never wandered skid row. I knew exactly where I was going! And I didn't know Joey was homeless. He lied and told me that cardboard box was a science experiment. How dare you bring that up! I'm not some low-level hoochie. So get your zig-zag straight. Because I know you don't want me to talk about your secret visit in a blond wig to an STD clinic. Fire crotch. Queen of the itch, itch."

My chocolate skin turned flaming red, and the South Central in my genes was two seconds from waking up and doing a drive-by sling. I swallowed, drank in two deep breaths, and reloaded with an exhale. "Listen here, Bubbles, do you have Botox leaking from your lips or something? Certainly you already know talking nasty to me is not an option, because I will take my Gucci-covered wrist and beat you into a smart moment. I'm sooo not the one! So I advise you to back up." I pointed my finger into her face and squinted. "All the way up."

"You better—"

"The only commitment I have to the word better, is that I *better* stay rich and I *better* stay beautiful, anything other than that is optional. Now you on the other hand, what you *better* do is shut your mouth, take your compact out and look at the pimple-face bearrilla growing on your neck!"

She gasped.

And I waited for something else nasty to slip from her lips. I'd had enough. Over. It. Besides, my mother taught me that talking only went thus far, and when you tired of the chatter, you were to slant your neck and click-click-boom your hater. But, never with the hands, that was so unlady like. Instead, one was to clip their nemesis with a threat that their dirtiest little secret was an e-mail away from being on tabloid blast. "Now, Spencer," I batted my lashes and said with a tinge of concern, "I'm hoping your silence means you've discovered that all of this ying-yang is not the move for you. So, may I suggest that you shut the hell up? Unless, of course, you want the world to uncover that freaky videotaped secret you and your mother hope like hell the Vatican will pray away."

All the color left her face and her lips clapped shut.

I smiled and mouthed, "Pow! Now hit the floor with that."

3

Spencer

I can't stand Rich! That bug-eyed beetle walked around here like she was Queen It when all she really was, was cheap and easy. Ready to give it up at the first hello. Trampette should've been her first name and Man-Eater her last! I should've pulled out my crystal nail file and slapped her big face with it. Who did she think she was?

I fanned my hand out over the front of my denim mini-dress, shifting the weight of my one-hundred-and-eighteen-pound frame from one six-inch, pink heeled foot to the other. Unlike Rich, who was one beef patty short of a Whopper, I was dancer toned and could wear anything and look fabulous in it. But I *chose* not to be over-the-top with it because unlike Rich and everyone else here at Hollywood High, *I* didn't have to impress anyone. I was naturally beautiful and knew it.

And yeah, she was cute and all. And, yeah, she dressed like no other. But Trampette forgot I knew who she was *before* Jenny Craig and *before* she had those crowded ass teeth shaved down and straightened out. I knew her when she was a chunky bucktooth Teletubby running around and losing her breath on the playground. So there was no way Miss Chipmunk wanted to roll down in the gutter with me 'cause I was the Ace of Spades when it came to messy!

I shook my shoulder-length curls out of my face, pulled out my compact, and then smacked my Chanel-glossed lips. I wanted to die but I couldn't let pie-face know that, so I said, "Umm, Rich, how about *you* shut *your* mouth. After all the morning-after pills you've popped in the last two years, I can't believe you'd stand here and wanna piss in my Crunch Berries. Oh, no Miss Plan B, *you* had better seal your own doors shut, *first*, before you start tryna walk through mine. You're the reason they invented Plan B in the first place."

I turned my neck from side to side and blinked my hazel eyes. *Sweet...merciful...kumquats!* Heather's mother's perfume had chewed my neck up. I wanted to scream!

Rich spat, "You wouldn't be trying to get anything crunked would you, Ditsy Doodle? You—"

"Ohmygod," London interrupted our argument. Her heels screeched against the floor as she said, "Here you are!" She air-kissed Rich, then eyed me, slowly.

Oh, no this hot-buttered beeswax snooty-booty didn't!

London continued, "I've been wandering around this monstrous place all morning—" She paused and twisted her perfectly painted lips. "What's that smell?" London frowned and waved her hand under her nose, and sniffed. "Is that, is that you, Spencer?"

"Umm hmm," Rich said. "She's wearing La-Voom, from the freak-nasty-rash collection. Doesn't it smell delish?"

"No. That mess stinks. It smells like cat piss."

Rich laughed. "Girrrrl, I didn't wanna be the one to say it, since Ms. Thang wears her feelings like a diamond bangle, but since you took it there, *meeeeeeeeow!*" The two of them cackled like two messy sea hens. Wait, hens aren't in the sea, right? No, of course not. Well, that's what they sounded like. So that's what they were.

"I can't believe you'd say that?!" I spat, snapping my compact shut, stuffing it back into my Louis Vuitton Tribute bag.

"Whaaaaatever," London said, waving me on like I was some second-class trash. "Do you, boo. And while you're at it. You might want to invest in some Valtrex for those nasty bumps around your neck."

I frowned. "*Valtrex?* Are you serious? For what?"

She snapped her fingers in my face. "Uh, helllllllo, Space Cadet. For that nastiness around your neck, what else? It looks like a bad case of herpes, boo."

Rich snickered.

I inhaled. Exhaled.

Batted my lashes.

Looked like I was going to have to *serve her, too.*

I swept a curl away from my face, tucking it behind my ear.

Counted to ten in my head. 'Cause in five...four... three...two...one, I was about to set it up—wait, wait, I meant set it off—up in this mother suckey-duckey, okay? I mean. It was one thing for Rich to try it. After all, we've *known* each other since my mother—media giant and billionaire Kitty Ellington, the famed TV producer and host of her internationally popular talk show, *Dish the Dirt*— along with Rich's dad, insisted we become friends for image's sake. And in the capital of plastics appearance *was* everything. So I put up with Rich's foolery because I had to. But, that chicken-foot broad London, who I only met over the summer through Rich, needed a reality check— and *quick*, before I brought the rain down on her.

Newsflash: I might not have been as braggadocious as the two of them phonies, but I came from just as much money as Rich's daddy and definitely more than London's family would ever have. So she had better back that thang-a-lang up on a grill 'cause I was seconds from frying her goose. "You know what, London, you better watch your panty liner!"

She wrinkled her nose and put a finger up. "Pause."

Did she just put her finger in my face?

"Pump, pump, pump it back," I snapped, shifting my handbag from one hand to the other, putting a hand up on my hip. My gold and diamond bangles clanked. "You don't *pause* me, Miss Snicker-Doodle-Doo. I'm no CD player! And before you start with your snot-ball comments get your facts straight, Miss Know It All. I don't own a cat. I'm allergic to them. So why would I wear cat piss? And I don't have herpes. Besides how would I get it around my neck? It's just a nasty rash from Mrs. Cummings' new perfume. So that goes to show you how much you know. And they call me confused. Go figure."

"You wait one damn minute, Dumbo," London hissed.

"*Dumbo?!* I'll have you know I have the highest GPA in this whole entire school." I shot a look over at Rich, who was laughing hysterically. "Unlike some of *you* hyenas who have to buy your grades, *I'm* not the one walking around here with the IQ of a Popsicle."

Rich raised her neatly arched brow.

London clapped her hands. "Good for you. Now...like I was saying, *Dumbo*, I don't know how you dizzy hoes do it here at Hollywood High, but I will floor you, girlfriend, okay. Don't do it to yourself."

I frowned and slammed my locker shut. "Oh...my... God! You've gone too far now, London. That may be how *you* hoes in New York do it. But we don't do that kind of perverted-nastiness over here on the West Coast."

She frowned. "*Excuse* you?"

I huffed. "I didn't stutter, Miss Nasty. I *said* you went too damn far telling me not to do it to myself, like I go around playing in my goodie box or something."

Rich and London stared at each other, then burst into laughter.

I stomped off just as the homeroom bell rang. My curls bounced wildly as my stilettos jabbed the marbled floor beneath me. *Welcome to Hollywood High, trick! The first chance I get, I'm gonna knock Miss London's playhouse down right from underneath her nose.*

But first, I had more pressing issues to think about. I needed to get an emergency dermatologist appointment to handle this itchy, burning rash. My heels scurried as I made a left into the girls' lounge instead of a right into homeroom. I locked myself into the powder room. I had to get out of here!

OMG, there was a wildfire burning around my neck. *Ooooh, when I get back from the doctor's office, I'm*

*gonna jumpstart Heather's caboose for her mother trying
to do me in like this.*

I dialed 9-1-1.

The operator answered on the first ring, "Operator,
what's your emergency?" Immediately I screamed, "Camille
Cummings, the washed-up drunk, has set my neck on
fire!"

4

Heather

My eyes were heavy.
Sinking.

And the more I struggled to keep them open the heavier they felt. I wasn't sure what time it was. I just knew that dull yellow rays had eased their way through the slits of my electronic blinds, so I guessed it was daylight.

Early morning, maybe?

Maybe...?

My head was splitting.

Pounding.

The room was spinning.

I tried to steady myself in bed, but I couldn't get my neck to hold up my head. ———

I needed to get it together.

I had something to do.

Think, think, think...what is it...

I don't know.

Damn.

I fell back against my pillow and a few small goose feathers floated into the air like dust mites.

I was messed up. Literally.

My mouth was dry. Chalky. And I could taste the stale Belvedere that had chased my way to space. No, no, it wasn't space. It was Heaven. It had chased my way to the side of Heaven that the crushed up street candy, Black Beauty, always took me to. A place where I loved to be...where I didn't need to snort Adderall to feel better, happier, alive. A place where I was always a star and never had to come off the set of my hit show, or step out of the character I played—Wu-Wu Tanner. The pop-lock-and-droppin'-it, fun, loving, exciting, animal-print wearing, suburban teenager with a pain in the butt little sister, an old dog, and parents who loved Wu-Wu and her crazy antics.

A place where I was nothing like myself—Heather Cummings. I was better than Heather. I was Wu-Wu. A star. Every day. All day.

I lay back on my king-sized wrought iron bed and giggled at the thought that I was two crushed pills away from returning to Heaven.

I closed my eyes and just as I envisioned Wu-Wu throwing a wild and crazy neighborhood party, "You better get up!" sliced its way through my thoughts. "And I mean right now!"

I didn't have to open my eyes or turn toward the door to know that was Camille, my mother.

The official high blower.

"I don't know if you think you're Madame Butterfly, Raven-Simoné, or Halle Berry!" she announced as she moseyed her way into my room and her matted mink slippers slapped against the wood floor. "But I can tell you this, the cockamamie bull you're trying to pull this morning—"

So it was morning.

She continued, "—Will not work. So if you know what's best for you, you'll get up and make your way to school!"

OMG! That's what I have to do! It's the first day of school.

My eyes popped open and immediately landed on my wall clock: 10:30 A.M. It was already third period.

I sat up and Camille stood at the foot of my bed with her daily uniform on: a long and silky white, spaghetti-strap, see-through nightgown, matted mink slippers, and a drink in her hand—judging from the color it was either brandy or Scotch. I looked into her ice-chipped blue eyes. It was Scotch for sure. She shook her glass and the ice rattled. She flipped her honey blond hair over her blotchy red shoulders and peered at me.

I shook my head. God, I hated that we resembled each other. I had her thin upper lip, the same small mole on my left eyelid, her high cheekbones, her height (5'6"), her shape (a busty 34DD), her narrow hips and small butt.

Our differences: I looked Latin although I wasn't. I was somewhere in between my white mother and mysterious black father. My skin was Mexican bronze, or more like a white girl baked by the Caribbean sun. My hair was Sicilian thick and full of sandy brown coils. My chocolate eyes were shaped like an ancient Egyptian's. Slanted. Set in almonds. I didn't really look white and I definitely didn't look black. I just looked...different. Biracial—whatever that was. All I knew is that I hated it.

Which is why, up until the age of ten, every year for my birthday I'd always blow out the candles with a wish that I could either look white like my mother or black like my father.

This in-between thing didn't work for me. I didn't want it. And I especially didn't like looking Spanish, when I wasn't Spanish when people asked me what was I? Where did I come from? Or someone would instantly speak Spanish to me! WTF! How about I only spoke English! And what was I? I was an American mutt who just wanted to belong somewhere, anywhere other than the lonely middle.

Damn.

"Heather Suzanne Cummings," Camille spat as she rattled her drink and caused some of it to spill over the rim. "I'm asking you not to try me this morning, because I am in no mood. Therefore I advise you to get up and make your way to school—"

"What, are you running for PTA president or something?" I snapped as I tossed the covers off of me and stood to the floor. "Or is there a parent-teachers' meeting you're finally going to show up to?"

Camille let out a sarcastic laugh and then she stopped abruptly. "Don't be offensive. Now shut up." She sipped her drink and tapped her foot. Her voice slurred a little. "I don't give a damn about those teachers' meetings or PETA, or PTTA, PTA or whatever it is. I care about my career, a career that you owe me."

"I don't owe you anything!" I walked into my closet and she followed behind me.

"You owe me everything!" she screamed. "I know you

don't think you're hot because you have your own show, do you?" She snorted. "Well let me blow your high, missy—"

You already have....

She carried on. "You being the star of that show is only because of me. It's because of me and my career you were even offered the audition. I'm the star! Not you! Not Wu-Wu! But me, Camille Cummings, Oscar award-winning—"

"Drunk!" I spat. "You're the Oscar award-winning and washed up drunk! Whose career died three failed rehabs and a million bottles ago—!"

WHAP!!!!

Camille's hand crashed against my right cheek and forced my neck to whip to the left and get stuck there.

She downed the rest of her drink and took a step back. For a moment I thought she was preparing to assume a boxer's position. Instead she squinted her eyes and pointed at me. "If my career died, it's because I slept with the devil and gave birth to you! You ungrateful little witch. Now," she said through clenched teeth as she lowered her brow, "I suggest you get to school, be seen with that snotty-nose clique. And if the paparazzi happens to show up you better mention my name every chance you get!"

"I'm not—"

"You *will*. And *you will* like it. And *you will* be nice to those girls and act as if you like each and every one of them, and especially that fat-pissy-princess Rich!" She reached into her glass, popped a piece of ice into her mouth, and crunched on it. "The driver will be waiting. So hurry up!" She stormed out of my room and slammed the door behind her.

I stood frozen. I couldn't believe that she'd put her hands on me. I started to run out of the room after her, but quickly changed my mind. She wasn't worth chipping a nail, let alone attacking her and giving her the satisfaction of having me arrested again. The last time I did that it took forever for that story to die down and besides, the creators of my show told me that another arrest would surely get me fired and Wu-Wu Tanner would be no more.

That was not an option.

So, I held my back straight, proceeded to the shower, snorted two crushed Black Beauties, and once I made my way to Heaven and felt like a star, I dressed in a leopard cat suit, hot pink feather belt tied around my waist, chandelier earrings that rested on my shoulders, five-inch leopard wedged heels, and a chinchilla boa tossed loosely around my neck. I walked over to my full-length mirror and posed. "Mirror, mirror on the wall who's the boom-boom-flyest of 'em all?" I did a Beyoncé booty bounce, swept the floor, and sprang back up.

The mirror didn't respond but I knew for sure that if it had, it would've said, "You doin' it, Wu-Wu. You boom-bop-bustin'-it-fly!"

"Good day, madam," my driver said as he held the limo's door open for me.

"Good day, Charles." I nodded as I walked up the red carpet toward Hollywood High's entrance. And just in case there were any paparazzi hiding in the bushes I threw my hips and silicone-filled booty pads in overdrive, rocking them from side to side.

I walked on cloud nine and the moment the doorman

opened the double glass doors and I walked into the school's marble foyer, I felt like ordering someone to signal the trumpets and announce that I'd arrived.

I made a brief stop into the headmaster's office and smiled at him. Mr. Westwick shook his head and pointed to the clock: 12:30 P.M.

"I had to get dressed." I smiled.

He didn't smile back; instead he simply nodded and said, "School begins at half past eight. But I will make an exception today."

"Merci. I forgot my schedule. What class am I supposed to be in?"

He perched his thin lips. "Miss Cummings, it's lunch time. The juniors are all dining in the Déjeuner Café."

I really was late. "Bonjour."

I threw my hips in motion and clicked my Manolo Blahniks toward the café, which could easily pass for any top-notch club in the city—white leather couches, reclining chairs, lava-topped tables, plasma TVs, white glove service. The glass doors slid back and I stepped into the room of the Who's Who.

Cliques were everywhere. And seated in the same exact place they'd be this time every day until the school year ended. And when the school year began again, they'd resume position.

There were the jocks, their cheerleaders, the glees, the wannabes, the newbies, who sat across from their rivals, the fogies, better known as old money. The foodies, who complained about weight all day, and the super skinnies—who complained about weight all day. The preppies who wouldn't be caught dead not wearing Polo. And the hip-hop crew who wouldn't be caught dead wearing Polo. The rock-star goth kids whose parents hoped would one day appreciate the sun, and the half-dead *Twilight* kids who wore pale white make-up on purpose and whose secret code words for cuties were "team Edward" and "team Jake." And they all had one thing in common: they were all rich, filthy rich. But the one thing they didn't have was access to the clique of all cliques: The It clique. The Pampered Princesses.

The Pampered Princesses sat in the center of the room, surrounded by peons. And these princesses weren't rich. They were wealthy. Quite a difference. This clique had money that defined infinity. They could easily lunch in Paris, have dinner in Spain, and then hop on their parents' private planes and be home in time for a nightcap. They were not the "Who's Who," they were the "Who." The *who* you wanted to be, wanted to be seen with, wanted to be associated with, and would lay on a table and sell your kidney to be friends with. If you were with this clique then you'd made it.

Period.

And lucky for me, they decided that Wu-Wu Tanner, the hottest teen star ever, was worthy of their company—even if they didn't really like me and I absolutely couldn't stand them. Well, I could halfway tolerate Spencer. She wasn't as judgmental as that loud mouth and ever-ready, throw-the-rock-and-fold-her-manicured-hands drama trick, Rich, or that Upper East Side–oh-this-is-how-we-do-it-in-New-York Buffy-chick, London.

But whatever. None of that was important at the moment. What was important was my fan club president, Co-

Co Ming, waving his tiny hand and dying to get my attention. I smiled and looked his way. "We love you, Wu-Wu!" he screamed.

I returned his smile and blew him and his clique, the Stalkers and the Gawkers, air-kisses. "Oh, doll, Wu-Wu loves you, too."

Co-Co Ming and his table screamed.

After signing a few autographs, doing my signature catcall, "Ahh Wu-Wu!" and moonwalking across the room, I finally made my way over to the Pampered Princesses. I fought with everything in me not to allow my eyes to inch toward the ceiling. I could feel myself about to roll them, hard. But, I didn't. I leveled them and instead shot a wide smile, all teeth. Besides, out of all of them *I* was the only one who didn't need my parents for star status. *I* was the star.

I snapped my fingers and said, "Meow." And don't ask me why but a heated rush came over me and I felt like breaking it down and busting it out! So I did. I moved my hips from side to side, snaked down to the floor, and did a booty pop, all while chanting, "Ahhh, Wu-Wu's in the house!" I popped up and repeated my routine. "I said, Ahhh, Wu-Wu's in the house! A pow-pow! I said, Ahhh, Wu-Wu—"

BAM! POP! DROP! "Ahhhhhhhh!" I screamed. Suddenly, my heels slipped from beneath me, and everything went black.

5

London

*O*h...*my*...*God! These Hollywood scallywags have to be sniffing Krazy Glue!* That's what I thought the minute Heather hit the floor and commenced to scream as Spencer stood over her wearing a pair of Gucci ski goggles, spraying a whole can of Mace in her face and going off like a wild woman. I'd never seen anything like this. And I definitely didn't think Spencer was the type of chick to set it off like that. But she proved me wrong.

"You low-down, dirty, stank-a-dank, skid row, Cracker Jack booger! You and your no-good rickety-crickety, drunken mother tried to ruin me! Why, Heather?! I've been a good friend to you. I'm the only one who knows you're walking around wearing booty bags and not once did I ever tell anyone that you're really a flatty-Patty. And when the girls made fun of you I never laughed. Even though I knew it was funny. I always snickered, but I never stretched across the floor and howled. I've always been good to you and this is how you bring it. Burn my neck up! I have no choice but to do you good for that!"

Heather screamed as if she was being flayed with a rusty steak knife.

"Ohmygod, girl," I snapped, feeling sorry for her. I looked over at Rich, who recorded the whole scene with her phone. "Aren't you going to stop her?"

"Me?" Rich blinked and pointed to her chest. "And risk some of that poison popping into my face? Oh no, I don't do that. And besides, why should I? What Heather and her wretched, ratchet, Crenshaw pigeon mother did to Spencer was downright sinful. You should never take advantage of the afflicted and they knew Spencer was—"

"Code Red, Code Red!" a voice blared through a bullhorn megaphone, cutting through the loud buzz in the café and cutting Rich off. "Wu-Wu down...repeat, Wu-Wu down. Need immediate backup!"

The Stalkers and the Gawkers rose from their seats, two of them even fainted once they saw Heather sprawled across the floor.

Rich and I looked at each other and cracked up, tears flowed from our eyes from laughing so hard.

"I repeat, Wu-Wu down!"

"What in the hell?" Rich and I said in unison.

"Move, move...get out the way. Co-Co Ming coming through."

The crowd stepped back and there stood this...this, I don't know what it was. All I know is he wore a pink ostrich hair floor-length coat over a sharp, brown Brooks Brothers suit with a pink tie and a pair of pink kitten heels on his feet, holding a bullhorn in his hand. "Drop the can, Spencer. And slowly back away from the Wu-Wu."

Rich and I looked at each other and resumed laughing.

"Ohmygod, who the hell is *that?*" I asked in between chuckles.

Rich waved me on. "Oh, girl, please. Pay him and his theatrics no mind. That's Co-Co, president of the Wu-Wu Tanner fan club."

Co-Co? Alrighty then...

"I said step away from the Wu-Wu. I'm warning you, Spencer. Drop the weapon..."

Spencer dropped the can of Mace, then dropped down to her knees putting her hands up over her head as if she were under arrest. She looked dazed.

Ohmygod, her goggles are fogged up!

"Don't shoot," she said. "I didn't wanna hurt her. I swear I didn't. I only wanted to teach her a lesson for burning my neck up. I really didn't wanna bust open a can of whip-azz on her and make it rain up in here. But she had it coming. Please don't shoot me."

I blinked.

Rich blinked.

Then we both burst out laughing as security escorted Spencer out of the café, and Heather was rolled out on a stretcher, screaming, "Wu-Wu took a lickin', but Wu-Wu still kickin'. I can't see, but I'ma always be me. Ohmygod, my eyeballs are on fire!"

"We love you, Wu-Wu!" Co-Co Ming screamed as he followed behind the stretcher. "Co-Co Ming has your back! Don't worry, I'll set it off for you, just like you did in the last episode when Jenny tried to attack you and you had to smack her. I got you, Wu-Wu!"

I'd never seen anything like this in my entire life. Back in New York, yeah, we were real catty. And, yes, we could be downright...messy when called for. We ruled the world. And you were lucky if we let you live in it. But, setting it off on the first day of school is, and was, a definite no-no. But, here it was only fourth period and I was already exhausted from all the drama I'd witnessed today. I needed a damn Cosmo!

"Girl, I can't," I hollered in laughter. "I can't believe Spencer took it to Heather's face like that. Nutty or not, that girl has heart."

Rich pulled out a Chanel handkerchief and dabbed at the corners of her eyes. "I can't breathe," she wailed in laughter. "Spencer said, 'I had no choice, no choice...'" Rich stuttered, "'...but to do you good!'"

I laughed and shook my head. "But wait, wait, did you see Heather, I mean Wu-Wu, drop down and sweeping the floor with it. She looked like a circus ho on E-pills. And what the hell is a *Wu-Wu*, anyway?"

"Oh, you don't know. I thought I told you. That's Heather's TV show character. The show is hot and popping. She's dubbed herself America's sweetheart. Whatever. All I know is that she doesn't know when to come out of character. Trust she gives new meaning to Trash TV."

"Poor thing. Bless her little raggedy, confused heart," I said, laughing again. "And this president of her fan club. Girl, he's a fashion nightmare. Who in the hell wears ostrich hairs in eighty-degree weather and kitten heels with a man's suit? Ohmygod he was dead wrong for that."

Rich chuckled. "Girl, Co-Co Ming is the king of *Project Runway*."

"Mmmph. More like Project Train Wreck. He looked a mess."

"Oh really?" Captain Sticky Pants popped up out of

nowhere, with his bullhorn to his side and his ostrich feathers blowing. He jumped in my face, snapped his fingers, and stomped his feet.

"Excuse you?" I said and frowned.

He wiggled his neck. "Yeah, ah, excuse you, boo-boo." He tooted his lips.

Was he trying to set it off?

He carried on, "Oh, you wanna talk about Co-Co Ming. Well, let Co-Co set you straight, sweetness. The only mess-up in here is you and that crystal ball, oh wait. That's your big-ass forehead shining like that. Don't do me, Miss Stink-Stink! I'm the president of the Wu-Wu fan club and I—"

"Little Geisha boy, I don't care who you are."

"Well you better care, Amazon."

Rich gagged, slapping her hand up over her mouth.

I leaned over toward Rich. "Ummm, I'm still trying to figure out who this RuPaul wannabe is talking to."

Rich bucked her eyes. "Well, he definitely isn't talking to me. Co-Co doesn't want it with me. So it must be you, boo."

I eyed him. "What you better do is run along."

He slammed a hand up on his hip, then neck rolled while jabbing a finger in the air at me. "No, Sweet Cheeks, what you better do"—he snapped his fingers and stomped his foot—"is take your high-rolling, jungle-booty, trick-ass back to Dirty Jersey where you belong."

Oh no this back-alley Snow Cone didn't!

This was definitely not how I had expected my first day of school to jump off, but it had. And I was two breaths from sealing this boy's lips shut. "It's New York, Egg Noodle. Don't get it twisted. And what you better do is skip along with all that finger movement in my face before you find yourself flat on your back looking up at the front of your eyelids 'cause I will shut your lights out in a New York minute. And you only get one warning. So take heed."

He snapped his fingers. "Oh, no, Miss Tuna. Put it back in the can"—he stomped his right foot again and placed a tiny hand up on his hip, waving the other hand in the air—"'cause I don't do fish. So *you* better take heed. Or get the Co-Co Ming reading of your life."

I took a deep breath, glanced over at Rich. "I really don't want to beat this Tootie-Fruity down, but he's asking for it."

Rich smirked. "Well, girl. You've already warned him. So give it to him. He'll learn."

But before I could decide what to do Co-Co Ming had grabbed someone's pomegranate smoothie off the table and tossed it in my face. "Tootie-Fruity on that!"

I blinked my eyes in disbelief as the cold slush clung to my lashes and dripped down onto my five-thousand-dollar blouse, staining the one-of-a-kind creation.

"Oh, no the hell he didn't!" Rich snapped, leaping up from the table at the same time I did.

"Oh, yes Co-Co did," he snapped back.

Rich looked at me.

I looked at her.

And, before he could say another word, it was lights . . . camera . . . and fist rocking. We tag-teamed his behind. Punching, slapping, and kicking him. He started running. And we chased him down. I caught up to him first and yanked him by the back of his coat and swung him around. Boyfriend wind-milled his arms, but Rich came behind him and kicked him in his back. He stumbled forward, twisted his ankle in his heels, then it was on. Heels and feathers flew everywhere.

The next thing I knew, Rich and I were being pulled off of him by four security guards and dragged out of the café. Here I was trying my damnedest to stick to the script and not like this girl. And there we were—two divas with our clothes tore up, hair all wild, heels broken off our shoes— being escorted to the headmaster's office on the first day of school. We were partners in crime. *Damn her!* Not getting close to her was definitely going to be harder than I had anticipated. She had my back. And now I was going to have to have hers.

6

Rich

I sat in the office lounge, closed my eyes, and did all I could to meditate my way into a painful vision. Something that grieved me worse than the thought of being banished to the mall and made to shop amongst the tourists and the commoners. Something that made my eyes swollen with tears. So that once Mr. Westwick, the headmaster, and Mr. Sharp, his assistant by day and drag queen mistress by night, switched their way in here I'd be able to freak out and transform into an overloaded panic attack; accompanied by Academy Award–winning tears and Oscar-worthy snot ooze and lip drool.

My plan was to have my glossless bottom lip hang and in between a series of incoherent *"Why me's?"* convince them that although Co-Co Ming had to be carted out of here by way of EMTs, that London and I were really the ones who'd been under siege. And that Co-Co Ming had simply gotten the beat-down that he'd asked for.

But the tears wouldn't fall. All that would fall were the

pink diamonds in my tennis bracelet, my earrings, and the right sleeve of my Burberry blazer that had hung on by an unraveling thread.

I shook my head, opened my eyes, and jumped. "Ahh!!!! Clutching my pearls!" I blinked, blinked, and blinked again. Who was that creature sitting next to me? For a moment I wondered if this was Lauryn Hill. This creature's clothes were tattered, it had a pair of broken heels in its lap, wore one earring, had red lipstick that sailed its way from its lips to its cheeks. Its false eyelashes were crooked and one had just fallen off and almost touched me. "Ugg!" I couldn't believe what I was seeing and that's when it hit me that this was London.

OMG!

I didn't know whether to laugh or stand and give a eulogy.

But one thing I did know was that Co-Co Ming was lucky I didn't really believe in violence or else I'd run into one of his parents' five-star sushi restaurants and kill him. DEAD.

London flipped her hair behind her ears and sniffed. "I don't believe this," she said more to herself than to me.

"Believe what?" I took my Chanel handkerchief and dabbed the sweat from her forehead and then balled up the cloth and placed it in her hand. "You can keep that."

"If this is only the first day of school, my God." She blinked and her remaining lash fell into her lap. "What the hell is tomorrow going to look like?!"

"Calm down," I said as I popped open my ruby compact and realized that my mascara was streaked across my face like war marks. "Today was highly unusual. Maybe this is how you sling it in New York, but we don't usually drop down low enough to have a physical slugfest. We usually let the blogs, and the TMZs, Popsugars, and the Perez Hiltons of the world do our dirty work."

"What?" She looked half baffled and half disturbed. "What are you talking about? This place has been popping off since I walked in the door. I'm not used to this." She wiped her face with the handkerchief. "This is too much for me! I can't do this!" She tossed her head back. "I'm not really religious, but one thing I know for sure is that you all need Jesus." She started to fall apart. "I have to get out of here!" she screamed. "I have to get out of here! Ohmygod! My blouse is ruined!"

I gasped. Here I thought Miss International had it together and yet, here she was acting like new money. I hobbled over to the door, one heel on, one heel broken, and closed it. "London!" I said tight-lipped. "Get it together. Right now." I shook her by the shoulders. "Get it together."

"I'm not used to this!" London repeated.

"What is wrong with you? The only thing we did wrong was allow Co-Co Ming to come close to us and inhale our air. He deserved everything he got today."

"Hollywood High is not the place for me."

"London! Listen. Once you understand how we do things around here you'll be fine. Just know that next time a freak approaches us, we don't get our hands dirty. We hire bodyguards to do that. We're ladies at all times."

London spat. "He tossed a damn smoothie all over my Chanel! I should have dug his grave with his head! My daddy is going to be so pissed and I hope like hell this doesn't make the press—"

"And why not?" I said taken aback.

"Because rocking the front page of the *Enquirer*, and *Star*, and *In Touch*, and whatever other disgraceful ran-by-a-prick magazine was not on my list of things to do today! I don't need that kind of press!"

My heart skipped a beat. Apparently she was really clueless. "All press is good press. Period. We don't run from the paparazzi. We welcome them. Around here popularity and ruling the press are more of a drug than Chanel could ever be!"

"What? And why is that?"

"Because the secret to survival at Hollywood High is to keep people talking. Be their dinner conversation. Little girls should look up to you. Mattel should offer to make a Barbie doll in your likeness, companies need to call and beg you to endorse their products. People need to worship you. And you know why?"

"Why?"

"Because you have pulled the infamous Jedi mind trick. And now you have fans, not because you're talented, but because you're famous. And you're famous for no *gawt-damn* reason at all. Now get it together! And I'm not going to tell you anymore," I said as I pulled out my iPhone and scrolled through the images I took of Spencer macing Heather, and the one I managed to take of London smacking Co-Co Ming to the floor before I jumped on him. I showed her the pics. "You see this?"

"Yeah," she said. "I almost forgot you were taking pics."

"Yep and let's not forget about the bonus." I hit the video button and the entire café brawl unfolded.

She sucked in a deep breath. Gave a nervous smile. "And what are you going to do with that?"

"What else? We're going to be the first to ensure that it gets all over the Internet."

"Why would you want to do that?"

I sucked my teeth and snapped my fingers. "London, I just broke it down to you, girlfriend. This is how we stay on people's minds and have our names coming out of their mouths!" I attached the pictures and video to an e-mail I typed to my publicist. The e-mail read:

> *Clair, you are to send this to everyone with the head-line that famous teen star Heather Cummings was attacked by crazed and jealous socialite Spencer Ellington, while London Phillips and Rich Montgomery were forced to save the day from psycho stalker, Co-Co Ming, son of the five-star Sushi King, Ying-Ming.*

I smiled and looked over at London. "Would you like to do the honors?" I pointed to the send button.

She sniffed, thought for a moment, and said, "Why certainly."

"Now welcome to Hollywood High." I smiled.

After we secured our spot on the front page of every magazine, blog, and gossip site, we giggled at the thought of the video going viral. In the midst of us planning our shero speech for the public we heard Mr. Westwick's heavy footsteps coming our way.

We sat upright. Still. And watched Mr. Westwick walk in, release a burdened sigh, and hand his briefcase to his assistant, who stood behind him. I could already tell that they'd thought of a million ways to punish us: community service, breaking up our café table and forcing us to eat among the masses. Uniforms.

I shuddered.

"Young ladies—" Mr. Westwick said.

Before he continued I screamed, "Oh God, Oh God, Oh God! Mr. Westwick, look at me, look at us!" I forced myself to cry and after a few seconds London caught on and joined me in falling apart.

"That alien jumped us! Attacked us!" I sobbed. "He tried to drown London!"

"I almost died!" London cried.

"And we did nothing. Nothing!"

"You beat him to a pulp!" Mr. Westwick said. "He's in the hospital, suffering from a designer beat-down! This is Hollywood High Academy not the University of Gang Bangin'! Your parents pay a lot of money for you young ladies to attend this school and instead of learning, you all have torn up the café and are now sitting here looking as if you've survived a tsunami! This behavior is unacceptable." He looked toward London. "And you, young lady, this is your first day and already you're in my office. And you, Rich, have been here since your freshman year, so you know the proper decorum here at Hollywood High!"

"Mr. Westwick, you're right," I agreed. "And you know that I've never had a brawl in school, so it had to be something critical."

He paused and cut his eyes over at London. "No, Rich, you've never been a discipline problem."

"She certainly hasn't." Mr. Sharp cut his eyes over at London as well.

"I was minding my business!" London said. "And that

cartoon puppy Co-Co Ming attacked me! What was I supposed to do? Where I come from we don't stand for that."

"That is why we have security," Mr. Westwick said. "We
don't take matters into our own hands and destroy the
place!"

Mr. Sharp added, "Someone has to pay for this!"

"Do you take black card?" London asked.

"Black card?" Mr. Westwick said, sounding borderline
offended.

"This way I could pay for the damages."

"And this could stay between us," I said and arched one
brow at a time. "No parents."

"And the café could be put back together by tomorrow."
London hunched her shoulders.

"And if you don't take American Express," I interjected,
"I have checks."

Mr. Westwick sat quietly. He stared at his assistant and
then stared at us. Back to assistant. Back to us. "You young
ladies have an image to uphold." He scowled. "Hollywood
High also has an image to uphold. Children here come
from fine families. Not animal farms. We only educate the
best, not the beast. And while I really don't want to upset
your parents, this behavior is unacceptable."

"Please, Mr. Westwick." London folded her hands in a
prayer position.

"It won't happen again," I assured him.

He paused. His eyes looked as if he were in deep
thought. He went into his desk drawer and pulled out his
personal credit card machine. "Just this once I will allow
you to pay for the damages without your parents' knowl-
edge."

London handed him her card. He swiped it and charged a hundred thousand dollars. Small change.

He looked at me. "You may make a check out for the same."

I smiled. "No problem."

Once we were done with our transactions Mr. Westwick said, "You young ladies may leave. No one wants to see you walk around here looking like Weapons of Mass Destruction! I will see you tomorrow."

"Thank you," London and I said simultaneously.

We rose from the Queen Anne olive green leather chairs, picked up the pieces of our clothing and loose diamonds. We hobbled out of the lounge and once we were out of Mr. Westwick's ear- and eyeshot, we looked at each other, leaned against the marble wall, and fell out laughing.

7

Heather

Black.

That's all I remember seeing before I passed out.

So how did I get here?

Where everything was white.

My heart raced as it dropped into my stomach. Sweat gathered in my palms. My breath was short. My skin was on fire. My eyes were swollen slits and everything moved in fast-forward motion as it danced before me.

I squeezed my eyes shut.

I think I'm dead.

No this was a dream...

I squinted.

Bright lights.

Bright yellow lights, with shadows in the distance calling me...

Oh...my...God...the light.

This wasn't a dream...

Someone had killed me.

I was dead.

My body stiffened and all I could do was open my mouth and scream at the top of my lungs, "AHHHHHHH-HHHHHHHH!" Tears slipped from the corners of my eyes and burned their way down my face. "I didn't want to die!" Snot oozed from my nose as I wailed.

"Heather," a gentle voice said, "calm down."

I hesitated. I felt like fire was lodged in my throat as I struggled to say, "Is that...Is that you, God?"

"No. I'm Nurse James and this is Dr. Turner."

Angels. "Am I in purgatory?" I said too scared to open my eyes. Tears slid into the corners of my inflamed lips. I sniffed. "I know for the last few months I've been doing some dumb, dumb things. And I know I should've gone to church at least once a year for Easter. But, I was on the set all the time. And my mother was always too drunk to take me. Don't hold it against me. Send my mother to hell. I'm just a child. And if you give me another chance at life I swear I'll turn into a religious fanatic. What do you want me to be? Muslim? Buddhist? Baptist? Jewish? Catholic? Please," I sobbed. "Please, Angels, put in a good word for me with God! I just need another chance. I don't wanna go to hell! Oh God, Oh God," I hyperventilated.

"Heather, calm down, please," the gentle voice said. "You're not dead, honey. Open your eyes."

"I can't."

"Look at me."

I took a deep breath and slowly opened my eyes. My vision was blurry but I could see a smiling brown face lean in next to me and from what I could decipher she wore a white nurse's uniform.

"You see." She smiled. "I'm not an angel. I'm Nurse James. And you're not dead. You're in the hospital."

"Are you sure I'm not dead?" I sniffed, ready to hyperventilate again.

"Yes, dear. She's sure. Of course you're not dead." That voice came from the foot of my bed. I opened my eyes wider and there was Satan.

Now I really wished someone had killed me.

"It's your mother, darling," Satan said as she crept over to the left side of my bed and kissed me on my forehead. "I'm so glad you're awake."

I almost keeled over. The last time I heard Camille call me "darling" I was five and she was a torturing stage mom. A vision of her telling me to sit upright and smile for the camera flashed before me.

I stiffened. Counted to three.

"Why am I in the hospital?" I struggled to ask. "Why does my skin feel like it's on fire and why are my eyes swollen?"

Camille stroked my hair away from my face the way she used to do when I was little and she was sober. "Sweetness," she said as tears filled her eyes and her voice trembled. "Those girls at your school are so cruel." She wiped the lone tear that streaked her right cheek and I thought about the last movie she'd starred in—where the character she'd played hovered over her daughter's body, with a lone tear making a trail from her eyes to her mouth, as she said the same exact line that Camille had just said to me.

If Camille's next words were, *"You know I only want what's best for you. So you have to leave those girls alone. They are not worthy of your friendship,"* then I'd know for sure that she was reenacting her Golden Globe–nominated role.

Camille cleared her throat and just as I thought, she said, "You know that I only want what's best for you..." She rambled on, completed her line and it took everything in me not to banish her from my bedside while screaming, "Sick ass!"

"Can you just tell me what happened to me?" I asked, annoyed.

Camille continued to cry. "At your cheerleading competition one of the girls' mother tried to kill you—"

"What?!"

"Oh, oh, that wasn't you. Wrong girl," she stammered, looking at the nurse and the doctor, who must've thought she was just as nuts as I knew she was. Camille continued, "Well umm, dear, when the school first called me I thought maybe a crazed fan had attacked you."

"So I was attacked?" My heart skipped a beat.

"Yes, but not by a fan."

"Who attacked me?"

"Heather, what do you remember?" the doctor asked.

"I remember walking into my school's café, signing a few autographs...I walked over to the table with my friends and that's it. I don't remember a thing after that."

"My poor child." Camille held me to her bosom. "It hurts me so much when I think about what that girl did to you."

"Who did what to me?" I asked, baffled.

Camille sniffed. "That Spencer Ellington maced you."

"What?!" I screeched. "What? When? Spencer? Spencer did this to me?"

"Yes. But don't worry I've already filed the lawsuit. And I've already arranged for us to have an interview on E! TV tomorrow. And you and I need to tell them everything."

"I'm not doing that!" I felt dizzy. *Spencer did this to me?*

"Heather," Camille leaned in and whispered, "You *will* sue her. And you *will* do that interview and you *will not* complain about it."

"Spencer is my friend!"

"You have no friends." Camille leaned back and stood up straight. "I've already told you that in Hollywood your friends are only as good as the last role you played!"

"Ms. Cummings, that's enough," the nurse said.

"I'm telling my child the truth," Camille carried on. "You don't know what it's like to be America's sweetheart one day and the next day be dashed away! I know what that's like, so I have to look out for my daughter. Especially since that little trickster, Spencer, has this incident all over the Internet!"

"What?" I said in disbelief. "Are you serious?"

"It's viral, Heather!" Camille smiled and then quickly erased the smile from her face and her thin lips took on a disappointed droop. "It's viral! All over the world they are laughing at you and every news circuit is reporting the demise of Wu-Wu. So you have to do that interview. We have to emerge from this, so that our career stays on track—"

"Ms. Cummings!" the doctor said sternly. "Enough." He took a deep breath. "Heather, a little of what your mother said was correct, those girls you're friendly with may not be your friends. You should take a look at how they treat you, because anyone who would mace you is questionable."

"How come I don't remember that?" I asked.

"Because," the doctor said, "it seems that after you were maced you fell to the floor, hit your head, and suffered a slight concussion. Which may contribute to your not remembering the incident. But the good news is the concussion is slight, nothing too serious and you can go home today. We flushed your eyes when you arrived in the emergency room, and gave you a sedative to help you relax. You may feel groggy for a while, and your skin may feel a little inflamed. But, by the time you get home, you should feel much better and your vision should have cleared up as well."

"Thank you, Doctor," I said.

"You're welcome." He turned to the nurse and said, "I'm going to prepare Heather's discharge papers. Please have the orderlies bring the wheelchair around."

"I'll call the driver to meet us out front," Camille said as she waltzed out of the room and I wondered if I was the only one who noticed that she wore a mink shawl and a long-sleeved red ball gown. In California. In August.

I was silent as we rode from the hospital to home. Camille stayed on the phone with our publicist demanding that she capture the moment and line up at least a month's worth of interviews so that she could discuss my "life and death ordeal" and cry about how it felt to almost lose her only child.

Strangle me.

The driver pulled into the circular driveway and I was so anxious to get away from Camille that I didn't wait for the driver to open the door, I let myself out.

I slid my bumblebee sunglasses on and walked up the overgrown grassy path that led to our bungalow. I was ex-

hausted and wanted nothing more than to chill and relax
with a hit of Black Beauty. My eyes were still swollen and
my vision remained a little foggy but there was no doubt
in my mind that with one hit of Heaven I would be able to
see clearly.

Camille clicked her off-beat heels behind me and her
laughter cackled through the sky like thunder as she raved
to the publicist about how this incident would be the
comeback that she needed.

Pathetic.

We walked into the house. I made a right and Camille
made a left to the bar.

Typical.

I opened the double doors that led to my platinum and
white vintage-Hollywood bedroom. I stepped into the
room and for a moment I wondered if I were in the Twilight Zone.

Yeah, that's exactly where I am . . .

I stepped backward across the threshold and pulled the
doors closed. My eyes had to be playing tricks on me.
Yeah, that had to be it. Especially since my bedroom,
which I kept spotless—mostly because I didn't want the
maid going through my things—was in a catastrophic
state.

Jesus . . .

I took a deep breath and opened the doors slowly.

Same shit. Different minute.

Clothes were scattered everywhere: on my floor, hanging out of my closet door, strewn across my dresser. My
all-glass high-boy drawers were hung open, with finger-
prints smudged all over the glass, causing it to look smoky
as opposed to its usual pristine.

My queen-sized sleigh bed was rumpled. My scripts were...scattered...everywhere. My signed and framed posters of Dorothy Dandridge and Josephine Baker were crooked, and my floor to ceiling all-glass bookcase was a total disaster.

My heart dropped.

Split in two.

The aorta clogged my throat while the rest exploded in my chest.

Sweat gathered on my forehead and ran down my temples.

I couldn't think. All I could do was react.

I rushed over to my bookcase, climbed the attached ladder and frantically searched the top shelf.

It's not here...

But this is where I keep it.

Calm down. Maybe you moved it.

But I never move it...

Hysterically, I searched the next shelf, and the next, and the next....

Knocked everything off and by the time I reached the last shelf, all I'd done was add to the mess.

I was queasy, seconds from throwing up or passing out, or both.

"Camille!" I screamed, as I stood to the floor and whipped around, prepared to go to war. And there she was, leaning against the doorway, smiling wickedly, with a drink in one hand and my bag of Heaven in the other.

"Would you happen to be looking for this?" She shook the ice in her glass and sipped.

I was frozen. Watched my bag of pills swing back and forth in her hand like a pocket watch. I swallowed, wiped sweat from my forehead and said, "How dare you come into my room! Who gave you the right to go through my things?!"

"This is my house!" she insisted.

"Your house was foreclosed on! I pay rent here! Now give me my things and stay out of my room!"

"I'm not giving you anything and I will come in here anytime I want to!"

I sprinted toward Camille, fist balled, and right hook ready to lay her down. I had every intention of knocking her in the head and snatching my bag of Heaven from her hand. But suddenly, as if I were remote controlled, I stopped in my tracks.

Camille smiled and took another sip. She narrowed her eyes on me and said, "Oh now, Wu-Wu's turned into Billie Jean Badass? Well, isn't this something? Instead of trying to attack me you should've handled Spencer. Because from what I saw on that video, after your little booty bags deflated, you were flat on your back and screaming for help. So don't try and get tough with me, young lady. Now, collect yourself and mind your manners!" She stuffed my pills into her bra.

I felt like she'd taken a knife and sliced me down the center of my chest.

I did my best to calm down but if I didn't get my pills back I was seconds away from having a psychotic fit! "Give it here, Camille!"

She didn't respond. Instead, she finished off her drink and then turned to walk away.

I followed her. She marched into her bedroom and attempted to slam the door in my face. I kicked it open and the door handle crashed into the wall behind it. "Give me my medication, Camille!"

"Medication?" She spun around and arched her brow. "Since when have you been on medication, Heather? The last I checked you didn't need any medication and as many times as I've tried to have you committed, I know firsthand that there are no pills for teenagers who treat their mothers like crap!"

"Mother? Is that some kind of sick joke? After what flop of a movie did you figure out that you were a mother? Or are you trying to make comedy a part of your comeback? If so, then get ready for failure number two. Now give me my things!"

Camille screamed, "I swear you're just like—"

"Like who?!" I screamed back at her. "Like my father? Oh no that couldn't be it, because you have no idea who my father is!" I walked over to Camille's vanity and started picking up pictures of her in different poses with different celebrities—mostly men. I screamed, "I'm just like my father? Well, who is he?!" I tossed a picture at her. "Is he Morgan Freeman?" I tossed another picture. "Is he Denzel Washington? Come on, Camille, tell me something!"

"Heather, put those pictures down!" She attempted to grab the pictures from my hand. I yanked my arm away, causing Camille to stumble backward.

"No!" I screamed. "Is he Will Smith? Idris Elba, or did you get really down and dirty with it and give up the golden goods to the mailman, the cable man, or the gardener? Huh? Or were you too drunk to even know! You're so evil! So nasty! You don't even know who my daddy is. You probably slept with every last one of them! Now who is he, Camille! Who is he!" I knocked the remaining pictures off of her vanity in one sweep. The glass from the pictures' frames shattered as they hit the floor.

"I said who is he!"

"He's Richard—" She stopped herself midsentence and covered her mouth abruptly.

I ran over to her and tried to snatch her hand away from her mouth. "Say it, Dammit! Tell me!" I screamed at the top of my lungs. We wrestled across the bed and fell to the floor. I wanted to stomp the truth out of her. For years I have wanted to know who my father is and she stopped midsentence, taunting me with a piece of my truth.

"You owe me this!" I spat. "Say his name! I'm tired of not knowing! I need to know!"

She overpowered me and pushed me off of her. "Heather, are you crazy? What do you want to know for? He doesn't want you!"

"Does he even know I exist?!"

"Yes he knows! He's known from day one and he's never wanted anything to do with you! He already has a daughter! I was supposed to abort you but when I got there it was too damn late!"

"So I was a mistake?" I asked, my legs feeling as if they were about to buckle and fold beneath me.

"Yeah, yeah, his! Now get the hell out of my face!" she spat.

I headed toward her. I was determined to kill her. I saw no reason why she should continue to live. She looked at me and laughed. "Do it. And I will call Officer Sampson."

I gasped and stopped in my tracks.

She gave a crooked smile. "You didn't forget that you had a probation officer, now did you? Should I call him and suggest that he give my junkie who tried to kill me, who held me at knifepoint—would you like me to add that—a drug test? Because you know I will. I'm looking for a reason to act. To tear your career down and let you know how it feels. 'Cause you have gotten a little bit too big and I'm just the person to bring you down, my dear. Now retreat to your corner, behave, go fix me a drink and act as if you have some manners."

Instantly fire raced through my body. I couldn't think and that's when it hit me. "Is that what you want?" I asked. "Because I will grant your wish!"

She straightened her nightgown and said, "Yes, dear, on the rocks."

"No problem."

I raced over to her bed, reached for the secret stash she kept under it, ran over to her bedroom window and sailed all five bottles of Scotch into the L.A. skyline. "If you want a drink go get it!"

"HEATHER!!!"

I twirled around. "I'm sooooo sick of you! Really, did you really think I would keep letting you do whatever you wanted to do to me! Huh, Camille?!"

I brushed past her, ran down the stairs, and into the great room. I made a left toward the bar and grabbed all of the bottles that I could. "You want a drink?!"

"Put them down!" she screamed.

"Then here you go!" I spat and my voice cracked from yelling at the top of my lungs. I picked up three bottles and hurled them toward Camille. She ducked and they smashed and shattered into the wall, leaving her dirty secrets running down to the floor.

"You're a drunk! A Hollywood nobody! Norma Marie!" I

raced toward the terrace—which was open to the great room. Camille grabbed my arm, and caused me to drop two of the bottles to the floor. They crashed into a zillion pieces and the liquor quickly streamed through the grooves of the terra-cotta tiles.

"Get off of me!" I snatched my arm away, sailing the bottles I held in my hand over the terrace's iron black railing and into the driveway. I dusted my hands and rushed back into the house.

"Stop it now, Heather! Show some respect!"

I growled at her, "You need to can the jokes! Respect? If anything you need to show *me* respect and watch how *you* speak to me, *Norma Marie*. I'm not the one you want to play with. I know all of your secrets before and after you changed your name to Camille!"

"How dare you!" She cornered me as I raced back to the bar. Seeing no way out, I took my arm and swept everything off the bar with my elbow. Camille lifted her hand in the air and I said, "You got away with hitting me this morning, but if you do it again I will be leaving here in handcuffs."

"You certainly will!" She sneered at me, her hand still in mid-air.

I huffed, unsure of whether I could completely take Camille, but certain that if she put her hands on me I would try. "Is that what you really want to do, Camille? Send me to jail? Have you forgotten that I'm the one paying these bills? You don't have any money. None. You don't contribute one dime to this eight-thousand-dollar-a-month rent! Not one dime to paying the driver, the maid, or anyone else around here! If it wasn't for an anonymous donor there'd be no way I could even afford to attend Hollywood High!"

"Shut. Up!"

"No. You. Shut. Up! You've never even asked how we're maintaining around here! Do you even care that the well is running dry? How much money do you think I make? We have lost our house and now we have an eight-thousand-dollar-a-month rent! I'm paying all the utilities, buying all the liquor you drink and you won't even tell me who my father is!"

"I will not stand for you speaking to me like that!" Camille said, reaching for the phone, which I quickly snatched out of the wall.

"I pay that bill, too!" I spat. Before I could say anything the doorbell rang and a tiny voice called my name. "Heeeeeaaaather! Are you in there?"

Ding Dong!

Camille and I were silent as the bell rang again.

Camille sucked in a deep breath and backed away. "You heard what I said. No pills. No drugs. No crap. And no more talk about your damn daddy who doesn't want you anyway. I don't need the stress. I'm trying to make a comeback! And before I have you around here high as hell and making me look bad, I'll have you on a plane to rehab so fast you won't have time to even think about your next hit!"

Ding Dong! "Heeeeeeeather!" whoever rang the bell called my name again. "I hear voices, are you in there?"

Camille continued, "So you better get yourself together and gather yourself real quick!" She turned away from me and slid her matted slippers toward the window and peeped out. "What is that snotty little trick Spencer doing here?!"

"Spencer?" I said. *What is she doing here . . . ? And how much of this did she hear . . . ?*

Camille grimaced at me. "I'll call the maid to come from the pool house and clean this mess up! You get the door and ensure that Kitty Ellington's little thugette isn't here long!"

8

Spencer

I stood at the front door of Heather and her mother's million-dollar Penny Lane Bungalow, clicking my heels in disbelief as I discreetly pulled out my cell and recorded the nasty argument between the two of them.

Sweetjigglebootypop! I can't believe that they're renting. Renting? How tragic! How will I ever look Heather in her eyes again, knowing she's broke, busted, and can't be trusted? Rich was right. They really are in the projects. Oh, this is scandalous!

I blinked. A part of me almost felt bad. First I had to mace her. And now I found out that, on top of it all, her mother's a fraudulent barnyard mess. *Poor thing!* I turned from the door and thought about leaving until I heard Heather's mother say to her, "You get the door and ensure that little thugette isn't here long!" My mouth dropped open. *Who in the world is she talking about? With a name like Norma Marie, I know that drunk isn't talking about me.*

I quickly shut my phone off and shoved it back down in

my bag as Heather came to the door scowling at me. I couldn't see her eyes because they were hidden behind her sunglasses. "Spencer, what do you want? I'm really not in the mood for your theatrics right now. I don't appreciate that stunt you pulled this morning, macing me in my damn face."

I giggled, tilting my head and touching one of my diamond earrings. "Theatrics? Heather, you're so dang silly. I'm not an actress. Actresses can't even keep jobs. I came here—"

She folded her arms across her chest, narrowing her eyes. "For what? To make sure you didn't blind me?" She tossed her sunglasses off and her eyes were red and practically swollen shut. "Well, as you can see, you didn't blind me. Now leave."

"Heather, I'm not leaving. I have been nothing but a friend to you."

"I cannot believe this," she chuckled in disbelief. "*You* think you've been a *friend* to me? Oh, this is priceless! Is *that* how you define a friend—by spraying Mace in their face?"

"Well I had to get your attention and let you know that you can't go around giving out your mother's cheap perfumes to people."

"So you couldn't talk to me about it, instead? You had to run down on me and steal on me? Really? Is that how you greasy skanks up on the hill do it?"

I rolled my eyes, putting a hand up on my hip. The nerve of her! "Well, at least I came *down* the hill. I asked Rich to come with me but she said she doesn't do the hood. But that's not the point."

"Well how about you get to the point because you're

wasting my time. And the sight of you is really making me sick."

I swept a curl from my face. "Ohmygod, Heather. That's not nice. Do you have any idea how embarrassing it was to be told your mother's perfume smelled like cat piss on me? Then have to walk around the school with my neck wrapped in gauze? Do you know how hard it is to bling out a bandage? Today's been hell, Heather."

"You know what, Spencer? Screw you, your blinged out bandage, and my mother's perfume!"

"No, screw you, little Miss Pissy-face. You got the wrong toolbox, boo. I don't get screwed. And you can go to hell in a gasoline-covered handbasket for saying that to me. I have blisters on my neck because of you, girlie. So if anything you owe me an apology. And you should be thanking me."

"Oh, dear God!" she snorted, shaking her head. "Thanking you?! For what?"

I frowned, pulling my shades up over my head and looking her in her puffy eyes. "For not suing you or your mother, that's for what. But you know what? It's not even that serious now. I came here to be the bigger person to forgive you for what you did to me."

"For what *I* did to *you*? Are you serious? You are really delusional. You have the audacity to dart your dizzy behind over here with this dumbness, talking about you forgive *me!* And that I owe you an apology? Oh, no. You are really tripping on stupid."

My eyes flicked for a few seconds, trying to figure out if she was trying to imply I wasn't the brightest shade of lipstick in the make-up caddy. But I let it go. She couldn't possibly be insinuating that. "Heather, I don't want to fight with you. So let's not turn this into a snotty cat-box fight."

"Tramp, you turned this into a fight the minute you jumped up and attacked me. And now you want to forgive *me*. *You* disgraced *me*. *You* told *my* business. I did nothing to you."

I flipped my hair. "Girl, are you crazy? What business of yours did I tell?"

"Trick, you practically told the whole school that I had no ass."

"Ohsweetbutteredbiscuits, now you're going too far, Heather. I did not. I said you wore booty bags. Get it right."

She huffed. "Same difference. You ruined me! You put me on blast in front of the whole damn school. No, matter of fact...the entire world! Yelling out that I wore booty bags! If I choose to pad my behind, that's nobody's business but mine. You're two-faced! And you wanna come over here and talk about forgiveness. Oh, you're dumber than I thought."

I took another deep breath. The balls of my feet were starting to burn from standing out in this horrid heat in these heels. I glanced around her yard, looking for a spot of shade. But the only thing I noticed was that there was glass everywhere and that the grass needed to be cut. *My God, they can't even afford trash pickup or lawn service! This is sinful!* I turned my attention back to her, giving her a saddened look. There was no way I could stay mad at her with all of this suffering going on around her. I reached out for her hand. "Heather, I really forgive you."

She snatched her hand back. "For what? For that video of you spraying a whole can of Mace in my face going viral?

Is that what you're here to forgive me for? Oh, oh, wait. I have some forgiveness for you. How about *you* forgive me for having to pay all the bills around here. And for having to spend almost four hours in the damn emergency room getting my eyes flushed out because you wanted to go psycho on me. Yeah, forgive me for that. Because I can clearly see here that you are clueless. Oh, and better yet. Forgive me for having to be friends with a bunch of nasty, conniving, hobags, including you, who don't even like me...."

Tears started welling up in her eyes.

"Heather—"

"You're not the one who everyone has their hands out to, looking for handouts, shaking tin cups up in your face expecting you to rescue them from their miserable little lives. Well what about my misery? No one cares about that. So don't talk to me about forgiveness. You're not the one who has to live trapped in a box. I'm sick of it! And I'm sick of people like you! And I'm sick of trying to be everything everybody else wants me to be, except for me. I thought you were different, Spencer. I thought I could kick it with you. I thought you liked me. Not Wu-Wu. But *me*...Heather! You knew that one thing about me. And today you yelled it out in front of everyone. Do you know how mortifying that was? Do you have any idea how badly you hurt me?"

I gave her a blank stare. I couldn't believe she was going off on me like that. Like really. Hearing all those nasty things she was saying made me feel like she had just sideswiped me, and knocked me over like I was a mannequin dressed in a cheap polyester suit and bargain basement jewels. I was the victim here! Not her. I was the one with the blisters on my neck wearing a god-awful bandage that

I had to turn around and hot glue loose gems on just to make it stylish. Clearly, she was confused. But since I had gone over there to forgive her, I had to pick myself up because I didn't have on polyester and my jewels were anything but cheap.

"No, of course you don't," she continued, eyeing me, "because—unlike me—you have the whole world at your fingertips. Everything you want is handed to you. And I have to practically beg, borrow, and pretend to be something I don't wanna be just to have a little bit of what you have. So you want forgiveness. Then, forgive me. Exonerate me, please. Yes, free me. Do me that honor, Your Majesty. And since you're gracious enough to come down the hill and into the *hood* to hand out forgiveness, I have one more thing to add to the list. Forgive *me* for tossing you off my property!"

Whaaaaaat?! Oh, she really tried to push her go-kart into my last nerve telling me to get off property she *doesn't even own!* I took another deep breath. I really didn't want to have to mace her again. But she was acting like a wild dog and I had a full can on ready if she didn't pump her brakes real quick.

She bit into her bottom lip and stared at me. Her eyeballs looked like little red balls wrapped in puff pastry. That's how swollen and red they were. We both just stood there under the blazing sun, looking at each other. Her lips quivered. Her eyes watered. I had really hurt her. Now I did feel bad. So I did what they always do on my mother's TV show when someone was about to start crying. I stepped up in her space and hugged her.

And then, on cue as if we were going on commercial break, I cried with her. Heather clutched me tightly. And right at that moment, I felt as if I could win a Daytime Emmy.

"It's all right Heather. It's going to be okay. It could have been worse, you know. I could have clawed your eyeballs out and stomped you with my seven-inch heels, but I didn't do that. I was reasonable."

"No. What you were was mean! How could you do that to me, Spencer? You're not the one shamed! You're not the one floating around the Internet looking like a fool! You could have talked to me."

I stepped back, touching the side of her face. "I'm sorry but my neck was on fire, and I needed you to feel what I was feeling. You didn't talk to me before you gave out your mother's perfume to tell me that it might break my neck out. So why would I want to talk to you?"

She moved my hand away. "Because I thought we were friends? But, then again, you just confirmed what I already knew. I don't have any."

She turned to walk away, leaving me standing there. And just as she was about to open the door I dug into my bag and pulled out the Swarvoski-studded special edition bottle of Rose Alize I had bought, holding it up to the sun so that she could see the two-thousand-dollar bling and said, "Hey Heather, how about we wipe the bulletin board clean and make up over drinks?" She hesitated, then glanced over her shoulder at me, narrowing her eyes. I smiled and batted my lashes. "Pretty please."

She paused. Took deep breaths, opened the door and said, "Come in."

9

London

My cell rang. I grabbed it and glanced at the screen. *Oh God, it's the drama queen!* I stared at my phone for a few seconds contemplating whether or not to answer. Especially since, dealing with Rich outside of Hollywood High was not the plan. I mean, really. Girlfriend had yanked my lifelines down. Stuck a Krazy Straw into my vein and siphoned out my emotional cup. I was drained. And exhausted from the drama ride I'd been forced to endure. Oh, no. I wanted no parts of her until tomorrow morning, when I *had* to deal with her. Otherwise, the rest of my night was already mapped out in my gorgeous head.

Starting with the luxurious bath I'd already drawn with my guiltiest pleasure—six feet, two-hundred-and-ten pounds of sweet, milk chocolate—who awaited me in my master bathroom suite, naked and ready.

But, before I could indulge I had to retreat to the wet bar and bring up another bottle of Perrier-Jouët champagne, toss back a few more flutes, slide down into the tub with him, then crawl up in my king-sized Baldacchino Supreme bed—the bed of all beds to make hot passionate love to my prince atop thousand-count sheets threaded with 22-carat gold. Oh, yes...it was going to be nonstop, body-rocking, spring-bouncing lovemaking going on up in here.

Then my prince and I would go down to the spa-style steam room so that I could continue to purify myself from the three toxins I had encountered earlier today: Rich, Spencer, and Heather. *Ahhh, Wu-Wu's in the house!* I shuddered. *What ahhh hot mess!* Ugh!

And lastly, after the spa, my sexy chocolate-drop and I would take a dip in the indoor, Olympic-size pool—naked of course—and make sweet love all over again.

Therefore talking on the phone to Rich was *not* in any way, shape, or form anywhere on my radar.

Thank God the phone stopped ringing and just as I went to turn it off, it rang again.

Rich.

I thought about sending her straight to voice mail, but then I remembered how she'd gotten down and dirty with me today, and maybe I did owe her at least one very limited phone conversation. I took a deep breath, glanced over at the French bathroom doors that held my prize behind them, then braced myself.

"Hello."

The drama started immediately. "Get your couture right, girl!" she yelled into my ear. "Get your stilettos out! Get your diamonds out! Let's go. Let's get it, get it! Because Hollywood is not gonna be the same after tonight! We're 'bout to shut it down, girl. It's over! Whoop-whoop! Lights out! Let's paint the town pink and make da booty clap-clap!"

What in the hell?! Apparently she is always on ten.

"Rich, what are you talking about?"

"Uh, hello?" She knocked against the phone. "Hello? Are you brain-dead, boo? I'm talking about hitting the club, girl. Let's party! Let's pop bottles! Let's celebrate!"

I can't believe this.

I blinked. "Rich, I'm trying to unwind. And here you're rambling like you need a bottle of Zoloft. You're talking a mile a minute about couture and diamonds and popping bottles, while we get it, get it and make the booty clap, clap. And I'm trying to relax and unwind. Clearly, one of these things is not like the other."

"Ewww, you did not quote *Sesame Street,* did you, girl? Oh my, clutching pearls. You really need to hit the scene. You can't go around saying things like that or you'll be dubbed the slow queen. And how would your publicist fix that—"

"Rich—"

"Now listen, we are too fine, too fly, and too damn fabulous to be sitting up in the house. We're about to boom, bust it. Pop it. Shake it. I'm ready to…own it. Serve it. Drop it down to the floor and work it. Get sexy with it—"

"Rich! I'm tired. I'm sore. I'm just trying to get my mind right and digest all the craziness from earlier today—"

"Beep, beep! Pull over for a minute, boo. And let me take the wheel 'cause obviously you're too busy driving down memory lane. What happened earlier is yesterday's news, that's not even on the Internet anymore. That is sooooo, seven hours and twenty-seven seconds ago! It's already forgotten, boo. So get over it."

I rolled my eyes. "*Get over it?* Girl, are you serious? I had some boy wearing pink heels and a godforsaken pink-haired ostrich coat toss a damn smoothie in my face, then I had to beat him down—"

"*We* beat him down—"

"You know what I mean. And then on top of that I had to toss out a hundred grand—"

"Small change. And besides we don't discuss money. We leave that for the newbies. I mean, really. You're stressing over a measly hundred grand? Please. We shop that away."

"The point is today was a mess!"

Rich huffed. "Look, we handled *Hello Kitty*. So snap out of it! Yeah, *we* had to tear up the café. But oh well. Miss Co-Co Lo Mein had to get it. And you know it, so stop with all the whining, girl. He had no business trying to breathe in the same air as us. "

"Still—"

"*Snap-snap! Still*, nothing, girlfriend. Let it go. The only thing we're gonna *steal* is a good damn time. Now this conversation is already old. So pull up your big-girl panties and—"

Click!

I disconnected the call. There was no way I could keep listening to that mess. Hmph, I was about to pop-pop-get-get all right! "Coming, boo!" I yelled toward the bathroom. Yet, before I could say anything more my cell rang. Again.

She's baaaack. I sent her straight to voice mail. And a

few seconds later she called back again. *Oh, for the love of God! This girl is relentless!* "Hello."

"Girl, were *we* disconnected?"

"Yeah. Bad connection," I lied.

"Well, we're reconnected, boo. So let's get it, get it! What we need to do now is get out and pop, lock, and drop it. And I have just the spot."

I need an Excedrin. This girl is about to wear me out!

"Rich, not tonight. Maybe—"

"*Maybe* you should hurry up and get ready. I'll be there at eight."

I huffed. "No."

"*No?* Oh, no boo. I don't understand the word *no*. What language is that? Ebonics?"

I sighed. "No, it's universal. And it's a part of the Rosetta Stone collection. It's used in all languages. And no means, *no*, I don't want to go out tonight."

"Ummm, noooo, it doesn't. I don't know a Rosetta Stone, but I know Rich Montgomery, boo. And that word doesn't exist in my dictionary. I only know *yes, I can* and *I will.* Outside of that it's *sí* and *oui*. So I'll *see* you in a few hours. We're shutting Hollywood down tonight!" *Click!*

I blinked, blinked again. *Whatever, she can come over here if she wants to, she'll be waiting all night long....*

I turned my cell off, then stepped out of my clothes, removed my black-laced bra while keeping on the matching thong. I slipped into a pair of seven-inch, red-bottom platform pumps, then strutted my way into the bathroom, shutting the door behind me.

"Damn, yo...what took you so long—" My prince looked up, taking in my beauty. He licked his lips. "Now, that's wassup. 'Bout time you get in here and handle ya man. Who were you on the phone with?"

"Who else?" I said as I dimmed the recessed lights. "The attention whore herself."

He eyed me, leaning back in the oversized tub. "So we still on?"

"I'm working on it," I told him, kneeling down, then taking the washcloth and washing him. My mouth watered as beads of water slid down over his muscled chest and chiseled abs.

He looked at me suspiciously. "You're not going soft on me, are you?"

I shook my head. "Of course not. I just need for everything to happen at the right time."

He sat up and pulled me toward him. "You need to make it happen soon."

"I will."

We kissed until I felt myself starting to overheat, getting lost in the moment.

He smiled, splashed water up on me. "So you gonna get in this tub, or what? Ya man wants some company."

I giggled, stepped out of my heels. My whole body filled with excitement. "You take them panties off," I teased, slipping a foot into the steamy water, then quickly pulling it back out and turning toward the door. I placed my hand on the knob. "I'll be right back."

"Yo, where are you going?" he asked.

"I don't remember if I locked my bedroom door. I don't need the house manager slipping in here. She tells everything."

"London—"

I turned back toward my baby and softly placed a finger up to his lips. "Sssh." I gave him a kiss, then poured him another glass of champagne. I handed him the flute. "I'll be right back." I walked out into the powder room area of my bathroom, staring into the mirror. I smiled at my reflection. Life was good! No, wait…better than good. It was great! No, scratch that. It was fantabulous!

I opened the bathroom door, stepped out into my bedroom, walked into the sitting area of the room to grab some candles and I…almost…died. "Ohmygod, Daddy!" I screamed. "You scared me!" My heart skipped four beats.

He sat on the edge of my chaise lounge in his custom-tailored blue pinstriped suit and his monogrammed white shirt. His Hermès tie hung loosely around his neck. He narrowed his eyes at me.

"Where are your clothes?"

Oh sweet merciful Jesus! Someone please roll out my coffin now, so I can throw myself in it! I am sooooo dead! I threw an arm up over my breasts, trying to cover them. "Daddy, give me a sec to put something on." I quickly spun around and raced back into the bathroom, shutting the door behind me. I ran into the tub and shower area. "Ohmygod, my father's here."

"Whaaat?!" my guilty pleasure snapped, hopping up from the tub. "Oh, daaaaaamn!"

"Sssh. Keep it down. Are you crazy? Do you want him to hear you?" I tried really hard to stay focused and keep my eyes from roaming his nude body. Under different circumstances I'd be ready to set if off, dropping down and licking the drops of water rolling down his body. But, my life flashed before my eyes so I checked my hormones, fast. I threw a towel at him, grabbing him by the arm. "I have to hide you." I opened the linen closet. "In here."

He gave me a confused look. "Are you serious? Look at me. You expect me to squeeze all of this body into that little closet."

"Either that or start writing your eulogy. 'Cause you know if my father catches you in here he *is* going to kill us both."

He huffed, stuffing himself inside the closet. "Can I at least dry—" I quickly kissed him, then shut the door in his face. I grabbed a robe, pulled a deep breath in, then stepped back out into my bedroom, practically out of breath. I slowly walked over to where Daddy sat and gave him a kiss on the cheek.

"Daddy, what are you doing here?"

He eyed me. "I live here."

I pushed out a nervous chuckle. "Oh, Daddy. I know that. I meant I'm surprised to see you. I thought you weren't getting back until the end of the week."

He leaned forward in his seat. "You mind telling me what you're doing half-naked at"—he glanced at his watch—"four o'clock in the afternoon?"

I felt my face crack, then explode into tiny little pieces. "I-I-I..."

"Take your time. Better yet, have a seat while you get your story together."

"Oh, that's okay. I'll stand."

"No. I *said* take a seat." I swallowed the lump in my throat and sat in the chair across from him. "Now, you were saying..." He interlocked his fingers, then cracked his hands back. I blinked. Uh-oh! Daddy only cracked his fingers like that when he was about to go off.

Think, girl!

"Daddy, you have no idea the kind of day I had. I've been cramping like crazy ever since I got home from all the drama."

"Try me."

"That school is a zoo, Daddy. First thing this morning, the fire alarm went off and we had to be dragged out of homeroom and stand outside for almost forty-five minutes. The firemen, police, and paramedics were all out there. Then I found out that girl, Spencer, you want me to be friends with was the one who pulled the fire alarm."

He raised his eyebrow. "Go on."

"Oh God, Daddy! Then she attacked that actress girl, Heather, during lunch because Heather's mother gave Spencer some perfume that smelled like cat piss. I couldn't believe it! That Spencer chick jumped up and maced her out of nowhere." I shook my head. "It was nonstop drama, Daddy. The whole mess had my stomach in knots. I just needed to get home, take me a nice hot bath and unwind. Those girls at Hollywood High are crazy."

"London, stop with all the theatrics. You're not any different from them."

I frowned. "Daddy, I beg your pardon. I'm *nothing* like those girls. They keep a lot of drama stirred up. I'm telling you, they're nuts."

"Then explain to me how your face ended up being plastered all over the front page of every online magazine with your breasts hanging out of your blouse."

I blinked. *Ohmygod, Thanks to Rich, I pressed the send button to my own grave.* "This boy in pink heels and make-up tossed a smoothie in my face." He tilted his head, giving me a look of disbelief. "I'm serious, Daddy. He calls himself Co-Co Ming. And he attacked me."

He stood up. "I don't want to hear another word of this nonsense. You've managed to get yourself caught up in a bunch of nonsense on the first day of school. You know better than that. Then you had the nerve to drag Rich Montgomery into your mess."

"*Rich?* Umm, excuse you. Are you serious? Newsflash, Daddy: Rich Montgomery was the one who set it *all* off. This was all her mess!"

"Watch your mouth. And watch your tone, young lady. Do *not* put any of that mess on her. I know you. And I know how your mouth and attitude can be. So stop with the Miss Innocent act. Rich's father is one of my highest paying clients. You do understand that, right?"

"But I wasn't doing anything."

"London, that's not what I asked you. I am not going to have what happened back in New York happen here, do you understand? That whole fiasco cost me millions of dollars."

"Daddy, this is different. You want me to be friends with girls I don't even like. They're effen crazy! I know Spencer's mother is also another one of your clients, but I'm sorry, Daddy. She's about as dumb and dizzy as a pail of seashells. That chick Heather looks like she's a walking billboard for rehab or a loony bin. And Rich likes to call the media on herself. Who in the hell calls the damn media on themselves? Ding, ding, ding...Rich, the attention whore, who else! And these are the girls you want me to hang out with. Ugh, I can't get with these crazy-behind girls and all of their histrionics. It is too extra for me. I have got to get back to New York, Daddy. Please."

"You're not going back to New York so you might as well get that idea out of your pretty little head. You understand me?"

"But Daddy," I pouted and folded my arms across my chest.

"It's not going to work. And another thing, why has Anderson been on my phone complaining about not hearing from you?"

"Because he hasn't heard from me," I said sarcastically.

"And why is that?"

"Because I don't want—"

"London, let me explain something to you, it's not about what you want. It's about the life your mother and I have planned for you. I have let you get away with far too many things, which is part of the reason we had to move across the country. Therefore I will not listen to anything that you don't want, because you will do what I tell you to do and that is not up for negotiation. Nor is this a debate."

Silence.

A few seconds later the house phone rang and Daddy walked over to the cordless phone that sat on the table. "So you might as well settle in." He handed me the phone. "Starting with your new friends. It's Rich Montgomery. Maybe she wants to hang out. Show you around your new hometown."

I stared at his hand. *Little does he know.*

"I mean it, London. Don't try me."

I rolled my eyes and took the phone from him. "Hello? Yeah," I paused. "Okay, see you at eight so we can bust it." I rolled my eyes at my father and quickly hurried back into the bathroom and locked the door before he could say anything more. Once I heard my bedroom door close I let my prince out of the closet.

My poor baby was all bunched up. "He's finally gone," I said with a drag.

"Damn, you had me all up in there bent up like a damn pretzel. Any longer and I was gonna end up with scoliosis."

"Look. My dad wants me to hang out with Rich tonight. But I don't want to."

He kissed me on the lips. "Nah. You need to go. Put that work in so we can get it poppin'."

I poked my lips out. "But I want to finish up what we started. I need you so bad, boo. I've missed you so much."

He pulled me into him. "And I want you, too, but in order for us to be together I need you to handle that tonight. So go hang with your peeps. I'ma lay low until you get back. You just need to sneak me up some grub."

"I can arrange that," I said as I untied my bathrobe and let it fall off my shoulders. "But can we at least get a quickie in before I have to get ready?"

He grinned, dropping his towel. "Oh, no doubt, baby. I'm all yours."

10

Rich

Melanie Fiona's "4 AM" played softly through the surround sound as I sat Indian-style in the center of my
oval king-sized bed, beneath the glittering lights of my crystal
chandelier. I did my all to focus on why my boyfriend
Corey's text clearly read that he'd be home from Belize tomorrow, but my private eye said that he'd arrived yesterday and was in the club boom-bustin' it up tonight.

Right now.

At this moment.

And even though I'd come up with a plan to creep up
on him—with London in tow—and slice his throat, that
still wasn't enough to maintain my focus.

And I wasn't thinking about tomorrow's headlines either, or the viral video of Co-Co Ming's beat-down.

And I didn't wonder when I'd finish my American literature, chemistry, or calculus homework. Hmph, Hollywood High was the last thing on my mind.

Instead, my head spun from something much crazier

than any of that—like why I couldn't stop thinking about my best friend, Christian, who everyone called by his last name, Knox.

Knox had been my brotherly-type boo since second grade, with only one interruption—well, two. The first one was in third grade when he wrote me a note and asked me to be his girl.

I checked the yes box.

It lasted for a week and then my mother ordered me to dump him; and not because he was ten and I was only eight. There was never an allowed-to-love-and-date age assigned to me. After all being taught to marry well started early. And in the world of wealth and success men were never too old, or too young, they were always just right. So that wasn't the issue.

It was much deeper than that.

Problem was Knox's trust fund wasn't deep enough, which meant his family wasn't rich enough. They had everyday money. Low millions. No more than seven. Not enough to last a lifetime. And to top it all off his father was Daddy's accountant, which my mother likened to the hired help. And although I didn't have many rules, never ever dating, sleeping with, and marrying the hired help or their young was definitely one of them.

So, I broke up with him and for the next few years we remained friends. Until this summer—July 4th weekend. My parents celebrated Independence Day at our home in the Hamptons but I stayed home alone in Beverly Hills. Knox's parents were in Myrtle Beach and he couldn't leave California because he was taking summer classes at UCLA.

So he came over to my house to celebrate.

Told me to give the chef the night off and he would barbecue.

So he manned the grill and I bartended the drinks.
Barbecue chicken, ginger shrimp, asparagus, orange Popsicle martinis and Jell-O shots were our specialty for the
evening. Hours later we were full and loaded. And I drunk-
enly confessed to him that despite my mother's wishes for
us to only be friends, that I'd been in love with him since I
was eight and no matter how hard I tried, my feelings
wouldn't go away. . . .

I lay back on my seven-foot white leather headboard
and squeezed my eyes tight. I had to stop Knox from invading my mind.

He wasn't important.

Running up on Corey and teaching him a lesson for attempting to play me was important.

Getting out of this bed and turning off this melancholy
music was important. Shaking this sad side of Rich
Gabrielle Montgomery and bringing back Rich the Party
Girl was important.

Snap. Snap.

I was losing it and there was no way I could allow my
thoughts to keep me off my square.

I sat up in bed and said to no one in particular, "Where
are you, Party Girl?"

"Over here," I answered myself.

I shook my head. This was stupid. But whatever—
'cause one thing was for sure and two things were for certain: I didn't do regret and blue most certainly wasn't my
color.

I hopped out of bed, changed my CD to Birdman's "I Run

This" and just like that I was amped again! I had twenty minutes to be at London's so that we could run up in the club real quick and if everything went as planned, we'd be able to bust Corey in the head, drag him home, and drop it to the floor at a whole other club before the night ended.

As Birdman chanted, I danced from my room to my dressing room and into my walk-in closet. I bounced over to my mirrored wall, tapped the center of it, and my holographic keyboard appeared. I typed in "black club dresses" and in the blink of an eye the section of black club dresses made their way down the automatic rounder and stopped before me. I chose my all black Gucci super-tight and ultra-mini dress.

Dabomb.

Perfect dress to bring Corey to his knees.

Birdman continued to blast through the surround sound as I spun around and broke out into a throwback dance—the Pop-Lock-And-Drop-It. I carried my routine from the closet and into my shoe room—which could compete with the chicest upscale boutique any day of the week.

It didn't take me long to choose my black, Gucci, hand-woven, peep toe boots that stopped midway up my thigh, and were so fly that they all but purred.

Meow.

I showered, dressed, confirmed with my private eye that Corey was still in the club tearing up the scene, and summoned my driver to take the Phantom. We picked up my girl, London—who was dressed just right to kill—red Chanel dress that dipped low in the front and stopped midway up her thighs, and six-inch black Tabitha Simmons chandelier sandals. And before I could drop the bomb on London as to why we were really going out she turned to me and said, "Are you and Corey really serious?"

That threw me. Where'd that come from? "Why'd you ask you ask me that?"

"Because," London hesitated, "I had somebody who I wanted you to meet. And I didn't want to be introducing you to him if you were really hung up on Corey."

"Well, who is he?"

"My boy Justice and he's *fine*." London popped her lips for emphasis.

"Fine," I said and sipped my champagne. "Anytime fine is said like that, it usually means that Mr. Fine is low money. And this princess doesn't do low money."

London rolled her eyes and refreshed her drink. "You just insulted me. I don't do low money on any level."

"Girl, now you know I didn't mean to insult you. You know that's not how we do. We came out to have a good time and that's what we're going to do. Now let's make a toast."

We clinked our glasses as we pulled up in front of Club Sixty-Six Paradise in Santa Monica. Better known as the newbies and the classless rich kids' hole in the wall.

Ugh.

A place where neither the paparazzi nor I would dare be seen—except for tonight of course.

But, I wasn't here to party or snatch a headline. I was on a mission—The Chin-Check-This-Playa-Playa Mission.

London and I finished our glasses of champagne as the driver pulled in front of the club. I frowned. There was no red carpet, no one taking celebrity roll call, and no velvet rope to separate the VIPs from the common folks. How gross!

"So where are we?" London asked as the driver rolled out the emergency red carpet that I kept in the trunk.

"Santa Monica," I said as the driver opened the door and assisted London and me out of the car.

"I know we're in Santa Monica," London said as she shook her hair and dusted invisible wrinkles from her dress. "I meant what's up with the club? What kind of spot is this?"

"Oh," I said and batted my lashes. "I almost forgot you didn't know." I quickly refreshed my gloss and popped my full lips.

"Know what?" She gave me a suspicious smile.

"That this is the spot we 'bout to tear up." I quickly clicked my heels toward the door. Obviously London was on pause so to help her along I turned toward her and said, "Girl, what are you waiting on?"

She blinked. Blinked again. And then hurried over to me. "What. The. Hell. Do. You. Mean. 'This is the spot we 'bout to tear up?!'"

"Girl, let me tell you." I slapped my right hand on my respective hip. "Corey's been lying. Again. And I swear I'm sooooo tired of his lying. It's like he just lives and breathes to lie, lie, lie. So when I texted him and he didn't respond to me for two days. And in that text he had the audacity to say, "I'll be home tomorrow night. Call you then." No 'hey baby.' No, 'I miss you.' Nothing. Just some whack 'I'll call you tomorrow night.' Oh hell no. I wasn't having that. So, I sicced a P.I. on him."

"A what?!"

"A P.I. I had to see what kind of slick-playa-playa moves ole-boy was trying to pull over on me. Besides, you always have to know what your investment is doing. And right now this is a losing quarter for me. So come on, let's go inside and make it pop-pop-get it-get it."

"O.M.G. this is just way too much." She shook her head and tapped her feet. "I don't believe this. When you called me screaming in my ear I didn't know this was the type of pop-pop-get it-get it you were talking about!"

"What, they don't make it pop in New York?" I curled my top lip. "The East Coast needs to get it together. Oh my."

"Rich, I thought we were coming to party, dance a little bit. Get. Our. Drink. On. You didn't tell me that we were coming here to run up on your boyfriend!"

"It's just a layover. We don't have to make this our destination. Trust. This will not take long at all. And right after this we can still get our drink on." I did a quick two-step and a booty bounce. "Ahh, see girl. When we leave here we gon' hit up this spot in Hollywood and bust it. Now come on." I took a step closer to the door and waved at a few cuties eyeing us. London was back on pause. I walked over to her and said tight-lipped, "Would you come on before somebody out here thinks you're slow?"

"Rich!" London called my name like she was crazy. "I'm serious! My daddy will flip. He's already warned me and besides, I didn't come dressed for this! The least you could've done was clue me in from the beginning and then I would've slipped on some jogging pants!"

"Eww." I heaved. "Clutching pearls. Please spare me the jogging pants visual, I have a phobia of those things." I shivered. "Believe me, London, we are not about to get physical. We're ladies, remember? So we'll be out of here and tearing up a whole other club before you can say 'Weezy!'"

Before she could continue with her protest I locked arms with her and practically pulled her into the club. Waka Flocka Flame's "No Hands" blasted through the D.J's speakers. There were people everywhere. Sweating. Throwing their arms in the air and yelling something about the roof being on fire. And all I could think was Cheesytothemax.org.

This little horrid spot was a sea of red, courtesy of the red strobe lights and the naked red bulbs that hung over the dance floor and illuminated the bar. The whole scene reminded me of an indie film gone wrong.

London and I were definitely overdressed and out of place.

"Hey," caught my attention. I looked to my right and there was a gold-mouth freak, standing before me grinning. "Y'all lookin' good."

I rolled my eyes toward the ductwork running through the ceiling. I could spot a wannabe gangsta rapper a mile away. "Ain't you Richard Montgomery's daughter? Yo, can I slide you my mix tape? And after that can I get your phone number? And my man over there was looking at your girl." He turned to London. "He wants to know if you wanna be the bust-it baby in his video?"

Instinctively London and I took two steps back. I frowned. "For real," I said and batted my lashes. "What's good with you? Like why are you in my space? Back up."

"Seriously," London said and looked him over. "'Cause the only thing you need to be mixing is a toothbrush and Colgate—"

"And a Tic and a Tac," I added as I flicked my hand and

London and I walked away quickly before this monster could say anything more.

We walked over toward the bar and I couldn't find Corey anywhere in here.

"Hold Up. Wait a minute," London said as she placed her right hand like a visor over her eyes. "Is that...?" She paused. "Is that...?" She paused again, and said more to herself than she did to me, "...Anderson?"

"Anderson?" I frowned. "Who is Anderson?"

I looked over toward where she pointed and boom, there he was: Corey.

"You mean, Corey?" I said as I stretched my arm toward the dance floor. "Oh hell nawl, I know this mofo is not walking around telling people his name is Anderson! What kind of whack mac-daddy game is that?! Oh I'm pissed. He's walking around calling himself Anderson!"

"Not him." She blinked and pointed both of her index fingers. "The one standing there with a bottle of champagne in his hand and breaking it down like a dog pissing on a fire hydrant!"

"Oh him." I shook my head. I was disgusted watching the dude London pointed to hold his right leg in the air and pump his pelvis into some hoochie's behind like a curbed dog. "His name is not Anderson," I said. "That's Corey's friend C-Smoove. Corey is the one over there shaking his bottle of champagne and doing the white-boy dance."

"I don't believe this," London said.

"Me either," I said as I watched Corey become sandwiched between two chicks. Then he took his bottle of champagne and passed it to the girl dancing in front of him. The girl took a swig and gave it back to him. Corey took a swig and then passed it to the girl behind him.

WTF!

I shook my head. Something told me to roll through there packin'!

"Oh hell nawl!" I spat, coming out of shock. I turned to London. "You see this?!"

"I don't believe Anderson."

"Didn't I just tell you that was C-Smoove!" I said aggravated, stomping my feet. "Would you get the name right!"

London curled her lip. "What the hell is a *C-Smoove*? His name is Anderson!"

"How do you know?" I asked.

"Because that's my boyfriend."

"Dr. Corny? *Whaaaat*?!" I screeched as my eyes popped open wide. "I would've never imagined him being your taste. You just messed me up, girl. Oh my, clutching pearls," I sighed. "Now we gon' have to bust 'em both in the throat!"

London gave me a blank stare.

"Why are you looking at me like that? Didn't you just say that was your boyfriend?"

"Yeah."

"Well we need to be making a move over there." I pointed to the boys. "They're over there poppin' bottles and trickin' up on these girls. Oh hell no. We have to do something about this—"

"Rich—"

"Don't worry, London, we'll still be ladies. And if for any reason we forget our manners then we'll just show up at the Catholic church and make a confession."

"But I'm not Catholic."

"Me either, but that doesn't matter, they'll still see you. Now let's go get 'em!"

"Wait." London pulled me back. "I really can't get into any more trouble, especially not tonight. If I do my black card and trust fund will be on the line."

"So what? We're just going to let them play us?"

"They don't have to play with you." A voice drifted over my shoulder. "But I sure want to."

I gagged. Another gold-mouth creature stepped to us and grinned. London and I eyed this thing so hard that he practically tripped out of our way.

"Now," London continued, as our distraction ran away. "As I was saying, we will keep it cute and keep it calm."

"Always," I agreed. "You know my motto: always be a lady. And that's exactly why I'm going to tap Corey on the shoulder and let him know that I will be politely busting him in the head."

"No you will not," London said sternly. "We will walk over there, tap them on the shoulders, tell them that the car is waiting, and they need to come on. All arguments will be saved for the ride home."

"What?" I shrieked. "Tap them on the shoulders and talk to them? What kind of mess is that?"

"Rich, would you just try it my way? I got this."

I hesitated. "All right," I agreed. "Okay, we'll try it your way."

We strutted across the club and onto the dance floor. I did my all to compose myself and remember London's plan but as this skank placed her hands on the floor and backed it up on my man in front of me, London's plan became a distant memory.

I yanked the girl out of Corey's face and wouldn't you know she shot me a nasty look. I took a step into her personal space and said, "I wish a hood-ho would." I looked her over. "Now lose yourself!" I pointed to the girl dancing with C-Smoove a.k.a. Anderson and said, "And take that floozie with you!" The girls sucked their teeth and scurried away.

I bucked my eyes at Corey. "Umm, we won't even discuss why you had a set of walking STDs in your face. But what we will discuss is why haven't I heard from you, Corey?"

He hesitated and then he said, "I just flew in tonight."

"And what's your excuse, Anderson?" London snapped.

Don't you know this clown C-Smoove twisted his lips and said, "I don't have an excuse, I just didn't call you."

Freeze…What did he just say?

London gasped and for a moment I thought about chin-checking this puppy real quick, but I didn't. I turned my attention back to Corey and he continued on with his lies. "Yeah, I got back tonight. An hour ago and then I came here to chill with my boy."

This is some straight up bull! "Corey," I said. "Corey, look at me, Coreeeee. Look. At. Meeeeee." I shook my head with every word. "Now what are you lying for, Corey?"

"Lying?" He looked pissed.

"Yeah, lies. Coreeeee. 'Cause I know and you know that you may have arrived at night, but it was last night. 10:07 last night. And then you pulled into your circular driveway at 10:47. You were in bed Coreeeee by midnight. And even though you didn't come to school you were up this morning by 8:03 A.M. Then you headed to the gym. And by one o'clock you were taking a nap. An hour later you were having tea with your mother, then you had a dip in the pool, and all of this was done by 3:15 in the afternoon. And not once did my phone ring because I was receiving a call from you!"

"Rich—"

I wagged my finger. "Don't interrupt me. 'Cause you and your boy, C-Smoove, or is it Anderson, tried to play me and my girl over here, and we won't be having it. You hear me, Coreeeee?"

Corey stood quiet and I could imagine that thoughts of losing me floated through his mind and had him speechless. I knew he was set to give me an apology and for a moment I thought about not accepting it. But then I decided that two wrongs didn't make a right, so I would forgive him, this time. Especially since this whole fiasco had to be an oversight on his part. But that was cool, too, because now I knew what I needed to focus my future-husband's training on.

I looked him in his eyes and just as I cocked my neck and prepared for him to beg my pardon he chuckled and said, "You effen crazy."

Pow!

Bang!

Bang!

Was I shot?

Did somebody just shoot me with a stun gun?

I looked over at London and she was still speechless. "Umm, Earth to London." I waved my hand in her face. "Don't you have something to say? Cute and calm was your idea."

London picked up her bottom lip and said, "What did you just say to me, Anderson?"

Anderson looked at London, frowned, and then took two tiny steps back as if her breath stank.

Oh he needs to be cut. I can't believe she doesn't have him in check.

Anderson carried on, "London, don't even look to get crunked over here."

"Spell crunked, Anderson," she snapped. "Now, as I was saying, I don't appreciate having to call you—"

"Don't call me!" Anderson spat and if looks could kill he would've murdered London with a double-barrel shotgun. "Don't call Anderson," his words slurred. "You ain't called Anderson all week and now you wanna run up on C-Smooth. I mean C-Smoove." He took a swig of his champagne bottle and wiped the excess from his lips.

Ill.

"Psst, please, I'm not having it," he carried on.

"Don't try to show off!" London said.

"Show off?" Anderson took another swig. "I'm not showing off, you *know* I haven't heard from you in a damn week. I'd been calling you and what did you do? You sent me to voice mail, 'Hello this is London, leave a message at the beep.' Beeep. Well here's the message, London. You and your psycho homegirl take your Jimmy Choos and step!"

"Yeah, beat it," Corey said to me as he and Anderson turned away from us, grabbed two new girls, and resumed dancing.

I couldn't believe this. I could've sworn that I was supposed to die before I went to hell, yet here I stood, six-inch-stilettos deep. I looked at London and said, "I thought you had the master plan? Now had we gone along with my plan and busted them in the head, they wouldn't have been able to sing all that yang. They'd be on the floor. Bleeding."

London blinked. And I didn't know if she was in disbelief or wanted this whole night to disappear. But whatever. I couldn't worry about that. I just knew that the night couldn't end like this. I looked at London and said, "You might wanna be at Burger King trying to have it your way, but they just played us like the dollar menu. Now what's next? Are we still going to keep it calm and keep it cute?"

"Yes." London drank in a deep breath. "Now follow me."

I complied and walked alongside of her as she went up behind C-Smoove and tapped him on the shoulder. He turned around, sucked his teeth, looked London over and said, "You still sweatin'—?"

Wham!

Bam!

Boom! A slap to the right cheek followed up by socking it to the left. London reached back and slapped C-Smoove so hard that spit sprung from his mouth and he stumbled two steps back, knocking the girl behind him to the floor.

I couldn't help but smile because that was all I needed. "Excuse me, Corey." I tapped him on the shoulder. He turned around. And as he twisted his lips to say something, I reared my hand back and took it to his gut! Corey's champagne bottle crashed to the floor and made a zigzag trail as it rolled away and he dropped like a stone.

Pow!

Code ten!

Man down!

And just as we saw security approaching, we tucked our clutches securely beneath our arms and strutted outside to where the driver waited.

London looked at me and said, "Here's my friend's number. Call him." She handed me a shiny business card with
the name Justice embossed. I ran my fingers across the
name and said, "Maybe I'll call him."

We eased into the car and as the driver pulled off leaving Club Sixty-Six Paradise in the distance, London filled
two flutes with champagne, handed me one, and said,
"Here's to keeping it cute."

"Amen." I batted my eyes and clinked her glass. "Next
stop Hollywood!"

11

Heather

A week later

The sun-dyed streaks in my chestnut hair dazzled in the window's reflection as I sat in the back of my British literature class. My eyes half-mast. Shoulders slumped. And the tips of my fingernails bitten into sore and jagged pieces.

I couldn't concentrate.

I couldn't think straight.

And the last thing I wanted to hear was Mr. Hammond pour his heart into a Shakespearean soliloquy, because at this moment suicidal Romeo and Juliet couldn't do a thing for me.

I didn't need medieval literature in my life. I needed New Millennium advice on how to shake whatever had my stomach cramping. And how to stop the sweats that made me feel as if I should've worn a bikini; or quench the dry mouth that made me thirst for a gallon of water. And I needed to know how to stop this eerie voice that eased over my shoulders and whispered faintly in my ears, "You need a hit." That's what I needed. Not this!

Ugh!

There was no way I could stay in here much longer.

I had to leave. I had to.

I'd already proven that I wasn't a junkie and could stop anytime I wanted to. So one hit to help me get my Wu-Wu back was nothing. It didn't matter that I'd been snorting Adderall—twice a day—for the last year, what mattered was that I had control over it. Adderall was like... like... my assistant. It helped me focus. Kept my lines together. Kept the stress of dealing with Camille and fronting for the Pampered Princesses at bay. Adderall was my ride or die. We understood each other. And it wasn't about chasing that first high. It had nothing to do with me needing more and more pills to maintain. It was about being sane. Because without Adderall to maintain it was only a matter of time before I lost my mind!

"He never wanted you... You were a mistake... I was supposed to abort you... He never wanted you... He knows about you... It's Richard... It's Richard..." Shaking Camille's voice from my head I turned to the left of me and there was Rich Montgomery, sitting there.

I wondered....

It's Richard....

No....

It's Richard...

No it couldn't be....

It's Richard....

I continued to stare at Rich until she looked over at me and frowned.

He already has a daughter....
I gotta get out of here.

Just as I slid my book into my backpack to bolt out of there, my phone vibrated. It was a text from my agent returning my call from this morning.

Finally.

I'd only been trying to reach her since last night.

I slung my backpack over my right shoulder and strutted out of the classroom unapologetically. And I didn't care if Mr. Hammond gawked. Given the way I felt, I would've smacked him.

My heels pumped out an angry drumbeat as I walked into the girls' lounge, quickly locked the door, and then hid in the last stall. I dialed my agent's number and screamed at the top of my lungs, "WHERE IN THE HELL HAVE YOU BEEN?!"

"Heather—"

"Don't Heather me, Diana! You work for me and you better remember that, so I don't expect to have to wait six minutes let alone six hours to hear back from you!"

"Heather, you called me at two o'clock this morning. I'm just seeing your text. I'm truly sorry."

"And that you are!" Sweat poured over my brow.

"Heather," she said, her voice making evident that she would be attempting to pacify me. "Just breathe and tell me what's wrong."

"What's wrong? What's wrong? I have a laundry list of things that are wrong! Camille waking up every day is problem number one. Problem number two are these shallow, superficial, money-controlled chicks that I'm forced to be friends with—"

"That's for your image."

"I don't care about my image anymore!"

Diana sighed. "Heather. Relax, please. I am working with Camille on her drinking. I am doing all that I can to get you on another show. A fresh start. A chance to show-case your true talents. All you need is to give me some time and it will all come together."

"When?!"

"Soon, dear, soon. And by the way have you taken a pill today?"

"No!"

"Well then you need one, maybe two."

"Don't tell me what I need."

"I just want you to be stress-free. And let me worry about your next move. And as far as the Pampered Princesses, just act as if they're family and all will be well."

Click.

I hung up on her! I simply couldn't take it anymore.

You need a hit....

"Shut up!" I kicked the locked door. I could feel water building in the back of my mouth and my stomach bubbling all over again.

Just one hit...

That's it...

Screw it. I sat down on the closed lid of the toilet and opened my bag. Then I quickly closed it.

My goal was seven days—pill-free.

I had two more to go and then I wouldn't have a doubt that I wasn't a junkie.

I stood up, unlocked the stall, and quickly walked to-ward the door. I unlocked the door and as I placed one foot on the other side I quickly pulled it back in, closed the door, and leaned against the back of it.

One hit. That's it.

I ran back into the last stall, locked it, and laid a dollar bill on the lid of the toilet. I placed two Black Beauties in it, wrapped the bill around it, and pounded the dollar bill with my fist. Two seconds later I opened it and snorted a breath of fresh air.

I lay back on the toilet and just as the golden gates of Heaven opened up and welcomed me in, the rushing sounds of footsteps bolted into the bathroom.

Didn't I lock the door?

My heart thundered as I climbed into a tight and still fetal position on top of the cold toilet lid. It was a good thing I was 5'2" or this would definitely be a problem.

Two sets of feet walked back and forth: one dressed in pink ostrich six-inch heels and the other in Marc Jacobs sneakers.

"Wait! Wait!" said a female voice belonging to a set of the unwelcome footsteps. "We have to make sure there's no one else in here."

Who is that? Is that . . . no that's not . . .

"Come on, baby," a familiar male voice said. "It's nobody in here. You don't have to check in every stall."

"But Corey, we have to make sure the Coast Guard is clear."

Corey? Rich's boyfriend, Corey?

"It's all good, baby. Trust me."

OMG, that is Corey!

"Are you sure?" the female voice whined and all I could think was, *I know for sure that ain't Rich. And I know that can't be Spencer. . . .*

"Come over here and let me show you how sure I am," Corey growled.

It took everything in me not to squeal in laughter.

After a moment of silence the couple was going hot and heavy, panting and kissing. I knew I needed to lie perfectly still but I had to confirm this creeping couple. I eased as quietly as I could off of the toilet and peeked under the door.

And...I...almost...died....

Straight flatlined....

Look at what we have here...Legally blond by morning and sex kitten by lunchtime: Spencer, and Rich's boyfriend.

Damn!

I took my phone from my purse, pressed record, and happily watched Corey's belt buckle hit the floor and his jeans fall to his ankles all while Rich's good friend Spencer dropped to her knees.

Ahhh...payback.

12

Rich

I slid the canary-diamond heart-pendant on my Tiffany necklace back and forth as I stared off into the distance. I hated that at the very moments I should've thought about where Corey was and why I hadn't heard from him, yet again, that Knox rocked my brain cells.

Me avoiding Knox since the Fourth of July weekend was intentional and not happenstance. So why my mind couldn't swing with that was beyond me. Instead, Knox ruled my thoughts and completely wrecked my flow.

Seriously, this was a situation that I was in and I didn't have time for distractions. Corey—who'd called me all week, begged for my forgiveness relentlessly, and promised me during our creep-creep pillow talk two nights ago that he would get his priorities in order and make me his number one—had pulled the infamous whooptie-wam on me and suddenly stopped returning my texts.

Like really?

Really?

Clearly, he had me confused. 'Cause now my level of pisstivity had risen from a simple slap-your-face-crunked-ten to a gut-punched-nunchucked-twenty.

And there you have it.

I was too through. How dare he ignore my texts since yesterday afternoon! And so what if I texted him a hundred and twenty-five times...okay a hundred and twenty-nine times, but so what. All he needed to do was respond to one. But instead I got nothing.

That just simply wasn't acceptable.

No way.

No how.

And it's not that I was so in love with Corey that I couldn't fathom not being with him. I mean he was fine but my mirror confirmed that I was much prettier. And it's not that Corey had my nose open or I was so caught up that I couldn't see the forest for the trees—the hoes for the stroll. I wasn't in love or in stupid. Psst, please. Spare me.

I knew Corey was a pimp. Ah duh, it was obvious. And that's exactly why my plan was to dump him. Can him. Say bye-bye, boo. But first I had to get him and *keep* him where I wanted him: sweatin' me. Dying to have me. Swearing that his life couldn't go on without me, and then I could dump him.

Boom!

After all, relationships weren't about love, they were about financial growth, potential assets. And being that last week his father's company was accused of allegedly running sweatshops in Guatemala, which caused their stocks to tank, ole boy had to get the boot. Problem was he didn't behave long enough for me to not only dump him but to

be certain that he would have a nervous breakdown behind it.

Life sucks.

"Hey, doll," London said as she walked over to our center table and air-kissed me. She flopped down in the pink
leather chair and said, "And why weren't you waiting for
me at your locker?"

"Girl," I said with a drag. "It completely slipped my
mind."

"How could something that we do every day slip your
mind? What's really the problem?" she asked, her New
York accent making her sound as if she had a head cold.

I rolled my eyes toward the heavens. "What do think is
the problem or *who* is the problem, I should say."

"Corey?" She frowned.

"Umm hmm. He's ignoring all my texts. Won't answer
my calls or anything. I'm soooo sick of this."

London rolled her eyes. "I wish you would just dismiss
him already, like seriously he is such a douche bag."

"Eww . . ." I curled my lip and crossed my legs. Sometimes when London opened her mouth there was no
telling what kind of gutter trash was bound to come out.
"Douche bag? That is so unladylike." I picked up my chop-
sticks and dipped my spicy tuna sushi into wasabi and soy
sauce.

"No, unladylike is you allowing Soulja Boy to play you.
You deserve better than that."

I blinked. Blinked again. Apparently she had me confused, too. "Of course I do. I know that. But first I have to
make sure he worships the royal ground I walk on before
I dump him. I need to make sure he is officially sweatin'
me. And when I know that he loves me enough to walk

the plank after I dismiss him, I will send him a text and tell him to never call me again."

London side eyed me and said, "Blank stare."

"Whatever." I waved my hand dismissively as we ate our lunch of varying rolls of sushi. "Anyway, did you peep the new embroidered and signature Louis boots?" I asked, excited.

"Straight sick."

"Cancerous. Meow! Snap. Snap. Oh, yes. And there are only two hundred in the world."

"Ohmygod," London said in a panic and reached for her phone. "I need to reserve mine. I have to call my—"

"Girl, put that phone down, you know I got you, boo. I had my stylist order four pairs. Two pairs for me and two pairs for you. A size nine, right?"

"Yup."

"They will be here in two weeks, just in time for us to shut Hollywood High down, again."

London and I cracked up and in the middle of us sweatin' ourselves and squealing about the perks of being born fly, Spencer cut across our conversation with a yay-wide smile and an extremely loud, "Hey girls!"

"And where have you been?" I looked at my watch. "Last I checked lunch started twenty minutes ago."

"Did it really?" She batted her lashes. "And did you count those minutes all by yourself, Rich? Or did you and Miss Upper East Side make that a joint effort?"

Did she just get nasty?

London looked at me and her eyes seemed to be asking the same thing. Before I could decide if I should let Spencer's remark slide she pointed to the chair where Heather usually sat and asked, "Where's Heather?"

London frowned. "Last I checked I wasn't her keeper."

"Ding dong the witch is dead. You're so bright, London. Not." Spencer shook her curls. "Stevie Wonder can see that you're not a keeper. This isn't a zoo. Although with the way you carry on, I most definitely understand the confusion."

I didn't mean to make a sound, but somehow "Meow" slipped out.

Spencer snatched her head toward me and then parked her neck at an angle. "Didn't I just tell Miss High Society, Miss Upper East Side, that this wasn't a zoo? Or did that go underneath your skirt, Rich? Over there making animal sounds. Jesus, Mary, and Jaheem."

Screech...now there was no question about it, this bimbo was straight bringing it to me.

"You have two choices," I said to Spencer, coldly with ease. "Either shut the hell up or buck."

Spencer looked at me confused. "Can you translate that? My ghetto is so rusty."

Ghetto? Oh those are fighting words....

I tucked my hair behind my ears, slid my diamond hoops off, and sat my Swarovski crystal-covered jar of Vaseline on the table. "Make a move."

"Rich," London called me.

"Don't worry. I'ma keep it calm and keep it cute."

"Rich," London snapped. "Forget the queen of classified." She pointed across the room to the athletes' table. " 'Cause look who I just found. Seems someone just walked right off the milk carton and into the café."

I followed London's finger and there he was: Corey. He took a seat and immediately started kicking it with his boys. I inched to the edge of my seat and, before I could get up, London said, "Don't do it, girl."

I paused and as I mulled over her advice Spencer took a bite into her sandwich, looked at me, and giggled.

What the hell...?

I waved her off and refocused my attention on Corey. "Text him now," London said. "And let's see what he does."

I frowned. It was one thing to play desperate when no one was looking but to be caught out there like this—in front of my friends—was something completely different.

"Text him," London repeated.

Reluctantly I texted him.

"Let's hope he responds this time," London said as she pulled out her mother-of-pearl opera binoculars and peered through them. "I need to see this up close."

A few seconds later London gasped, "That no good mother—"

"What?!" I snatched the binoculars from her hand and looked through them. "Did he...oh no he didn't...." I watched Corey frown as he slid his phone back into his pocket.

I couldn't believe this. Oh, he had to pay. "I'll be right back," I said and stood up.

"Rich!" London called.

"Don't worry, I'll be a lady."

I clicked my way over to Corey's table, slammed my hands on my hips, and as his entire table became quiet and all eyes were on me, I said, "Yeah, umm hmm, Coreeee, you didn't expect to see me did you? Oh this is how you want to boom-bop-drop-it, Corey Othello Marshall the Fifth?"

Corey looked at me and frowned. He hated when I called him by his whole name.

"Now," I said, "I need to have a word with you."

"You better go on, Coreeeeee," one of Corey's teammates said, mocking me. "Or her royal highness is gon' lash you!" And although I didn't think the remark was funny Corey's whole table laughed, except Corey. He simply snickered.

I was three seconds from settin' it off. L.A.-style.

I took a deep breath and said, "Corey, did you hear me?"

"I heard you," he said pissed. "Now what you want and make it quick."

Screech! Rewind. "I don't know what you think this is, or why you think you can show off in front of your friends, but I don't appreciate me texting you and you not responding!"

"I didn't get 'em," he said nonchalantly. "I don't know what you're talking about."

Oh...my...God...It took everything in me not to scream, "Off with his head!" Instead I said, "Corey. Corey. Look at me, Corey. Here you go lying again. I can't do this with you."

"Did you just say I was lying?"

"Yes, lying. Because just three minutes and twenty-five seconds ago I watched you through London's binoculars pull out your phone, look at my text, and ignore me!"

"Binoculars!" he screamed. "Yo, you real crazy. Straight buggin'. And when you start blowin' my phone up like that I'm not going to answer."

"And why is that?"

"Because you be on some bs. And I ain't beat for hearing your lips yappin'. Now go on and go back to your table. I'll call you and kick it to you later."

Pause. *What?* Blink. Blink. What just happened here? What did he just say to me? I turned around toward London, who was still sitting at our table in the center of the room, and motioned my index finger for her to come near.

It took her two-point-five seconds to scurry her heels over to me. She instantly took position beside me, looked Corey over and said, "Is there a problem over here?"

Corey eyed London as his phone buzzed, signaling that he had a text. "Nah," he said reading his screen and smiling. "Ain't no problem. I need to get this. Now go sit down, Rich. And like I said, I'll hollah at you later." He spun off, leaving the sound of his rubber soles screeching behind him. I couldn't believe this.

London and I stood silent for a few seconds, eyeballing the space where Corey once stood. I swear I didn't know what to do.

Should I stand here or should I run away?

I looked around the café and spotted Co-Co Ming snapping pictures and waving. I turned back toward the athletes' table and they were all stretched out in laughter. I wanted nothing more than to bolt out of here. But I had to play this carefully or my entire reputation would go up in scorned woman flames. So I looked at London and with nothing else to say, we locked arms and sashayed back to our table, while I did everything I could to keep my knees from buckling.

13

Spencer

"Spencer, wait up, boo," I heard in back of me as I was making my way out the door into the gleaming California sun. My heels clicked excitedly against the cobblestone pavement. The only thing I wanted to do was get home—oh, yes, home, where it was all about the zip code, *not* the area code—and wait for Corey to call me so we could pick up where we'd left off this morning in the bathroom. But this time with him sprawled out in the middle of my bed. Mmmph, he was finger-licking good, right down to the last drop! And I wanted me another taste of all his sweet, gooey goodness.

I glanced over my shoulder, and smiled. It was Heather. I stopped and waited for her to catch up to me. "Heeeey, Diva. Where've you been all day?" I said as we air-kissed. "You didn't even come down for lunch. And you know Rich and her pet silverback were trying to get it snapcrackling."

She rolled her eyes, pulling her Chanels down over her

eyes. "Sugar Snaps, both of them ho-rags can bite me. I had more important things to do than looking up in their whore-painted faces today. So how was *your* day? You seem to be glowing. Did you use a new face cream or something?"

"Oh, my day was just peaches and cream, boo. And no, I didn't use any new face cream today."

She smirked. "Oh. Well, knowing you, I bet it was filled with more *cream* than peaches."

I tilted my head. "What was filled with more cream than peaches?"

"Your day, sweetness."

I giggled. "Ooooh, you know me so well."

"Oh, trust me. I sure do, boo. I got your number."

Now, Heather's a dang liar! And how was I supposed to trust a liar, a broke one at that. She didn't know Jack-in-the-Box about me. Truth is, none of them cluckeroos did. Yeah, they thought I was some dumb blonde. Like, really. I don't even have blond hair. So how ridiculous was that? Still, I wasn't as clueless and airheaded as I seemed. I mean, really. Who cares about whether or not your elevator is going up to the top floor; or if someone doesn't have the brightest lightbulb in their socket? I know I don't care about stuff like that.

I waved her on. "Of course you have my number, silly. It comes up on your caller ID every time I call or text you."

Heather turned and looked at me, not saying a word. Behind her shades, I could see her eyes rapidly blinking as if she had dust in them. *Her contacts must be drying out.* She sighed. "You wanna hang out later?"

"I can't. I have something to do tonight."

"Like what?"

Tying Corey's hands and feet to my bedpost, then...
mmmph!

A chill of anticipation crept down my spine. Oh, I know sleeping with Rich's so-called man and doing all the little freaky things we did behind her back was messy and deliciously scandalous. Oh, well. It was a nasty job. But someone had to get down on her knees and do it. And it might as well have been a friend of hers. Keep it in the clique. After all, that's what friends are for. Besides, Rich ran through boyfriends like she did stop signs, at least two every three months. So taking her imaginary future hubby-boo was like snatching bananas from a baby chimp. Easy as one, two...have your man doing things he thought he'd never do; three, four...when I'm done with him, he won't be your man no more! Heheheheee.

Oh sure, Rich would probably have one of her full-blown hissy fits. Or even better, a mini nervous breakdown, like the one she had last year after she caught one of her many exes steam-pumping his hips into the heiress of a Fortune 500 company in a chalet at Ski Dubai. Oh, how delish it would be seeing Rich hauled off in a strait-jacket, being locked away in a padded room at some god-awful nut farm. I savored the thought. And, baby, Corey Lebron Richardson—or whatever his real name was—with all of his delicious swag juice—was worth the blowout. Like I said, *I* was the Ace of Spades of messy. And pushing Princess Pikachu down into her own trash bag is what I lived for. Because *that* was exactly what she was—hot gutter trash.

I looped my arms through Heather's as we walked. "I have a few projects to do. And like a ton of homework."

"Boooooring," she said, holding the back of her hand

to her forehead. "Ditch the homework, boo. And let's do drinks." I spotted her driver as he made his way around the winding road in their 2008 limo. *Oh, dear. How late model is that? They can't even afford an upgrade.*

"Let's hold the umbrellas for a rain check, okay?"

She sighed. "Umm, knock-knock, boo. They don't use umbrellas for rain checks."

I flicked my diamond-covered wrist. "Well, I do. Anyway, you missed the featured attraction today at lunch."

She raised her arched brow. "Oh, really?"

I nodded. "Yup. And it wasn't even listed on today's menu selection. Rich got her face crunched out in the café by Corey. Right in front of all his boys, he played her like the skid row trash she is."

"Do you mean cracked? Like in, her face was cracked?"

I tossed my hair to the side, letting out an exasperated sigh. I hated when they did that. Corrected me as if I didn't know what I was saying. Geesh, I'm not stupid. "Yeah, it was cracked, too, especially after he walked off, leaving her standing there looking like a raggedy-old dust rag. The whole table was laughing at her, snapping pictures and sending texts around the school. Poor thing had to call London over for backup to help her pick all the pieces of her face up."

Heather glanced around the campus, pulling out her phone as it chimed. A grin slid across her face as she read a text. I tried my darnedest to cut my eyes over at the screen to see who the text was from, but she quickly dropped her phone back into her bag. "I'm sure the look on her face must have been priceless."

"Oh, it sure was. And you missed it."

I handed the valet attendant my ticket as Heather

pulled her shades up over her head, cupping a hand over her eyes like a visor. "Boo, you better get your popcorn, get your Twizzlers, get your Sour Patch Kids, and a tall, cold drink, 'cause it looks to me like the real show is about to begin any minute. And I'm gonna have me a front row seat. I love it."

"What show are you talking about?"

"The 'Let's Make Up and Grind' show."

I frowned. "The what show? Is that something new coming on one of the prime-time networks?"

"No," she said, pointing. "It's Rich and Corey over there by the gazebo, lip-locking it up."

"Whaat?!" I lifted my shades, following the direction of her finger.

I squinted.

When my eyes zeroed in on the scene before me, I gasped. Did everything I could do to keep my ankles from snapping in half, and toppling over in my heels.

I blinked as my mouth dropped open. *That lowdown, dirty, no-good, slobbery, lying pound puppy told me he was going to drop that Chipette today. And the only thing he's over there dropping is his spit and tongue all down in her throat!*

Heather stepped off the curb as her driver opened the car door. She slid into the backseat, then rolled her window down when the driver shut her door. "Hey, Spencer, pick your face up, boo."

"Unh."

"Your face, sweetie, pick it up." She snapped a picture of me, smirking as she rolled up her window and the driver drove off.

I stood there shocked. Corey had his six-foot frame

pressed up against Rich's big ole nasty buffalo-booty with his arms wrapped around her waist. She backed it up on his crotch, bent over, then grabbed her ankles. *Nasty ho!* I kept my eyes on them, fuming as she turned to face him. I watched as she put her arms up around his neck. Then they kissed as he snaked his big, strong, basketball-playing hands down around her waist. They dropped down on her dimpled skank-a-dank. *Ohmygod, I'm gonna be sick! He was supposed to dump that oversized crack baby! Not do her! How dare he play me like this!*

"Hello? Hello? Earth to the wannabe bad girl," I heard someone saying. But I was too stuck on stunned to know who it was. A finger snapped in my face. Then snapped again, finally bringing me out of my fog.

"What?" I asked, blinking. It was London. She was standing in front of me with a smirk on her shiny, painted lips. I glanced down at the Kroell crystal clutch she held in her hand, then back up into her mink-lashed eyes. *She's probably bald-eyed; always wearing fake lashes!*

"You're holding up the line." She paused, raising her clutch up to her chest. "Oh, my...Rich wasn't exaggerating when she said you tear up all of your cars. The side of your car is all banged up. How in the world did they even give you a license?"

I frowned. Right now was not the time for her to try to get it funked up with me. I was already pissed. And I was not in the mood for any of her trick-box snobbery. "Excuse you? The same way they gave you that happy-snappy clown face you wear, that's how."

"Girlie, don't do it. I will beat you down in a New York minute."

I scrunched my nose up at her, then went...off! "You

know, London. Your breath smells like hot dog poop. Get over yourself and go brush your gums. I don't know how you trick-a-boos do it over on the East Coast, but you're in Hollywood now. And I don't give a hot damn about you or your New York minutes. The last thing I'm gonna do is let some uppity chicken ruffle my skirt. Oh, no, boo. You can go cluck yourself right on back in your coop."

She gave me a blank look as if I said something that didn't make any sense to her. "Listen, girlie. I don't know what your problem is with me, but I'm not in the mood. And I'm not the one."

"You must have cracked your coconut if you think I'm going to let you be all up in my cake mix. I'm not the two, three, or four, okay. But if you think I'm gonna let you come out of your fly trap and disrespect me you have another thing coming, *Miss New York*. Don't even know where the hell you're at. You're on the West Coast, you dumb bunny. Ever since Rich introduced us, you've done nothing but look down your nose at me. And turn your broke nose up at Heather. And I do mean *broke*, like snap, crackle, pop, broken-glass broke." I swung open my car door, sliding behind the wheel. I slammed the door. "Get your billions up before you come stepping to me, millionaire. Miss Low Money."

She opened her mouth to say something, but I cut her off. "Now open your mouth, and suck on my exhaust fumes, you poor gutter rat!" I pressed down on the gas and zoomed off, flying past Rich and Corey. I sideswiped two cars as I flew around the winding road. "Get the hell out of my way!" I yelled at the parked cars. I wanted to get as far the hell away as I could from Hollywood High, that pauper London, and any ugly memory of Rich and that dirty, two-timing Corey licking and lapping it up.

"I'm gonna light your fire, Corey Richardson, or Corey Othello Marshall!" I screamed as the speedometer-thingy shot up to eighty. The wheels of my Benz slid back and forth over the curvy road. "I'm gonna tear your boxers down for the world to see, you no-good, dirty weasel! And when I'm done with you, you're gonna wish your burnt butt never laid up on that grill!"

Somehow I lost control of the wheel. I slammed on the brakes. *SCREETCH!* My car flipped up in the air. *BOOM!* It landed on the roof. And I was upside down, screaming at the top of my lungs.

"Aaaaaaaaaaaaaaaaaaaaah!!!!"

14

London

*W*aaaaaaaaait *a minute! Reeeeeeeeeewiiiiiiind.* Hold the hell up! Did that hussy straight diss me? I looked around and all that was left of Spencer was the smell of burning rubber and smoke.

I kept myself composed as I waited for the valet attendant to bring my car around. Poised and camera-ready, of course. Just in case someone felt the urge to take a photo. *How dare that self-righteous skank call me broke!* My mother was worth over seventeen million alone. And Daddy was worth close to four hundred million. That was surely nothing to sneeze at. But Spencer practically pissed on it. And what made things worse is that I could've sworn I heard people snickering in back of me. I started to turn around and give it to anyone I saw with a simple smile across their inflated lips. And when I was done with them I'd slap Spencer into having common sense, because apparently for her to come at me crazy—the little I thought she had didn't exist. *But Daddy said I had to get along*

*with her and that I couldn't get into any more trouble,
but umm, hear this, if she says anything else slick that
chick has a stomp-out coming to her real soon. I mean
that!*

The valet attendant pulled up beside me, stepping out
of my car. He held the door for me, then closed it once I
slid in behind the wheel. I tossed him a twenty, then
pulled off, catching this couple going at it like wild sex
beasts over by one of the gazebos.

I slow-rolled by so I could get my nosey on. I blinked.
Wait. Is that Rich? Ohhhhhhhhhmygod, she was practically sucking Corey's face off! *What a damn trick! They
need a short-stay, and fast!* I sped off, disgusted. There
were two things money couldn't buy: class and common
damn sense. And sometimes, it appeared Rich was lacking
in both.

Halfway down the long winding road, I spotted tire
tracks stretching across the road. There was a tire and the
bumper of a car in the middle of the road. It looked as if
there had been an accident. Again, being nosey, I slowed
down, then stopped the car, getting out. I walked toward
the edge of the road and looked down. *Ohhhhhhhmygod,
it's an accident! Who was the stupid fool driving that
car? And how in the world did it end up on this side of
the road?*

I didn't immediately recognize the car. But when I
heard a female's voice screaming for help, I knew right
then who the car belonged to. I ran back over to my car
and pulled out my cell, calling Rich.

"Yesssssss, London. Is this an emergency? 'Cause if not,
you're straight boom-wrecking my flow."

I frowned. "Your friend . . . is down in the ditch. And you

better come down here to get her because I'm not breaking a nail to do it."

"*Whaaat?* Who are you talking about?"

"I'm talking about your girl Spencer. You know. The one who called me broke and told me to suck on her exhaust fumes. That's who I'm talking about. Her car is flipped upside down."

"She did what? She called you what, broke? Oh, no. Those are fighting words, girl. I wish a mofo would call me broke. Oh, no. She gotta get done in the dark for that. I'm sorry, that's a back-alley whooping for sure. Broke? Oh, she cursed you, boo. She tore her drawers all the way off with that one. That's when I have to drop all my ladylike manners. And bring it to her head. What you wanna do? Make an appointment to drag her? 'Cause I'm free next Tuesday at seven. And we can do her in, girl. 'Cause she done went too damn far this time, calling you broke."

"Appointment? Are you serious?"

"Yeah, girl. I'm busy. I have my stylist coming. I gotta get my hair done. Nails gotta get done. I have a lot going on."

I huffed. "Rich? Rich? Can you please shut the hell up for one minute?" I paused, pressing my forehead with the tip of my fingers. A headache was starting to pound its way to the front of my head. "You know what. Forget it. I don't even like the girl. And the girl doesn't like me. So if I don't ever have to deal with her again, I'm cool with it. So I'ma let her stay right here where she belongs, stuck in the damn mud. I'm out."

In the background I could hear Corey asking, "What happened to Spencer? Is she okay?"

"Oh my, boo is so sweet. He's all concerned."

I rolled my eyes. "Um...riddle me this: why the hell are

you with that snake? Didn't he just play you in the cafeteria today? And the other night at the club? We need to have a real heart-to-heart, fast."

Rich sighed. "You wouldn't understand. But, it's not what you think."

"Well since it's not what I think, then what you need to do is hurry up and get down here and see about this upside-down trick because I'm about to leave her here."

"Girl, then leave. Shoot. Nobody has time to be playing around with Spencer. She came at you sideways, so go. She's had an attitude all day, like she had hair on her chest. Even in the cafeteria she was trying to bring it-bring it. Where's Heather? Aren't they let-me-mace-you-and-get-over-it-the-next-day type of buddies? Let her save her."

"Rich, you know what? It doesn't even matter. I don't know what they are. And I don't. Care."

"I already told you to leave her in the ditch then, and call nine-one-one when you get home. 'Cause right now I'm about to get-it, get-it with my boo."

"Nah, we need to see about Spencer, babe," I heard Corey tell her.

"What?" Rich snapped in my ear, going off on him. "Go see about her? You must have banged your head. I don't think so. And then she called London *broke*. Oh, no. She's going to wear that. And the last thing you need to be concerned about is Spencer or any other ho down in some ditch, unless you're trying to get in the mud with her. She could be stuck in damn quicksand for all I care. You just told me, it was all about me and you. So why the hell are you standing here wanting to go help Spencer? Back it up, back it up...explain that. London..." I sighed, letting her rant. "I think you're going to need to come back up here to hold my clutch, 'cause I'm about to forget I'm a lady and set it off on this mofo."

I pulled the phone away from my ear and put them on speaker, listening to them go at it. How sickening!

"Now c'mon, baby. Why you tryna fight when we just finished making up? You know it's all about you. But I'm sayin'..."

"Oh, what you sayin', Corey? What you saying, Coreeeeeeeey? 'Cause all I hear is a bunch of yip-yap about you worrying about some other trick. As far as I'm concerned the word *she* should never part your lips in front of me."

"Go 'head with that. I'm not worried about no other trick. Spencer's supposed to be your girl, so you say. Yo, I'm only telling you the right thing to do. I don't really care what you do. You makin' a big deal out of nothing. You wanna leave her down there, then leave her. Something happens to her that's on you. I'm outta here."

I rolled my eyes. *Good riddance. He is such a damn loser!*

"Whatever, Corey. Oh, you wanna leave now? Oh, really? Is that what you really wanna do? Then go. Run along like you always do. Always running off somewhere. You make me sick with that!"

I screamed into the phone, "Rich, will you shut the hell up and stop sweating him! If he wants to go, then let him! I'm sick of this back and forth. The dude is no. Damn. Good."

"Slow down, London. You pushing it too far, boo. Maybe you don't believe in second chances, but I do."

"Well, he's had about three chances that I know of, but who's counting. So do you, sweetie. But anyway, why are we arguing about him? Bottom line, what the hell do you want to do about this chick down in this muddy hole? Because I am not about to play "Save a Ho Who Can't Drive," not today, boo!"

"Wait a minute, London. Stay put. I'm on my way to assess the situation. Don't leave until I get there."

"Well, hurry up 'cause this whole scene is boring me." I disconnected, tossing my phone back into my bag.

The whole time this was going on Spencer was groaning and yelling for someone to help her. I walked back over to the edge of the ditch and yelled, "Speeeeeeeeeeeeeeencer, are you still there? Or are you dead yet?"

She moaned.

I rolled my eyes.

I looked in back of me and saw Rich speeding up. She slammed on her brakes, stopping in back of my car. I was too damn through when I saw Corey hopping out of the passenger side of her Bugatti.

"Ohhhhhmygod!" Rich snapped, running up toward the edge of the road. "Clutching pearls. Girl, you didn't tell me this was newsworthy. How do I look?" She blew her breath in my face. "How's my breath? You didn't call the paparazzi yet, did you?"

I frowned. "No, I didn't call them. I don't do that."

"Good, girl. I'ma text my publicist the scoop right now. This way we have time to get down—"

She stopped in midsentence when we heard Spencer screaming. "GET AWAY FROM ME! DON'T COME NEAR ME! YOU NO-GOOD-FOR-NOTHING SLIMEBALL! YOU'RE THE CAUSE OF ME ALMOST KILLING MYSELF! NOW YOU WANNA HELP ME? YOU CAN HELP ME BY GETTING THE HELL AWAY FROM ME!"

Corey stopped in his tracks with his ear pressed to his cell.

Rich yelled down to him, "What do you need, a cape, Corey? What are you down there doing, Corey? Saving another girl, like you were at the club the other night when you were giving them drinks from your bottle? Don't think I forgot that, Coreeeeeeeeey. Now what are you doing, trying to get an S on your chest?"

I sighed.

WTF?! Is it me? Or is this whole scene a problem? This chick is all over the place.

I yanked Rich by the arm to get her attention. "Will you pull yourself together, girl."

"I said get away from me!" Spencer carried on as Corey was bent down. "I don't want you anywhere near me!"

"Wait one damn minute," Rich yelled. "I wanna know what you're down there doing, Corey. And why the hell is Spencer yelling at you like that? Spencer, why are you yelling at my man like that?"

"I don't want him touching me!" Spencer yelled back. "And why are you standing up there instead of being down here helping me? I need help. And not from Corey!"

"Yo, chill," Corey said to her. "If you'd calm down you'll see that all I'm doing is calling nine-one-one."

Rich looked at me and grabbed my arm. "C'mon, London. We need to get down there before the police get here. 'Cause he's tryna make the news."

"Huh? You'd think he'd do that?"

"Mmmph. I don't trust anyone when it comes to making the headlines, not even a man. Do you know how many times the headlines have been snatched from me?

Oh, no. Not this time. Kick them damn heels off and let's get down and dirty with it."

I was hesitant. I knew this was a bad idea. And it made absolutely no sense. But since I was commanded by my daddy to play nice with the Tinseltown queens of dramedy, I knew that there was only one thing to do—take off my jewels, kick off my shoes, and follow Rich down into the ditch.

"Now listen," Rich whispered as we climbed down. "We're gonna drag her out of the car and we'll both smack her one good time for all that slickness she was saying today, especially after she's called you broke. We're gonna show her how broke people do it. Real Section Eight-like. Corey, get away from her. London and I will take it from here."

Corey shook his head. "Nah, you don't need to be trying to move her. That's what I was trying to tell her, but she kept yelling and screaming at me."

I sucked my teeth, eyeing him. "Don't worry about it. We got this. You can go move along. She doesn't want you here anyway."

He frowned at me.

I rolled my eyes.

"I heard you were looking for some slow-singing and flower-bringing," Rich said to Spencer as she leaned over and banged on the door. "You ready to get it pop-pop, huh?"

"What? Slow-singing? I don't want you singing to me. What kind of games you playing, Rich? I want help."

"No, what you want is a beat down. You're the one who's been playing games. What was that she said to you, London?"

"She called me *broke*."

Rich kicked her door. "How dare you make fun of the financially afflicted? It's not her fault her parents are only worth a measly three hundred and eighty-five million dollars."

"Now wait a minute," I said, putting a hand up on my hip. "Who are we supposed to be coming for, me or Spencer? 'Cause it sounds like you're trying to *boom-bop it*, too."

"Girl, you know I got you. I'm just saying. It's not right what she said. I'm the one taking up for you, what are you getting all crunked with me about? Don't be getting sensitive now. You're still living up on Holmby Hills, so what's the big deal?"

I shook my head. There's no winning with this girl. She's going to always try to have the last word. "Whatever, Rich."

"Don't whatever me, boo. You might be a lot of things, trying to be all goody-two shoes and Miss Proper and all 'cause you're from New York. But broke isn't one of them. I know it and you better own it. But obviously someone forgot to fill this trick in. She's insulted all of your daddy's hard work, and pretty much called your mother a Walmart floor model. So, now...what's it gonna be? How you wanna handle this? You wanna keep it cute, or do you wanna go Section Eight on her? She got you all the way confused. She basically called you Culver City trash."

"Oh, hell no," I snapped, letting Rich get me all gassed up. The next thing I knew I reached inside Spencer's car and started pulling her out by her hair.

Rich yelled and dropped down, then popped back up

and said, "Now that's what I'm talking about, boom-bop that ho. Make it drop. Right hook her."

Spencer screamed, "Aaaaaaah, what the freak are you tricks doing to me? Get your nasty hands off of me. Have y'all lost your damn minds?"

Rich slapped her face. "And that's for talking all greasy to my man when all he was trying to do was help you."

Spencer swung, trying to fight back. "I didn't want your man helping me."

In the background we heard the sirens blaring. And we immediately stopped attacking her. As if on cue, Rich fluffed her hair. "I think I hear the media coming," she said. "Quick, act like we're saving this ho."

"Help me! Someone help! These girls are attacking me!"

"She's delusional," Rich snapped, pulling her by the arms through the dirt. "Spencer, snap out of it. We're here to help you, boo. Not hurt you."

"Don't talk," I said, grabbing her by the legs as the police were coming down to where we were. "Save your energy."

Rich broke out in tears, dropping Spencer, then dropping down to her knees, raising her hands up in the air. "God is good. He's not there when you need Him, but He's always right on time!"

I didn't know if I should burst out laughing, or pass the collection plate. So I did neither. I simply hummed and waved one hand in the air as the paramedics came down behind the police officers.

They lifted Spencer up on a stretcher, then carried her back up the hill.

"Somebody help me up," Rich said. "I think I'm stuck in this mud. I'm so exhausted and weak. London, you okay?"

"Yeah, girl," I said.

"Spencer?! Spencer?!" Rich yelled up to her. "Are you all right, girl?!"

"Nooooooooo, I'm not okay. You two swamp-donkeys tried to jump me!"

Two strapping police officers scooped Rich and me up into their arms and carried us back up the hill, our hair flowing in the breeze. And just as we reached the top of the hill is when I saw the whole world watching. There were cameramen, news reporters, and every gossip columnist and blogger known to man out there.

As Rich cracked a smile for the cameras, a news reporter yelled out, "Hey, Rich Montgomery. I think it's quite noble of you to save the very best friend who is also sleeping with your boyfriend. How do you feel about them being caught on tape in the bathroom this morning?"

I gasped.

Rich's eyes bucked. Then blinked as if she couldn't believe what she had just heard. "Repeat that?"

Just as the reporter was about to open his mouth, Co-Co Ming jumped in front of the camera and said, "The Pampered Princesses are more than a muddy mess. Who would ever think they'd be sleeping with each other's men."

Rich jumped out of the police officer's arms and started running. "Spencer! Where are you?!"

I yelled for the police officer to put me down and started running behind her.

Rich continued yelling. "Spencer, where are you?! How could she do this to me? Coreeeeeeeeeeeeeeeey?!"

I caught up to Rich, grabbed her by the arm, and spun her around toward me. "Rich, you need to pull yourself together." I shook her like a rag doll.

Rich continued to scream, "Coreeeeeeeeey! I CAN'T BELIEVE THIS! I CAN'T BELIEVE THIS!" She growled. "I'M GOING TO KICK SPENCER'S—!"

WHAP!

I hated to slap her but I had to. That was the only thing that would get her attention and have her focus on me. "Rich," I said and shook her shoulders once more. "Listen to me." I leaned into her face as close as I could and clenched my teeth. "We've got cameras zoomed in on us. Everywhere. Half the school is out here, watching this whole fiasco. And you're out here spinning out of control. Co-Co Ming is doing interviews and snapping pictures. I'm two seconds from wrestling him down to the ground! We're fighting for our image here! Get. It. Together. Now. Quick fast and in a goddarn hurry."

Rich blinked and looked as if she'd returned from space. "London, where am I? Am I in the middle of the war zone? Did someone just attack me and say that Spencer was sleeping with my boyfriend? Huh, London?"

"Yes—"

"I'ma kick her—"

"No, you're not!"

"Why not?"

"Because we need to play this right."

"Play right? That ho wasn't playing right when she slept with my boyfriend. No, she was playing me!"

I took a deep breath. "Rich, listen to me. You are too beautiful for this. Corey doesn't deserve you. You are fierce, fly—"

"And fabulous," Rich sniffed, wiping her eyes.

"Exactly. So I need you to see that Spencer is not the

ho-bag we should be going after. Corey is the real problem here. And he's the one who needs to be handled."

"You're right." She cleared her throat. "I want to take that mofo and peel his face off! I don't believe this. How could they do this to me? I'm so humiliated. Ohmygod, ohmygod...I can't breathe. She was supposed to be my friend. She broke all the rules."

"Yeah, that whore Spencer broke cardinal rule number two: Thou shall not ever sleep with a friend's boo—"

"'Cause that sin's reserved for the enemy." Rich wiped her eyes.

"So, yes, that needs to be dealt with swiftly, but in private. But, there is something more pressing going on here. And that is cardinal rule number one—"

"Thou shall never let them catch you slipping."

"Boom! Now what are we going to do? Are you going to stand here looking all kinds of crazy or are you, better yet are we, going to, as you would say, 'boom-bop, drop-it' on him?"

She sniffed again, pulled mud from out of her hair, then straightened her back. "Let's snap, crack pop it drop it! And let's go hunt him down!"

15

Rich

London wasn't talking to me. She paced from one end of the holding cell to the other, mumbling to herself. We had on no shoes and our clothes were tattered.

I was curled in the corner on a cold, steel bench. There was mud caked between my toes and somebody in here had an odor. It was only two of us in the cell and I smelled like Prada Candy parfum.

I was too afraid to move, and London hadn't stopped pacing long enough to even console me, after all I'd been through today.

How selfish.

I had a good mind to tell her off, but I couldn't uncurl myself long enough. I may have been in jail but my mother was going to be the one who shanked me! This was not the plan she had in mind for me. And all London kept mumbling about was her daddy. Which I didn't understand, because if he was a lawyer he should've been getting us out of here.

I tried to suppress my cry but I couldn't help but wail.

"SHUT UP OVER THERE!"

"Did you just tell me to shut up? Oh, you have anger is-sues. This is why we're in here in the first place."

I had to get out of here. This place was the size of a shoebox. A cheap one. I swear I could stretch my arms and touch both walls at the same time. And the walls, oh…my… God…were chipped, painted gray, with "Pookie's World" etched into the paint. There was a dirty little metal sink tucked in the corner and a nasty toilet with brown water sitting out in the open. No door. No draperies to cover up your business. And no toilet paper in sight.

My Gawd.

Clutching pearls.

Until I met this New Yorker I'd never been arrested be-fore and now I was a criminal, with the electric chair and some big burly woman with hairy arms and whiskers forc-ing me to wash her dirty drawers in my future.

"Ohmygod…Ohmygod…I can't breathe!"

London spun around on her bare heels and charged over to me! She grabbed my face between her index finger and thumb and squeezed my cheeks. She clenched her jaw and said, "Do you want your face slapped again! Huh? Well then shut up!"

I opened my mouth and screamed, "I'm in here with the devil!"

London let my face go, backed up, and said, "You're really pushing it! Over there whining and complaining and my fa-ther is going to *murder* me! *Cold. Blooded. Murder.*" She arched her brow. "And when I die, I'm going to haunt you for the rest of your damn life. I had enough of you and your ruckus! I have never been locked up before."

I gasped and placed my hand in front of my mouth in theatrical shock. "Really, London! I thought all you New Yorkers went to jail, at least once."

She narrowed her eyes, still inches away from my face. "Keep it up and I'm going to take your face and mop up this dirty floor with it!"

"Ahhhhh!" I screamed and sweat instantly ran over my forehead. "London! What's that critter crawling across your feet!"

London looked down at her feet and shrieked. She hopped up on the bench with me, grabbed my hands, and we screamed, rocking back and forth.

"I'm so sorry, Rich!" London cried.

"I'm so sorry, too, London. What did we let Spencer get us into?"

London contorted her face and sniffed. She paused, cleared her throat, and scooted back a little. "That conniving, ratchet, head-boppin' sleaze! She set us up. She crashed into the ditch intentionally."

"She knew I was an attention whore! And she knew I would call the media!" I attempted to wipe my eyes but realized that my hands were filthy. Nasty. Dirty. And the beds of my fingernails were black. I did all I could to keep myself calm. "Had she never slept with my boyfriend none of this would have ever happened!"

"No, had your boyfriend not slept with your friend this would have never happened! You know he seduced Spencer!"

"She was still wrong."

"She was but she's not smart enough to be that devious!"

"You're right. That's why I had to take it to his chest and

you followed up and cock-popped his eye in! Blood every-where!"

"But you didn't have to snatch that microphone and bust him in the face with it."

"I told you I was going to peel his face off. What did you think was going to happen?!"

"I just thought—"

"Phillips, Montgomery, get your stuff and let's go!" I blinked and blinked again, as a police officer marched her-self in front of the cell and opened the door. London turned her back and I sat up, crossed my legs, and said, "We're not going anywhere with you. You've been nasty to us ever since we've been in here and I've had enough! And as soon as we leave here we will be suing the state, the po-lice department, and you personally for treating us the way that you have! Trust. You will be brought to your knees!"

London twisted back around toward the officer and cocked her neck for confirmation. "We are not common trash!"

"Okay, you must not want to leave," the police officer said. "Enjoy your new cell mate!"

Don't ask me how or where this girl came from, but out of nowhere appeared this six-foot-tall, four-hundred-pound, no, four-hundred-and-fifty-five-pound, Rick-Ross-looking chick with the biggest hands I've ever seen. She looked at London and me and growled. Mean-mugged us. London and I grabbed hands, said a silent prayer, and put our game faces on.

The officer slammed the door. "I'll let your lawyer know that the two of you are not ready to leave."

"Oh no, we never said that!" London and I said simultaneously as we hopped up and slid past the Incredible Hulk, who looked me over and took a seat.

As the officer opened the door to let us out I looked at Rick Ross and said, "Yeah, you're lucky I'm leaving! 'Cause my name is Rasheeda and I'm in here for murder!"

16

London

*O*ur Father who art in heaven...
I lowered my head.

"Mr. Phillips, you don't know how happy I am that you freed me and London from Alcatraz. That place was horrid."

I look to you as I weep...
Please give me a chance to freshen up...
Before Daddy lays me down to eternal sleep...
I pray the Lord my soul to keep...

"Is that so?" Daddy said, slicing me with a side-eye glare as he gripped the steering wheel of his Maybach and zigzagged through the streets of Hollywood. I looked down at what was left of my one-of-a-kind designer blouse to see how much blood I had lost so far. This was like the third time Daddy had cut me with his eyes. And the gashes in my flesh were deep, jagged reminders that it was soon to be lights out for me. I shifted my body closer to the door, praying he'd leave me with enough blood so that I could at least live long enough to see my seventeenth birthday next year. But judging by the way the muscles in his jaw twitched, his nostrils flared, and the vein in his neck popped out, I knew Daddy wouldn't let me bleed to death. He'd finish me off with his bare hands, instead. And the more Rich yapped her smelly gums, the more convinced I was that my life was slowly coming to an end. She had sealed my fate.

I flipped down the visor, slid open the lighted mirror, and glared at her, hoping she'd get the damn hint. She didn't!

She gasped. "You have no idea. And they were so nasty to us. Ohmygod! But London and I gave them a piece of our minds. Oh, we let them know who they were messing with. Didn't we, London?"

I didn't respond.

"I don't know why you're sitting up there all quiet, girl. Don't be shy now. You woulda been so proud of her, Mr. Phillips. Whew, London doesn't take any mess. She knows how to set it off when it's necessary. You and Mrs. Phillips trained her well. I told her, we're always ladies, first. You know. Keep it cute and classy—that's her word, though. But when it's time to get down and dirty, London is always ready to boom-bop it..."

"Oh, she's Miss Boom-Bop It, huh?"

"Well, I'm the original Miss Boom-Bop, but I'll share the torch with my girl, London."

I clasped my hands in front of me.

"Mr. Phillips, I don't mean any harm here. But, London brings it like a real New Yorker, real hardlike, straight from the gutter. If she hadn't told me to go over there and handle Corey instead of Spencer, I don't know what I would have done. Thanks to her, Corey got taught the lesson he deserved. London is my home girl, for real...."

Please let my death be swift...

The more Rich talked, the deeper my grave got.

I blinked my suddenly watery eyes.

"She really put it down for me today. She was my hype-woman, for real. She crunked it all the way up to ten. Have you ever seen her skills, Mr. Phillips? This girl is wicked with the hands. When she reached back and punched Corey in his face, I knew what I needed to do next. It was freeze, pop, jump, make it crunk."

I eyed Daddy out of the corner of my eye, wringing my hands. He pulled in his bottom lip, then clenched his teeth. "Oh, I'm sure she did."

Forgive me for all of my sins...

"Ohmygod, I need an emergency manicure and pedicure, fast. This is tragic! London, do you want me to make you an appointment, too? I know your feet have to be on fire from all that pacing you were doing. Those heels of yours must be hard as bricks by now...."

I dared not say a word, hoping Rich would finally buy a vowel and get a damn clue to...shut. Up.

I glanced at the digital clock in the console. *My Lord!* It was 9:23 P.M. *I can't believe we sat in that funk-tank for almost six hours. Six long, torturous hours!!!* And now I had to sit in this car and be tortured again by not only Rich's stank breath, but her violent underarms and that cesspool smell that seeped out of her pores, too.

Rich had the audacity to lean forward in her seat and whisper, "Girl, you need to make sure you wash down real good when you get home. I smell you all the way back here. And it's not pretty, girl."

I ignored her, cutting my eye over at Daddy, wondering how he could leave me in jail all that time. And why the hell wasn't Yuck Mouth picked up by her own parents. But as Rich continued to rattle on with her incessant chatter I wished like hell that he would have left me in jail. I'd had rather rot in that dirty hole than have to face Daddy's wrath, and deal with this garbage mouth.

I felt sick to my stomach.

"...I'll be so glad to get home to exfoliate, luxuriate, and put this whole nightmare behind me...."

Oh, for the love of God! I wish Rich would shut the hell up!

Daddy rolled all of the windows down and opened the sunroof. We were immediately assaulted by the cool night air, whipping through the cabin of the car.

Rich leaned up in her seat, again. "Ooh, Mr. Phillips, it's gotten awful chilly in here. Do you think you can roll up the back windows some? All this wind is tearing my face up."

"No," Daddy said, curtly. "The air will do you *and* London fine."

"Well, yeah. I guess you're right," she said, then eased up alongside my ear and added, "See, I told you. You need to take a long, hot bath and soak that bottom real good. It's funk central, girlfriend."

And you smell like the back of a garbage truck!

The next thing I heard was her talking to someone on her cell making travel arrangements to Paris for two. She hung up. "London, pack your bags, girl. Get your Chanels out. Paris in the A.M. Milan in the P.M. We're gonna do it up, boo. We deserve it. After Spencer and Corey, and the way all the newscasts tried to drag us through the mud today, girl, we need to do it up." She reached over and tapped Daddy on the shoulder. "Mr. Phillips, can you please make sure you handle those charges while London and I are gone because we don't need anyone looking for us while we're out of the country? I know you're good and all, Mr. Phillips, but I just want to make sure that everything's handled. You know how it is, Mr. Phillips."

"No. I don't know how it is. And before you and London start whisking off into the clouds, both of you need to handle your own charges. And you better hope the two of you only get community service."

Rich smacked her crusty lips. "Community service? What? I don't do that. I ain't Lindsay Lohan. I service the community by dressing them. You know. Donate my last season's wardrobe to the needy. Everyone needs a little Chanel in their lives."

I imagined Daddy rolling his eyes up in his head as he pulled up to the humongous Montgomery estate. He waited for their handcrafted entry gate to open, then practically told Rich to get out. I was surprised he didn't at least drive her up to their front door. But, I guess, like me, he had had enough. "Tell your father I'll call him. And I'll fill him in on your travel plans," Daddy said to her as she stepped out of the car. He waited for her to shut the door, then walk through the gates. When they shut behind her, he drove off, rolling the windows up.

I swallowed.

Guttermouth, funk-box and all, now I really wished she had stayed a little longer. It was me and Daddy. Alone. There was nothing but air between us. And the silence was deafening. I kept having visions of him pulling over onto the side of the road, dragging me out of the car by my hair, and tossing my body over the cliff into the Pacific Ocean, then pulling off like he didn't have a care in the world. I tried everything I could to keep my heart from beating out of my chest.

"Daddy, can I—"

He shot me a look, gripping the steering wheel. "London. Not. A. Word."

Uh-oh. This is... really, really... catastrophic!

I felt myself starting to hyperventilate.

I started rocking. "Daddy, pleeeeeeeease. Can we talk about this? I know you're upset with me—"

He sliced me with another glare. "Upset? Upset doesn't even compare to what I am feeling at this moment. Upset is when you're getting a bad grade or me finding out that you've charged a hundred grand on my credit card on the first day of school to pay for damages. Upset is when you don't follow the house rules. This right here is beyond upset."

"I know, Daddy. I know, I—"

"You don't know a damn thing, little girl. Just be quiet. There is nothing you can say. You and your little Boom-Bop It twin—whatever the hell that's supposed to mean—are all over the damn news. Every channel I turn on, there you are. This is the second time you've done *boom, bop-bopped* it to the damn ground. We just had a conversation last week about your behavior. I told you then that I didn't want any more foolishness out of you. But, you simply disregarded everything I said..."

"Daddy, that's not—"

"Hold up. Who do you think you're cutting in on? I'm talking. You're to listen. Do you understand?"

"Yes," I said meekly.

"From what your little Miss Boom Bop and Drop home-girl, for real-for real, said, you're the damn ring leader here. And I believe her. Now since when did you become a damn gangster? "A Thug in Chanel" as the headlines read. You wanna be some hood urchin in the street? Is that the kind of life you want, huh?"

He raised his voice. "Answer me." As I prepared to respond to his question he told me to shut up. "I'm always thinking your mother is too hard on you. Well, hell... maybe she's not hard enough. Maybe, you're playing me like she says. Yeah, that's exactly what it is. You're playing me. And I don't like it. And I won't stand for it. Whatever happens with these charges, you better hope like hell—or better yet, pray—that I get over this quickly. Because it's gonna be a long damn time before I trust you again. From this point on, you will be on a very short leash. That car that I've shelled out all of that damn money for that you left in the middle of the damn road so you could go out and *boom-bop, drop it* with your home girl is a thing of the past. You will be dropped off and picked up wherever you need to go...."

The more Daddy spoke, the louder his voice got. And the more he looked like he was foaming at the mouth. "Unless you're choosing to be on the streets..."

He swerved over to the side of the road, stopped the car, then told me to open the door. I looked at him and hesitated with confusion in my eyes. "I said, open your door. 'Cause I don't know who the hell you are. But you are not my daughter. Not carrying on the way you've been. I'm out here trying to make money so that you can have the best life possible and you want to piss it all away on some BS. I have too many other things to be doing than running behind you and your nonsense. And your little pop-pop-drop-it friend making travel plans to France right in my damn face, like the two of you don't have a care in the world. Both of you are out of control.

"But she's not my concern. You are. In all the years I have worked with Rich's father, I have never seen that girl in any other kind of news except for her being somewhere drunk. But now she's all over the front pages getting arrested with *my* damn daughter. Videos going viral, bloggers talking nonstop, practically obsessed with the wild antics of London Elona Phillips, daughter of the high-powered entertainment attorney and here you're getting more spotlight than me. How do you think that makes me look?"

"But Daddy," I tried to explain, "Rich is the one who called the media. She loves the attention. That's what she lives for."

"I don't care. Obviously you live for it, too. You're making a name for yourself real quick. And it's nothing nice. You want fame for the sake of being famous? You want to be a fame whore? Well, now it's going to cost you, starting with you being grounded. All of that hanging out, getting your party on is over. You are to go straight home after school. On the weekends that your mother and I have to go out of town, you will come with us. You will not be left unattended or unsupervised, period. You can't be trusted, and I am going to treat you as such.

"I've spent a lot of time taking up for you, arguing with your mother, believing that she was overreacting. And here I am trying to give you the benefit of the doubt. And the only thing you've done is make me look the damn fool. And this is how you repay me. All on the news, again, assaulting someone else. Thinking you don't have to take any responsibility. But I'm gonna tell you this. And I'm only going to say it once. I'm not bringing home no little gutter-rat media-ho. If that's who you wanna be, then you can boom, bop, drop it over at the Montgomerys' because *I* am not having it."

I looked at him with fear, surprised that he was threatening to put me out on the road in the middle of the night. I've done a lot of things, but Daddy has never, ever, threatened to throw me out of the car. Right then...I made a vow to myself to get my life together. London Phillips was turning over a new leaf. There would be no more running wild for me. It wasn't worth losing my life.

I looked at him with tears rolling down my face. "Okay, Daddy. I understand."

He eyed me long and hard, then narrowed his eyes. My whole world had crashed around me. I held my breath.

"Now shut the door."

17

Rich

Eww, I can't believe Mr. Phillips was sooo rude. The nerve. No door-to-door service?

He knew our shoes were stolen.

So umm, he had to notice that I didn't have any stilettos on.

Oh God, look at my feet.

Yet he dropped me off at the bottom of the hill, like that was the move.

Who does that?

Obviously, Mr. Low Budget.

And then he made us ride with all the windows down, like it was ninety degrees out, when it was only about sixty. Maybe he needed to have his overheating, or should I say overeating, problem worked out. Like lift some weights and stay away from the plate. And no he wasn't that big, and yeah London claimed he worked out. But, from what I could see he had twenty extra pounds that made that belly of his a little round. And whenever the Phillipses came over here and had dinner with us, Papa Bear. Got. His. Grub. On. And easily threw three, four plates of food back. Okay. Snap. Snap. But whatever, that was not my problem, being cold was.

I stood at the bottom of the hilly driveway and our estate, which my mother had lovingly named "The Promised Land," looked massive. French chateau inspired with huge dramatic windows that towered from the first floor to the second-story ceiling and were on both sides of the forty-foot all glass and rhodium trimmed double doors. The platinum fountain of the Greek god Zeus was the crowning jewel of the English rose garden that welcomed you into paradise where there were sculptured bushes, an Olympic-size pool, a tennis court, a small golf course, and sprawling and plush green grounds that went even farther than the eye could see.

And all I could think was if my parents killed and buried me, no one would ever find me.

Damn.

At least my brother would miss me.

I smiled hesitantly at the servant crew, who were leaving out of the side entrance. "Good night, Miss Rich." They smiled and headed to the guests' garage, where their cars were kept.

Instinctively I wondered what time it was, because I could've sworn that the night staff didn't get off until midnight and last I checked it was 10 P.M. I swallowed.

Hard.

Now I knew for sure I was about to be dragged. Because my mother never ever let the staff go home early. Ever.

Know what, this is a dream. Yup, exactly. A dream. I

pinched myself just to test my theory and all I felt was pain shoot up my arm. It wasn't a dream. It was a nightmare.

Know what, maybe, maybe my mother had worried herself to sleep and my father was tucked away in his office and was relieving stress by writing a song. This would allow me to creep into my room, lock the door, and come up with a plan by the time the maids arrived in the morning.

Or maybe, maybe when I crept passed my parents' wing there would be slow music playing, then I could creep into my room and let them enjoy their groove. And when they woke up in the morning they would still be on their midnight high and would let this whole deal slide.

Boom!

But what if they're up?

And Ma is massaging Daddy's shoulders and working the kinks out of his neck when I walk in...that would be a clear sign of premeditated murder....

I got it. I'll blame it all on London.

After all, she did call and invite me to get it crunked. I'm a lady. I don't do crunked. And I already had a plan to get rid of Corey. I didn't need her assistance.

And if that doesn't work...?

Then...I'd beat my parents to the punch and cop to their famous lines that I was spoiled, self-centered, and needed to get my life together. Boom! And it didn't matter if I knew that none of that was true. What mattered is that they fell for it.

Now that I had my mind right and my plan intact, I squared my shoulders and strutted toward the front entrance.

Dang, I don't have any keys....

Think...think...think...

"Don't *think* if you take all night to come up in here—"

Freeze.

Did someone just put a gun to my head?

My mother continued as she stood in the doorway with her hand on her slender hip and her neck contorted, "—That your father and I will be tucked away somewhere and you'll be able to creep into your room, excuse me, *my* room that I allow *you* to sleep in, in peace. Because peace is a privilege. And your privileges, Miss Jailbird, have been stripped."

I swallowed again.

Extra hard.

There were two ways I could handle this: Say nothing and go down quietly, or raise up and let my mother know that I was sixteen and if she put her hands on me that it was gon' be a problem.

There it was. Solution number two.

I boldly put a little motion in my ocean, walked up to the front entrance, looked my mother over, strutted past her, and left her standing there with her mouth dropped open.

Now hit the floor with that.

But instead of hitting the floor my mother laughed. Wickedly. Now that scared me. She wasn't supposed to laugh, especially since I knew that when she laughed like this, she was ready to get it poppin'. This was when having parents that were originally hood rats before they were bourgeois snobs went straight to the left.

Maybe it's not too late to rewind my plan.

Yeah, that was it. *Reeewiiind...*

I turned around and said, "Oh hey, Ma. I didn't even see

you standing there." I walked back over to her, daringly kissed her on the cheek, and turned to walk away.

"If I were you," she said coldly, "I'd stand still until somebody told me to move."

Ummm...does that mean plan number one wasn't a good look either?

My mother walked up behind me, spoke evenly over my shoulder and said, "So you wanna be a thug, huh? You wanna rep a set now? And be like a common criminal, sluggin' it out on the street. Is that what you want to be?"

Blink...blink...and blink some more. What the... "I don't stink—"

"Are you talking back to me?" She rushed in front of me and shoved her face into mine. "Huh? Are you really bringing it to me? Answer me!"

"No."

"I didn't think so. Up in here smelling like garbage! Nasty. Sweaty. Stankin'garbage and I will not have it in my house!"

"So is that code word that we're going to end this conversation so that I can luxuriate in a bath? 'Cause I had a hard day, Ma. London is full of drama. And Ma, Ma, you know I have never been in such trouble since I hooked up with that girl. She is a typical New Yorker. Always ready to set it off. Always willing to—"

"Shut. Up. So now what you're saying to me is that you're a follower. So I'm raising a follower, who's willing to do anything that anyone tells her to do, and especially a *typical* New Yorker? Is that what you're saying to me? So I swam through the swamps of Watts, dodging bullets, ducking drive-bys, trying not to toss up gang signs, and hustled my way to the top, to have a daughter who's a *fol-*

lower! Are you sure that's what you're telling me? That all my hard work was in vain?" She mushed me in my temple and made my head jerk to the left. "Because if that's what you're telling me, then I'm telling you that where I come from that level of disrespect calls for a beat-down. And if you're trying to be a jailhouse thug then you need to know that! Now tell me." She slid off one stiletto and then the other. "Is that what you're saying? That you want me to whup you?"

"Ma, let me explain."

"Explain what? What part, how you were all up on the news and the blogs carrying on and fighting over a boy?"

"That was Spencer's fault—"

"Now this is Spencer's fault?"

"Yes. Hers and London's. And Corey's. 'Cause had Corey been faithful—"

"No man is faithful. You know that. And don't say that to me anymore!"

Pause... "Well. Umm, had Spencer not been a slut, sleeping with Corey. Then none of this would have happened. And had London not called me and invited me to toss it down—"

"Now London invited you to toss it down? I should willy-whop you. Now you're insulting my intelligence."

"Ma—"

"Don't cut me off again! Now you know how you're supposed to act and what I expect. Men will cheat. So that's not the issue, you deal with that in private. You don't ever embarrass your man by fighting in the street. That's the move of a woman who will forever be number two. Is that what you want? Always the mistress never the wife, well then you keep it up because you're on your way—"

"Logan," my father called from the distance. "Turner just called and said he dropped Rich off at the bottom of the hill. She should be in here at any minute and I want her in my office immediately! Do you know she had the nerve to make travel plans to go to France? Your daughter is out of control! Yeah, when she steps in here let her know that I'm waiting."

I wonder if they'll bury me in all black Chanel...

My mother peered at me. "Okay, Richard. I'm waiting right here for her." She continued, clenching her teeth, "When you speak to your father you better shut your mouth and listen, because if you even look at him crazy, I'ma bring it to yo' chest. Simple. Because now you're messing with my husband. And three things I don't play with: my money, my man, and my children. And in that order—"

"Ma, let me just say—"

"Say? You can't say a thing to me. Now you keep trying me, little girl, and see what's next. And I don't care if you are our daughter, or Daddy's little princess, you will play by *mother's* rules, and not your own. And rule number one in mother's handbook is: Going to jail is a no-no. Rule number two: There will be no fighting in the street over some lil boy, who may be hot right now but, given the financial state of his family, clearly will not be rich forever. And rule number three: Never break rule number one or two.

"Now you go upstairs and take you a quick shower. If I find out that you are trying to luxuriate, I'ma beat you out

of the stall. Now go rinse yourself and you have ten minutes to get back down here and you better know how to
speak. All that laffy-taffy, boom-bop-drop, you better keep
that out on the street. Now get out my face!"

I felt frozen in my spot.

"Rich Gabrielle Montgomery, did you hear what I said?"
She slid her earrings off and turned her eleven-karat diamond solitaire toward her palm. "Or do we really need to
handle this another way? 'Cause the way I feel I will beat
you like a woman in the street. Since you're grown as hell.
Now you have an option, get the hell out my face or I'ma
peel your face off!"

I felt my knees giving way. I had to go to the bathroom
and I knew if I kept standing here I was seconds away
from the drops of pee that had wet my panties to a full-
fledged stream making its way to the floor. I squeezed my
inner thighs. I knew my mother had dismissed me from
her presence. But, I also knew my mother well enough to
know that if I moved too quickly or turned away from her
too fast, she would swear that I was snatching away from
her and the next thing I would know she'd be taking a
Watts-certified sledgehammer to my throat. Not. An. Option. So I simply looked at her and rocked from side to
side, barely holding my pee. Before I could say anything
my mother said, "You've wasted two minutes standing
here, now unless you're going to bring it, you now have
eight minutes to get back down here odor-free!"

I zipped upstairs, barely making it to the bathroom.
This was nothing like I expected my day or night to be.
The last time my mother ran up on me like this was a year
ago.

I think I need Jesus.

I hopped in the shower and hurriedly washed. I hopped
out and changed into a champagne-colored lounge outfit
and slippers. I hurried back downstairs to my father's office with forty seconds to spare and I still felt dirty. I stood
in the doorway and watched my mother massaging my father's broad shoulders and working the kinks out of his
neck. For a moment I wondered if jail with Rick Ross was
a better look than this.

I looked at my mother and her eyes clearly said, "You
are finished."

"Hey, Daddy," I said hesitantly, wishing I could run
away. My father looked at me disgusted and pointed to the
twin set of leather wing chairs that sat before his mahogany desk and said, "Sit down."

I felt like I walked on glass. I tipped over, sat down, and
swallowed.

*Don't say a word. Just listen. Don't even move. Don't
even blink.*

After a moment of silence and them both staring at me,
not blinking, my father popped his neck and said, "I have
seen the news and I have read the blogs. Now, what's your
version?" But before I could say anything he said, "And
don't start that fast talk, cause the moment boom-bop
comes out of your mouth I'ma let you know exactly what a
boom-bop means."

My mother slid from behind my father's chair, pulled
her hair back into a ponytail, and cocked her neck to the
side. "I dare you," she mouthed.

Immediately my left leg started to shake and I felt like I
had to go to the bathroom again but I knew I couldn't

move. I swallowed and said, "See what had happened was. Ummm...yeah...ummm, yeah, see London came to Hollywood High bringing all this ra-ra—"

"Start over." He sat up completely straight and leaned forward.

My mother reached across him and moved his glass of cognac to the side. "Just in case you need to leap over."

My father cut his eyes at my mother and she resumed massaging his shoulders.

My eyes dropped back to my father. Veins ran across his forehead like a road map. He peered at me and said, "Now, I said start. Over."

"See, yeah, what the problem really is, is Spencer—"

"Start over again." He rose from his chair and sat on the edge of his desk. My mother was wringing her hands.

I broke down and started crying.

"Rich, those tears are not working with me, so suck 'em up and sit up straight," Daddy demanded. "You played yourself on national TV, all the headlines are reading that my daughter has turned into a thug in Chanel and I know, and you know, and your mother knows, that you don't know nothing about being a thug. Yet still you're out in the street carrying on—"

"Daddy, it just happened so fast. I let London talk me into fighting Corey, when I knew it wasn't right. And I knew that Mommy always said to be a lady. And I am a lady, but this girl just has a way of getting everybody—"

I paused. Swallowed. The look on my father's face reminded me that I was going too far to the left and needed to bring it back, quick, so I said, "So, Spencer, who I thought was my best friend since kindergarten, was sleep-

ing with my boyfriend. Did you see the video? Straight
porn star—"

"The only video I saw was you acting straight hood." He
rose off of the desk and the next thing I knew he stood in
front of me.

"I don't want to hear anything about London, Spencer,
or anybody else. All I'm concerned about is you. And you
do remember who you are. But then again maybe you
don't, so let me remind you. You are the daughter of
Richard Gabriel Montgomery Sr., founder and CEO of
Grand Records. Do you understand what that means?"

"Apparently she doesn't," my mother added and I
wished I could tell her to shut her mouth. But I didn't,
mostly because I didn't dare to.

"Well, let me school you," my father continued. "You
don't have a right to embarrass me. Actually you don't
have a right to breathe without me giving you permission." He paused. "And then I had three, four lawyers call
here asking me if they could sample your voice screaming,
'I'ma peel his face off!' Really? Rich? Who you supposed to
be? Queen Bee? Ill Na-Na? You ain't put no work in. You
haven't done anything but be a snotty-nose little brat, who
thinks she has the world at her fingertips. And the only
reason why you have that world is because I've given it to
you. This is my money, my house, my fortune, my reputation and I'm not going to have you and your behavior
tryna do me. When I was on the street, people have disappeared for less than that. Now what you think I'ma do to
you bringing lawsuits to my doorstep?"

My eyes popped open wide.

"Yeah, Corey's parents want money for you *'peeling his
face off!'* "

He continued, "And if we have to settle out of court, the money will come out of your trust fund, and you better hope it doesn't deplete it. Now from where I'm standing you have some serious thinking to do. Because if you can't get it right, you will be up out of here. There are plenty of boarding schools. Now I didn't have these problems from your brother and I'm not going to have them from you. Now get out of my face!"

I quickly rose from my seat and I could feel my top sticking to my back and my pants sticking to my legs. For a moment I wondered if I'd left a puddle of sweat in the chair.

"And know this," my father said as I stepped toward the door. "You are on punishment. And you will apologize to Spencer and Corey."

Psst, please. I wish I would. I'm Rich Montgomery, I don't do apologies.

"We will finish this conversation later," my mother said to me as I closed the door.

As I stepped away I heard my father raise his voice and say to my mother, "You have spoiled her way too much! This is your fault."

I hurried away from the door as my mother started fast-talking and explaining why I act the way I do, and from what I heard none of it made any sense.

It was close to midnight and I couldn't get any sleep. I tossed and turned thinking about a million things. The moonlight streamed in from the crack in my French doors that led to my terrace. I eased out of bed and walked over to the terrace and leaned against the doorframe, looking out into the night. The cool air bathed my face and just as

I closed my eyes and thought about everything that had happened today my phone rang.

Knox.

I hesitated. I knew what hearing his voice did to me... it took me away from everything we were supposed to be—friends. He was like, like the bag of chocolate that I knew was good, and I didn't need it, but I wanted it. Bad. And although I wasn't used to being told no, I had to tell myself no in this instance because it was the best thing for both of us...whatever the hell that meant. I closed my eyes and the phone again.

Forget it. Maybe his voice was just what I needed. "Hello?"

"Hey wassup, Love."

I closed my eyes, absorbed the beauty in his voice, and a vision flashed before me of Knox kissing me along my collarbone and me melting into his embrace. I shook the vision, twisted my lips, and said. "Nothing." I paused. "Just thinking about how rude it is to call people after ten o'clock at night."

Knox chuckled. "Yeah a'ight. Whatever. What, did your phone just start working?"

"What? No."

"Oh, so you just haven't called me on purpose?" he asked.

"You're the one who's always busy, Mr. College Boy."

"Yeah a'ight." He laughed and I found myself laughing, too. "So what's good with you?"

"Nothing."

"Oh here you go with that again. That's that bull."

I chuckled and said innocently while twisting my index finger into my left cheek, "What are you talking about?"

"Okay, Miss Innocent. Now stop twisting your finger in your cheek."

I couldn't help but smile at how well he knew me. "I'm just tired."

"Why are you tired? From all your media festivities. You're a real celebrity, huh? Real thug in Chanel, all the little girls will be boom-boppin' it. Everywhere. I bet you coined the phrase 'I'ma peel his face off.' "

"Oh you got jokes."

"Nah," he cracked up, "I'm leaving all the jokes up to you. How long before you think they drop a rap song, 'I'ma...I'ma...I'ma peel your face off!" He rapped and as hard as I tried not to get caught up I couldn't help it. So I dropped an old-school human beatbox behind his playful lyrics. And as he continued rapping, "I'ma peel your face off," I made scratching sounds and drumbeats with my chest.

We cracked up laughing so hard that tears had come out of my eyes. "Yo, come outside."

I hesitated. "Come outside?"

"And I'm not taking no for an answer."

I sighed. "Give me a minute."

I quickly changed into a pair of denim short-shorts, a white spaghetti-strap tee, and a pair of pink flip-flops. I walked out of the servants' entrance and eased down the driveway, praying that the gate didn't make too much noise as I opened it.

It didn't.

My heart dropped to my stomach the moment Knox filled my eyesight. I bit into my bottom lip, doing all that I could not to lick it. He leaned against his black Jeep Wrangler. His chestnut eyes sparkled in the glow of the lit pavers and the gas street lamp. He wore slightly baggy black jeans, with a black San Diego State University hoodie, and a pair of white Air Yeezy sneakers. His skin was the color of melted milk chocolate and his frame was broad, built, and sexy. He stood about six-three and it took everything in me not to run over and kiss him.

"I see you checking me out? Oh, you like what you see."

"What?" I said, trying not to blush, as I walked over to him. "Boy, please. I mean, you look all right. But you're not cuter than me."

He laughed. "Yeah a'ight." He looked me over and opened his arms up and said, "So you're too cute to give me some love. You haven't seen me in a month." He lifted my chin to meet his gaze. "Damn, it's good to see you. I missed you, girl."

I smiled, laid my head against his chest and breathed in his scent. "I missed you, too."

He slid his hands in my back pockets and pulled me in closer. I loved the feel of being in his arms, but I knew that we couldn't get caught like this again, so I slid his hands from my pants and placed them at his side.

He looked at me and smiled. "My fault."

I playfully rolled my eyes to the sky and sucked my teeth. "So where you been?"

He looked at me confused and said, "You know where I've been. I been at school and you been on the news. The question is when you gon' make time for me? Or do I have to keep creeping up at night, using the servants' entrance?"

"I always have time for you."

"A'ight show me. Come see me this weekend."

"At school and a whole hour and a half away?"

"Yeah. I would do it for you. I did it for you. I'm here."

I laughed. "You know you just left ya mama's house eating dinner and doing your laundry, 'cause I still smell chicken on your breath. And I bet you I open your car door and it's laundry on the backseat."

"A brother gotta eat and wash. And then I came through to see you."

"Awwl, I feel so special."

"You are special." He stroked my cheek.

We paused and an awkward silence filled the air.

"So umm," he said. "Maybe I should—"

"Yeah, get going."

"Yeah, I have a long ride."

"Get back safe."

I could tell by the look on his face he had more to say and so did I and just when I thought that maybe I was bold enough to say it, I changed my mind.

Knox kissed me on the forehead and said, "Later."

I watched him pull off and for a few moments I stared at the space where he once stood.

I turned toward the house, punched in the gate's code, and as it closed I was immediately greeted with a backhand across my face, causing me to stumble backward, hitting the ground.

As I tried to get up my mother stepped over me, one leg on each side and said, "I see you haven't learned yet!" Her hand kissed my face again.

18

Spencer

"I'm leaving now, Beautiful," Vera, my loyal and devoted house manager, announced in her thick Trinidadian accent as she walked into my suite. Vera—or Auntie Vera as she insisted she be called—was a short, stocky woman with wide hips and full breasts that had been my resting place many nights when I needed comforting. Vera had been in my life since I was nine. And I loved her. She didn't take piss for the cotton from anyone. But she had a platinum heart and loved me as if I were her own. "Do yuh need anyting else before me leave for de night, Sweetie? If you're hungry, me have yuh dinner in the microwave. Me made yuh favorite. Macaroni pie, stewed chicken, stewed okra, and callaloo. And if yuh eat your veggies there's a currants roll on the counter waiting for you."

I looked at her and gave her a wide smile, slipping back to when I was five. "Ohmygod, I love you so much. You always know how to put a smile on my heart."

"Who loves yuh?"

Definitely not the egg and sperm donors who created me!

"Auntie Vera does," I said with forced enthusiasm. I knew she really cared for me. But at that very moment, I didn't feel an itsy-bitsy spider's web worth of love.

"That's right." She gave me a long stare. "What does Tanty Vera always tell yuh?"

Against my will, I smiled. "That I am beautiful. That I am talented. That I am loved. Always."

"Always," she said. "Now tell me chile. What's troublin' yuh?"

"Nothing."

She placed a hand upon her wide hip. "Nah yuh know me know yuh like yuh was me own. And me lookin' at chu and know sumting weighs heavy on yuh heart. Whappen?"

"Nothing happened," I said, shifting my eyes.

"If it's about de car, don't vex. Yuh get another."

"It's not about the car, Auntie."

"Well me hope it's not about those fast girls. Dey frontish. And dey more hot than dey sweet." She sucked her teeth long and hard. "No worry with that."

"Please. I'm not thinking about them hooter-cooters. I know they're always stirring stuff up. They're nothing but hoggish pot hounds anyway."

She chuckled at me calling them rude stray dogs. "Be nice, chile."

"Always."

"Uh-huh. Leh go."

I shook my head.

"Come now. Get off ya bamsee and get ya tings. I'm takin' yuh home wit' me, like me used to."

I felt a pang in my chest. "Auntie Vera, I really miss those times."

I smiled, then quickly felt sadness sweep over me, remembering the festive holidays I'd spent with Vera and her family over the years when I wasn't spending them in France with one of my boarding school friends' families. And then that one time when I spent it with Rich and her family in Aspen for the winter break. And she had caught me and her brother, RJ, talking real heavy with our naked bodies. And we were having a good conversation, too, until she burst through the door with a blackmailing smile on her face. Miss Yappity-Yap couldn't wait to go tell her parents on us and spoil all of our fun. So that ended that. Still, my memories of the holidays, summers, and short breaks were bittersweet; all of the laughter and love... spent with everyone else's family except my own.

Vera smiled. "Me miss dem, too. Come now."

I smiled back at her. "That's all right. I'm fine right here. I'm sixteen and grown now. I'll be okay."

"Well, would yuh like for me to stay a while longer?"

I shook my head, crossing my arms in front of my chest. "Have you heard from my mother?"

She nodded. "Yes. I spoke wit' she twice today."

"Is *she* coming home?" Why I asked this was beyond me. I mean, really. I haven't overdosed on stupid. I already knew the answer. Still I kind of hoped for a different answer, just this once. Vera gave me a solemn look that told me what I already knew. Kitty had no interest in seeing about her only child.

"I'm not sure when yuh muddah is due in. When I spoke to she earlier, she said she'd try to get in this evening. If not, she'd definitely be here by the end of the week."

My eyes widened, then narrowed. What else was new?
It has always been about Kitty. Kitty this, Kitty that. *Kitty-
cat, Kitty-cat, stuff her in a hat.* I felt like snatching her by
her fluffy-butt tail and swinging her out of a window, just
to see how many lives she really had. But, knowing her,
she'd have more than nine lives and land on her hoofs. I
had 199 problems, and Kitty was one.

All she ever does is put herself before me. I hated that
crap. I have always been second to her career, third to the
guest on her show, fourth to her charities, and fifth to any
other mess she deemed important. I might as well have
been a Safe Haven baby she dropped off since she left me
with everyone else to take care of me. I had never been
her responsibility.

Whatever! What else do you do when you're married to
an old wealthy coot with no children? Simple: You give
him a baby, then let him figure out what to do with it. And
his solution: Hire a house manager and nanny and let
them raise it. Oh, and forget the fact that neither of those
women spoke fluent English. Oh, no. That wasn't of concern. Keeping a bouncing baby out of sight, except for
photo ops. Oh, oh, in front of the cameras and in all of my
childhood photos you would think I had been their bun-
dle of pride and joy. Nope. It was all an act.

So any memories of being kissed on the forehead, or
hugged, or told I was loved were from my Spanish and
French caretakers—Esmeralda and Solenne, during the
first three years of my life. My first steps, my first tooth, my
first words spoken, shared by them. I learned to speak
Spanish and French. And my concerned mother, oh, she
had no idea what I spoke. She thought it was gibberish.
And as a matter of fact, she had me evaluated, thinking I

was developmentally delayed, or had some kind of neuro-
logical problem. But the laugh was on her, because all of
her fancy doctors and expensive evaluations came back
with the same thing. There was nothing wrong with me. In
fact I was more advanced than most my age. The gibberish
she thought I was speaking was actually me speaking in
French and Spanish, sometimes at the same time. After
Mother made a fool of herself, she made their lives miserable, causing both of them to quit. She chased the only
two women who cared anything about me out of my life.
She knew they were both the closest things to a real
mother that I had known. And she took that away from
me. No one else in this house spoke French, or Spanish.
So I had to be forced to learn English.

Then what does Mother do the minute I turn twelve?
She ships me off to Le Rosey—a prestigious boarding
school in Switzerland—and leaves me there to fend for
myself because she couldn't be bothered with the needs
of a prepubescent girl. That's what she did. So, I purposefully took all of my studies in French since students there
were given the option to take their studies in either English or French.

I glanced over at Vera, who was looking at me as if she
knew what I had been thinking. "Don't yuh swell up yuh
face now. Yuh muddah will come."

I huffed, "Yeah, right. When has she ever?" I felt myself
about to go off. Just once, you'd think Kitty would pretend
to be concerned about me. I was almost killed today in a
car accident, attacked by two backdoor-bronchos, then
played like an old tossed salad by that lowlife Corey. And
where was Kitty?

I touched the side of my bruised face where London

had punched me. And pulled in my swollen lip where Rich had hit me. The pain was a reminder of how messy and lonely life could be. They wouldn't know the minute, nor the second, but I was gonna make them pay if it was the last thing I did. But I had a more pressing matter. Kitty Ellington! The neglectful mother!

If she were asked what my favorite color was, or my favorite movie or song, she wouldn't have a clue. If you asked her what my bra size was, or when I started my cycle, Miss Shitty Kitty wouldn't be able to tell you. That's how much Miss Mother of the Year knows about me. Not a cold damn thing! I promise you. It'd be a hot day in hell before she ever knew anything about me.

I run my own life. And do what I want! That's how it's always been. And that's how it'll always be. Screw Kitty! I hope she drowns in her litter box. If she doesn't watch her claws, I'll be chopping down her cherry tree next.

I looked over at Vera and shrugged. "I don't care if she does or not. You go on home with your family. I'll see you in the morning."

She walked over to me and gave me a kiss on the forehead and told me to call her if I needed anything. "You know, Tanty Vera loves yuh."

I smiled as she wrapped her arms around me and pulled me into her bosom the way she used to when I was younger. A part of me wanted to go home with her. To be where it was safe, and filled with love. But her home wasn't mine. Her family wasn't mine. Truth is, I had no family. And this wasn't a home. This was a cold, empty estate that meant absolutely nothing. I had no grandparents, no aunts or uncles, or cousins—that I knew of because Kitty had cut them all off long before I was born. And I have no rela-

tionship with any of my seventy-eight-year-old, free-spir-
ited, yoga-bending, loin-clothed father's family.

Vera gave me another hug and kiss, then headed toward the door. She looked back over her shoulder and
gave me a wide smile, then walked out. I watched as she
disappeared behind the closed door.

If Vera would have stayed a moment longer I know I
would have lost it.

I balled up on my chaise, then without warning I burst
into tears. Here I was in this big, two-story, majestic
Mediterranean-style mansion with all of its arch-topped
windows and fancy trimmings with no one here to hug me
or console me or even show me love.

I stared over toward the flung-open glass doors of my
two Juliet balconies that overlooked the courtyard, feeling
empty. I'd give up everything to have parents. As much as
I couldn't stand Rich, and as much as I despised that uppity London, and as much as Heather ruffled my nerves,
the one thing that they all had in common was parents—
well, in Heather's case, *a* parent, even if she was a drunk
and had burned my neck up...at least Heather still had
someone to come home to. Me? I had a mother more committed to her TV show ratings and her twenty-eight-year-
old boy-toy who she thought I didn't know anything about
than she was to me. And a father with his old rickety, ancient self, over in the Himalayas chanting to a Higher
Power and too busy chasing the Fountain of Youth. Who
was here for Spencer? Nobody.

I envied Rich, London, and even Heather. And wondered what my life would have been like if I had had parents who loved me, and tucked me in at night, and kissed
me on the forehead. Parents who had told me that every-

thing was going to be okay even if it wasn't. Parents who had cared enough about me to discipline me and set rules that I could break even if they didn't make sense. Parents who loved me enough to care about what I was doing. I've always wanted to know what that would be like. To be wanted.

I wasn't a Daddy's girl.

I wasn't a Mommy's little angel.

I was abandoned.

I was an orphan.

I was Spencer Ellington. Unwanted, unloved.

Oh, well... it's too late to cry over fried onions now.

I shut off my lights and crawled beneath the cold sheets of my bed. Doing my damnedest to pull it apart, I mean, together. But I failed again.

As always.

19

Heather

*A*ddress me as *Your Majesty!*
Kreayshawn on deck.

Shots of Patrón in the air.

Skittles at the door.

Black Beauty in the bag. Crushed and ready to go.

And three bitches brought down with one rock from a slingshot.

You can kiss the ring... Kreayshawn chanted as Co-Co Ming and I bounced across Club Eden. A small rooftop spot that had the best raves and Skittle parties outside of Hollywood.

Clearly the place to be.

The music was right and everyone in here knew me. Co-Co Ming and I were droppin' it low. And poppin' it high.

This was Wu-Wu's night. Not only had I daringly changed my looks and put hot pink highlights in my hair but I had a black Chinese dragon tattoo on my right arm with Wu-Wu blazing through his mouth like fire.

I was hot.

Sizzling.

Boiling over with joy.

My Wu-Wu was back.

Swag was in check.

"Ahhh, Wu-Wu's in the house!" I tossed up five hundred singles in the air and made it rain in the center of the dance floor. Puddles everywhere.

This was Wu-Wu's world and there was nothing anyone could do to ruin my night.

"Bust it, Wu-Wu!" Co-Co Ming spun around on his strappy heels while his matching Burberry blazer and tie floated in the air. His plaid shorts were super tight as he did a Rockette's kick and waved his arms in the air. After a few minutes of dancing Co-Co Ming topped it off with what he called the Wu-Wu duck walk. A mix between the Pop-Lock-and-Drop-It and the Wheelchair.

"Roll it! Ride the chair!" I yelled, dancing in my rainbow sparkling seven-inch platforms and canary booty shorts. My cleavage was busting out of my tiger bra top, ready to be shook free. "Do it, Co-Co! Make it work!" I shook my shoulders. "Who loves you, baby! Pop them hips! Vogue with it, Co-Co! Shimmy, shimmy, Co-Co, pop!"

Co-Co did a fly kick and landed into a Russian split. He started pumping the floor and the crowd who'd been dancing around focused their attention on us and started egging us on. "Ain't no party like a Wu-Wu party!" Co-Co and I sang simultaneously as we got lost in the movement of our bodies.

This was the truth.

The hottest party ever.

"Hey Wu-Wu," the D.J. called me and said from the D.J. booth. "Come say a little something and hit us with a freestyle!"

The crowd cheered as Co-Co Ming encouraged me to go and spit something on the mic. I was definitely not a rap artist but when I was feeling this good I was willing to dabble a little bit. I bounced my way over toward the D.J., took the mic, and said, "I need you to drop that classic Game beat from 'Put You on the Game.'"

The beat boomed from the speakers. All eyes were locked on me. And the vibrations of the beat went through my bones.

"One time for your mind!" Co-Co Ming yelled, slinging his hair back and forth. He was smiling so hard that his eyes sank into his high cheeks.

I waved my arms in the air, directed the crowd which way to sway, and rapped:

Let me tell you how…
I brought the Gucci clique down…
Click, click,
With the camera…behind the bathroom door
And smiling away.
Thought they could get away with the dirty tricks
*   and their best friend's boyfriend.*
Little did they know I was recording on the other
*   end!*
Click, click…

"Two times for your mind!" Co-Co yelled. And the crowd chanted, "Ahh, Wu-Wu's in the house!"

My rap continued:

And then I pressed send.
Brought their world right to an end.
Next thing I know Spencer got whupped down in
*   the ditch.*
Rich found out she was tricked by the dizzy bitch.
London got caught up in the matrix.
And the Gucci clique was clearly not ready for war!
Click. Click...

"Ahh, Wu-Wu's in the house!" the crowd chanted. "Ahh, Wu-Wu's in the house!"

I bunched my shoulders and slid across the stage. The crowd went wild and as I went to take a bow the crowd shouted, "Go, Wu-Wu...Go Wu-Wu!" And the next thing I knew I was taking a handful of Skittles to the head and spitting my rhyme all over again.

20

London

Early Saturday morning found me lying in my man's muscular arms, basking in the afterglow of the hot, steamy, body-rocking lovemaking session we'd just had. Forget the fact that I was on Daddy's Ruin My Daughter for Life list. Let's forget that he had practically grounded me until my thirtieth birthday. Well, okay, not that long, but long enough—at least until he had to fly out to London for business in a few days. I was supposed to be locked away in my room thinking about my behavior. A teenager's version of a time-out. But Daddy would absolutely flatline me if he even caught wind that I had snuck my Boobie into my bedroom two nights ago and was lying up with him right under his nose, underneath his roof. Yeah, I knew I was playing Russian roulette with my life *and* my inheritance. It was a dangerous game. But, like with everything else in life, love was a gamble. There were people in this world who were addicted to gambling. Then there were people like me. Addicted to love. Strung out on fairy tales and happily-ever-after. Caught up in the thrill of doing something you knew you shouldn't be doing all for the sake of experiencing that same exact rush you felt the very first time you did it.

Yes, love had me. And it had me betting high. I was taking a big risk. But when you're with the sexiest man on the face of the earth, who makes your heart flutter and your body shake—when you experience the kind of euphoria I was feeling with my man being in my bed, his hands roaming my body—you threw caution to the wind, tossed your chips up in the air and let them fall where they may. With Lady Luck on my side, nothing could ever go wrong. I was in it to win it.

Nothing else mattered to me. Not Daddy's wrath. Not the threat of being shipped off to a convent, or the threat of a nuclear war. I was feeling good...no, great! No, scratch that...fabulously on top of the world.

Then why am I feeling like the rug is about to be pulled right from underneath my baby-soft feet?

"I love you so much, baby," floated from my Boobie's lips, as he nibbled on my ear. He whispered it again. And the uneasiness that gathered in the center of my chest slowly vanished. He caressed my face, then lightly kissed me on the lips. "You know you my world, right?"

I lifted my head off his chest and looked him in the eyes. For a brief moment I wondered if he loved me in the same way that I loved him. Would he risk losing every ounce of who he was for me if the diamond were on the other hand?

He kissed me on the tip of my nose.

"What you thinking about, baby?"

I shifted my eyes, trying to keep my insecurities from sneaking up on me. "Nothing."

"Yo, c'mon, London. Don't play me. You know I can tell when there's something going on in that pretty little head of yours. Talk to me."

"Do you love me?"

He scrunched his face. "Of course I do. What kind of question is that? Didn't you just hear me tell you how much?"

I nodded. "I know what came out of your mouth. But did you mean it? Do you feel it?"

"Yo, word up, baby. Don't do that. After all we've been through, do you even have to ask?"

I ran my hand over his smooth chest. "I just don't want anything to change between us, that's all."

"Baby, stop. Nothing's gonna change with us, ya hear? We're in this together, thick as thieves, for life. You and me against the world, baby. You're the Bonnie to my Clyde." He took my hand and placed it over his heart. "Feel that?"

I nodded. Beneath, his hard pecs felt like the thundering of horses.

"That's us, baby. One heart, one beat...one love. Nothing can ever change that. But if you're feeling some kinda way about what we've been planning, then we can squash it all.

"Everything?" I asked, surprised, feeling a tinge of relief and guilt wrapped up in one.

"If that's what you want, hell yeah."

I eyed him. "And you'd be okay with that?"

"Damn straight, baby. I'll give it all up for you. I don't want you doing anything you're not feeling. If you say it's a wrap, then eff it. That's what it is, real talk."

I lowered my head. I loved my man. And I was willing to do anything for him. But there was a nagging in the back of my mind that told me it could all blow up in my face, leaving me to pick up the pieces, again, if I wasn't careful.

I could feel tears rimming my eyes.

He lifted my chin. "Baby, listen. I'd cut out my heart before I ever hurt you. Your happiness is all that matters to me. So it's whatever."

The tears started falling.

"Damn," he said, taking my face in his hands. He leaned in and kissed my tears as they fell. I closed my eyes. "Don't cry." He kissed my right lid, then my left. "I'm right here, baby." He kissed the tip of my nose. Then my lips, taking his hand and gently wiping my tear-streaked face. "I'm not willing to lose what we have."

"I know. I didn't mean to be selfish."

"You're never selfish."

I sighed. "It's just that I'm risking a lot."

"We both are."

"I know that. I only want to be sure that we're in this together."

He pressed his lips softly against mine. "That's how it is. That's how it's always gonna be."

"I don't want anything to go wrong."

"Me either, baby. Life is about chances. Look at us. We were built on chances. And we're still standing. I remember the first time I peeped you, sexy. You remember that?"

I couldn't help but smile. "Yeah, it was Fashion Week."

"And you had just finished tearing the runway up. You were mad sexy..."

My eyes drifted off to the distance. As beautiful as the

memory was, it was equally heartbreaking. I tried to not
think about how that was the last time I was on stage. And
how that was the last time my mother looked at me with
pride beaming from her eyes.

You're nothing now. You'll never be anything.

He stroked my hair. "... You hear me, baby?"

"Yeah... yeah, I hear you."

"Then why you looking all sad?"

I stared into his eyes. My stomach was aching. "I'm
scared and nervous."

"You have nothing to be worried about, baby."

"But I am. I'm worried that you're going to not want
me anymore. That someone is going to take your love
from me."

He pulled me into his arms. "Never that, baby. You're all
I want. All I'll ever want. We've been through too much together for that to ever happen. I'm all yours. In mind,
heart, and in body. I don't see anyone else but you in my
life. Ain't nothing gonna ever come between us. You're my
heart. I love you, girl. You hear me?"

I let out a sigh of relief, nodding. The fear of him leaving me, not loving me, all pressed down on my chest. I
knew he was here with me. Knew I was in his arms. Knew
that we had just finished making love, but still there was a
nagging sense of doom that gnawed at my spirit. I could
feel it, could smell it; could almost touch the heartbreak.

"What, baby, you don't believe me?"

"It's not that I don't believe you. It's—"

He cut me off, climbing out of the bed. "I was tryna wait
to do this..."

"Do what?" I asked watching as he walked over to his
weekend bag.

"I wanted to get things right for us, first. I've been walking around with this for about a week."

I giggled. "Walking around with what for a week?"

He walked back over to me holding a small Tiffany's box in his hand.

"I love you so much, baby. From the moment I saw you I knew you were the one. I never thought you'd check for a dude like me, but you did. It was never about how much money I had. Or what I did or didn't have. It was about me. It was about us. We're a family, baby."

He dropped down on one knee. I quickly sat up in bed, feeling overjoyed. *Ohymgod, ohmygod, ohmygod, he's about to...*

"London Elona Phillips, will you marry me?"

21

Rich

The early morning smog hugged my view of the Santa Monica Mountains as I sat on my terrace, sipped vanilla chai, and struggled like hell to figure out my life. Like how and when did it become so complicated? Yet tucked and fluffed so neatly below the crystal chandeliers and platinum guise of me having it all. When really, I had nothing. It all belonged to two egomaniacs: Richard Montgomery—a high school dropout, turned rap star, turned billionaire businessman; and Logan Montgomery neé Shakeesha Logan Gatling—a ridiculous groupie turned rich Stepford wife.

My life was nothing about me.

It was *all* about them.

Their money.

Their image.

Their dreams.

Their wishes.

Their plans for *me*.

They were the puppeteers and my little diamond-laced strings were to dance, move, groove, and love...however they wanted them to.

I'm tired of loving you and not getting anything back....

I shook Knox's voice from my head. The last thing I needed was to be haunted by one of his late night I'm-tired-of-only-being-friends guilt trips. I just wanted to skip to the next track of my life instead of being stuck on the same eight-year-old crush.

Damn.

I bit into my bottom lip.

I should run away...

I nodded.

Yeah...I should...

But then again... I thought as the chef sat my silver-dome breakfast tray on the small café table before me and smiled. *Maybe not...I don't think I'd have enough money for the chef to come with me. And if I didn't have a chef how would I eat?*

"Good morning, Miss Rich." The chef smiled and waved his hand toward the dome as if he'd just delivered a grand prize. "Hopefully you'll join your parents at breakfast in the morning. Two days away from the table is much too long."

I frowned. "I wasn't missed."

"Quite the contrary." He grinned—all teeth. "The table seemed rather dull and besides I missed you telling me how hot and boppity boom—"

"It's boom-bopped."

"Well how hot and *boom-bopped* I made the food this morning. And your parents looked rather sad. Particularly your mother."

Good. Let me them feel my wrath.

I lifted the dome and pointed to the plate of strawberry and banana crêpes with whipped cream, eggs, and bacon—fried hard. After money—oh and the press—food was definitely my main boo. "Bam!" I said with glee. "You boom-bopped dropped and popped it this morning, Chef Jean." I snapped my fingers and broke out into a slight dance in my seat.

Chef Jean giggled. "That's my Rich. And I knew crêpes were your favorite. Now tomorrow if you change that frown into a smile and join your parents at the breakfast table I will make chocolate chip pancakes."

I simply smiled. I guessed now wasn't the time to tell him that I'd planned to never speak to my parents again.

"Maybe," I said as I placed my linen napkin across my lap and picked up my fork. "Maybe."

Chef Jean smiled. "Good day, Miss Rich."

"Good day."

"Is it a good day?" my mother bogarted onto my terrace. She smiled at the chef as he left and kissed me on the forehead. Then she had the audacity to take a seat at my small pink table with me.

The nerve of her!

I started to tell her to run along, that her suite had a much better view so she didn't have any reason to be all up in here with me. All up in my space. But I didn't. I didn't want to take the chance of her bringing it to my face again. So, I took another route and punished her with my silence.

That always killed her.

"Richie-poo," my mother said as she scooted her chair next to mine, placing the Tiffany bag she held around her wrist in the center of the table. "Are you still mad at Mommy?"

Pissed. Off. I know going to jail wasn't the thing to do but I'm sick of you and your husband telling me what to do, when to do it, and how to do it. And I didn't appreciate the way you or your little gang-star ran up on me like that was cool.

No matter what I thought I didn't say a word. I simply picked up a forkful of eggs and placed them in my mouth. Then I looked at my mother and chewed . . . slowly.

"Don't be like that," she said. "I hate when you shut down. It makes me feel terrible."

Duh, that's the mission.

She reached in my plate and took a piece of bacon. "You know I love you."

No, you love the perfect daughter. You don't love me.

Silence.

I stared at her and it took everything in me not to smile as I saw the screws of guilt driving deeper into her. But whatever, she needed to feel guilty. She and my father were completely out of pocket.

"Richie-poo, your father and I aren't trying to hurt you."

I started to roll my eyes, but instead I did one better—I dabbed at the corners of them. Of course they were dry. It took a lot for me to cry, but my mother didn't know that.

"Awwl, Richie-poo." She leaned over and pulled me into her bosom. "I know you think that your father and I were hard on you. And maybe we were. Just a little. But, you have to understand you're not just *anyone's* daughter. You are the daughter of a high-profile figure and people are watching everything you do. Everything that you do matters. It matters to us. It matters to the public. And it should matter to you, first and foremost."

I dabbed my eyes again and sniffed.

She continued, "We only want what's best for you. It may not make sense to you now but it will in the end."

Whatever!

"If you just do what we tell you to do. You will see how much better things will be. I promise you one day it will all make sense."

"And when will that day be, Ma?" I blurted out and immediately shook my head. *There goes the silent punishment.*

My mother gave me a relieved smile, as if something in her mind told her we were friends again. Not.

"When you become a mother," she said.

"Well, I don't want to wait that long," I said.

My mother released me from her embrace and eyed me. She took a deep breath, and said, "Exactly what are you talking about?"

I shook my head. "Nothing. You never listen anyway."

She leaned forward in her chair with one brow raised. She tilted her head. "No, I'm listening. Now go on."

I hesitated. The sound of her voice let me know that I could handle this one of three ways. I could either retreat to being silent and postpone this for two more days, be the sweet sixteen-year-old who batted her eyes and did what Mommy said while being rewarded with a kiss on the forehead and a gift, or two. Or I could throw a tantrum.

Before I could decide what to do my mother said, "But... let me warn you. Watch what you say and watch how you say it."

"So you don't really wanna know how I feel then. You

just want me to be mechanical," I said, knowing I was pushing my luck. "Okay, okay, so I'll be a robot. I'll be the sixteen-year-old with no opinion of her own, who only listens to what you tell her to do. Who obeys your rules and gives no backtalk and no drama. Is that okay?"

"Exactly," my mother said snidely. "And you will also be the sixteen-year-old who gives me no reasons to even *think* about slapping her face again or tossing her over the cliff." She pointed toward the mountains.

I swallowed. I forgot about the cliff. And bigger than that, I forgot that my mother was crazy enough to knock me over it.

"Now, I love you," she continued. "But you will do what I say."

"You were never this hard on RJ. He did whatever he wanted to do and still does!"

"RJ *listened*. You are caught up in some warped power struggle with your father and me."

"No I'm not. I just want to live *my* life. After all it is *my* life," I pouted.

She chuckled. Looked me over and placed her hand on her hip. "You've been misinformed, honey. You have no life, darling. I planned to have you. I gave birth to you. I named you. And I raised you. *You* are *my* child and your life is one that I orchestrate. Now you have access to a lot of things: money, trips, diamonds, parties. Things that I could only dream of at your age. And there is no way I'm going to watch you piss it all away behind some broke-down little boy because he's fine and good in bed!"

"This has nothing to do with Knox!"

"This has *everything* to do with Knox! And lower your damn voice!" She clenched her teeth. "Now you hear me and you hear me well. Everything that feels good to you is not good for you."

"See, I told you, you didn't listen. You didn't wanna hear what I had to say. You only wanna hear what you wanna hear."

She crossed her legs. "Oh, I heard you and I'm listening. I'm just giving you instructions on what to say and how you better say it. Or do you suddenly have nothing to say and are waiting for me to kiss you on your forehead and hand you the diamond Tiffany bracelet that I had your father pick out for you?"

I glanced over at the bag and then turned back to my mother. "Diamonds aren't always a daughter's best friend."

"Well it better be chocolate cake then. Because it will not be the offspring of the hired help."

"I should be able to make my own decisions!"

"Are you raising your voice at me? Do you really want to escalate this to another level? Because as long as I cover your bank account, I make your decisions. So here are your choices." She opened the Tiffany bag and removed a chocolate and pink diamond bangle. "Diamonds or nothing. Now you decide." She dropped the bangle back into the bag and stood up.

"Ma—"

"Be quiet. Because I will have the last word. Now if you want your life to be a living hell, then let me know and I will start the fire roaring." She stared at me for a few moments and I decided to let it go because it wasn't worth her drama. Not when I was going to do what I wanted to do anyway.

I was grown and had always been grown. And she had run my life long enough.

"Okay, Ma. Whatever you say."

She bent down and roughly grabbed my chin. "Now you're trying to be sarcastic." She thrust her face into mine and I could smell the morning chai on her breath. "Rich, don't try me." She looked me deep in my eyes as if she were trying to burn her message into my soul. "There will be no you and Knox. So you better go run along and find yourself another little love interest because if I even hear that you're back messing with him again, I will not be as nice as I was this summer. You hear me? And you better say yes."

"Yeah, Ma, I hear you."

"I *said* say yes."

I paused. Swallowed. I wanted to snatch away and tell her to get out of my face but obviously that wasn't the safest thing to do. "Yes, Ma."

She kissed me on my forehead and said, "That's more like it. Now your father is off to New York with Turner. They have business to attend to. And I'm headed to Scottsdale. Your auntie and I have a spa appointment. I need to work out some stress."

She pointed to the Tiffany bag and smiled. "Diamonds are always a daughter's best friend."

I watched her walk out of my room and slam the door behind her. I picked up the throw pillow in the chair she'd sat in and tossed it toward the door. This was my life!

When you gon' let me love you!

"I can't!" I screamed at the sound of Knox's voice that invaded my mind. "But I want to so bad."

Skip it. I'm tired of thinking and I can't sit here like this anymore. I jumped out of my seat, left my half-eaten plate behind and hopped into the shower. The rain spout ran over my body and in mind's eye all I could see was Knox standing behind me...I could feel his hands on my body and...

Stop it!

This is crazy!

Shaking my thoughts, I ended my shower, quickly blow-dried my hair, and left my Chinese bob uncurled and fashionably blunt. I slipped on a pair of tight-fitting and curve-complimenting AG cigarette jeans, a crisp white rhinestone T-shirt from my private collection that read MADE THE HEADLINES TODAY?, a pair of five-inch denim Jimmy Choos, then tossed a soft pink Tori Burch frilly scarf around my neck. I put a pair of pink diamond studs in my ears and clasped my new bangle around my wrist.

I grabbed my Hermès hobo bag, descended the stairs, and slipped out the side door. I didn't know where I was headed; all I knew is that I had to get out of Beverly Hills before I lost it. Completely.

How did I end up here...?

I leaned against the doorframe and wondered what I would say to him. And what would he think of me being here. All I knew is what he wanted and what I could give him.

Which were two different things.

Maybe I should leave...

But I wanted to be here. And for now, at least for today, I wanted to pretend that this was right. That there was no mother, no threats, no balancing act of what I felt and what I was told to do. No worry about tomorrow. Tomorrow was too heavy, too much to contend with. In order to follow through with this I had to live in the moment.

I knocked again, hoping like hell he would hurry and answer before my nerve took flight and I fled.

I waited a few seconds more, nervously leaned from one foot to the next and bit the inside of my cheek.

Just leave.

I turned on my heels and made up my mind to hurry down the hallway but before I could take two scurrying steps he called, "Rich?"

I turned around and gave him a shy smile. "Oh hey, Knox. Umm yeah, it's me." I shrugged. "I, umm, was in the neighborhood."

"Oh really?" He folded his arms across his chest; the thin nylon of his Lakers jersey highlighted the muscular definition of his hard pecs. My eyes glazed over his baggy gray sweats and a sly smile swept its way across my face. I quickly tucked my lips in and dropped my eyes to the floor, hoping he couldn't read my blue thoughts.

"Long drive just to be in the neighborhood," he said sarcastically.

I lifted my eyes. I was so not in the mood for his cynicism but since he wanted to take it there... "Not really." I batted my lashes. "Being as though I usually drive past here. This was a short trip. Trust."

"Rich, please. You and I both know that you don't drive more than five minutes outside of Beverly Hills. Seriously, did you forget who you were talking to?"

"Whatever."

"Yeah, I got your *whatever*."

Silence.

"Now, did you come to kick in the hallway or would you like to come in?" he asked.

I didn't answer. I simply walked past him and stepped

across the carpeted threshold and into his small three-bedroom apartment that was a horrifically messy, royal-purple-and-mustard-gold homage to Knox's fraternity, Omega Psi Phi.

There was Que paraphernalia everywhere: wooden plaques on the wall, rugs on the floor, throw covers on the back of a nasty black and white checkered couch—that was clearly a seventies nightmare. And behind the couch was a picture of a bulldog with a giant nametag that read: ATOMIC DOG.

There were wooden beads that separated the galley kitchen from the compact living room and Bob Marley's "Jammin'" played loudly. One of Knox's roommates sat nodding his head—heavy-metal hard—to the music and the other sat with a video game remote in his hands and his eyes on me. He smiled at me but before I could give him the screw face, he looked over to Knox and fell out laughing. "You da man," he chuckled. "You da damn man, big homie!"

Knox gave him a sly grin. "It ain't even like that."

"Like what?" I interjected, curious to know what the hell this gooch was laughing at.

Neither Knox nor his roommate answered me. Instead, Knox's roommate said to him, "Oh word? Then you need to hook a brotha up." He looked me over and licked his lips. "They call me Midnight but you can call me all night."

Knox's smile quickly faded. "Yo, play ya game. Come on, Rich."

"Don't be like that. You 'spose to share, Knox!" His roommate cracked up as I walked behind Knox and followed him into his room. "You 'spose to share!"

"Knox," I said. "What was he...talking..." I paused.

Blinked. "Who is this?" I asked, stopping in my tracks, my eyes quickly zeroed in on the girl who sat on Knox's bed with her back against the wall. Immediately my mind told me she'd been here for hours.

Suddenly, I felt played. Smacked across the face. Disrespected. It took everything in me not to lose it.

I swallowed and I could tell by the look on Knox's face that he'd read my mind.

"Rich," Knox said, locking eyes with me. "This is Nikki. Nikki this is Rich."

"I heard so much about you!" Nikki said a little too chipper, flashing her Colgate smile. She stood up and extended her hand.

I stared at her and instead of quickly dismissing her I was unexpectedly stuck on how pretty she was.

She had flawless chestnut colored skin, unlike me— who every other month had a bout with acne.

She had a short and tapered Kelis-inspired haircut; the exact same haircut that I wanted. But, I wasn't sure if hair that short would look good on me. So I played it safe and settled for a Chinese bob.

She was petite; I struggled with my weight.

I couldn't believe this was happening. And I knew this was silly, and crazy, and made no sense. And of course I remembered the elementary school lesson of never comparing yourself to anyone: "Everyone's different."

Yet and still...I couldn't help it.

And yes, I knew I was stunning...curvaceous...had a dimpled smile...eyes the color of light brown marbles... and thick, bouncy, jet-black hair that could be styled effortlessly.

And yes, I knew I was fierce, and fabulous, and fashionable. Yes, I really did know all of this…problém was at this moment I didn't feel it, because if I did there would be no way that I'd be standing here—feeling as if I held my heart in my hand—and wondering if Knox thought that Nikki was prettier than me.

This was sickening.

A steel lump settled in my throat.

I wished I could place this moment on pause, rewind it, pretend that this never happened, and go back to a time when I thought I was the only one on Knox's mind. Now I knew I was wrong.

I turned to Knox. "If I caught you at a bad time I can leave."

He looked over at Nikki, who'd dropped her hand back to her side. She smiled at him and said, "No, it's cool. You two go on. I need to get to work anyway. Call me later, Christian."

Christian…

She walked over to him, gave him a hug, and then a kiss on the cheek. Knox eyed me the entire time she was in his arms. I couldn't believe I had driven an hour and a half to witness this. This was nowhere on my radar. It was not the escape I imagined. I eyed Knox as he walked Nikki to the door and I overheard him say, "I'll call you later. Enjoy your day."

Immediately I felt sick to my stomach. *I need to get out of here.*

He closed the door behind her and turned to face me.

"Who was that, *Christian?*" I asked, tilting my head. "And what was she doing here?"

"Whoa, hold up," he said, frowning. "I just told you that was Nikki. And she was here because I invited her here. Now wassup with all the attitude?"

"The question is wassup with you inviting me to come down here and you got some chick all up in your room?"

"First off, that attitude is straight outta pocket. Second of all, anytime I've ever asked you to come down here you always have some excuse and you never show up. Now all of a sudden you wanna *peel your face away* from the mirror, take a break from your fan club and the press, and fit me into your life schedule. Then you have the nerve to pop up—without calling—and wanna question me? Do I look like Corey? Nah, I don't think so."

I didn't respond to that. I couldn't. Because if I did I would've responded with a slap across his face. I grimaced, folded my arms, and fought against my insecurities. "So umm, was all that production because that's your little girlfriend?"

"Are you my little girlfriend? Did your mother give you permission? Is that why you're here?"

I don't believe he said that. Tears rushed to the back of my eyes. *Don't cry. Don't cry. You better not drop a tear. What you better do is read him.* "Let me kick this to you real quick—"

Knox walked up to me, leaving no personal space between us. "Yo, what's your problem?"

"I don't have a problem! I just don't appreciate being made to look stupid."

"What?" He looked at me confused. "Stupid?! What are you talking about? You are being real silly right now."

"I'm not your groupie. You got the wrong one! You could've told me that you were seeing somebody else!"

"I don't have to tell nothing. You're not my girl, but it's obvious that you wanna be." He stepped even closer. Brushed my hair from my face. "You wanna be my girl? Just say the word and I might let you be."

"Boy, please." I waved my hand. "If I wanted you I could have you. Let's not forget about this summer."

"Rich."

"What?"

"Shut up," he said sternly as he surprisingly pressed his lips against mine, forcing our tongues to drip in heated delight. Knox ran his hands through my hair and instantly my knees buckled as he pressed my back against the wall. I placed my hands on the nape of his neck and continued to kiss him passionately. Our tongues flicked back and forth and I felt as if we were fighting a love war.

His hands roughly cupped my behind and just as I lifted my leg to meet his waist, he broke our kiss, grabbed my thigh and said, "Are you done playing games yet?"

What? Did he just . . .

"Come on, Knox," I said, sounding as if I was seconds away from begging. "Not now." I pulled him closer to me and attempted to kiss him again. "We can talk about this later. I promise." I lifted his shirt and ran my hands over his pecs.

He pushed my hand down and pulled his face away. "Nah, there's no later. You need to let me know what this is now. 'Cause if all you're offering me is a piece of you then I gotta say peace to you, 'cause I'm done with the games."

Why was he doing this? Damn. I felt desperate. I needed him, in more than one way. And I needed him today, right now, at this moment. I needed to be in his arms and yeah,

I wanted to stay there forever, but given my life I didn't know how I would do that... if I could do that... But judging by the look in his eyes I knew that it was all or nothing. So I did what I had to do, which was tell him what he wanted to hear before I lost him for good. "I love you." I looked deep into his eyes. "And I wanna be with you." I lifted his shirt above his head and kissed him on his neck. "Always."

"Then you got me." He reached over me and flicked the light off.

22

Spencer

"Spencer, Spencer, Spencer..."
Ohsweethoneyblossoms...

I lay perfectly still in my bed, wondering if this was the beginning of a nightmare. I lifted my eye mask up over my head. There stood my mother tapping the side of my bed with a rolled up magazine in her manicured hand. She was immaculately dressed in a tailored pencil skirt and sleeveless blouse. Her arms were toned from years of Pilates. I knew her matching blazer was somewhere not too far, ready to be slipped into. Her light, honey-brown hair was cut into a sleek bob. I blinked. Surprised she had cut and relaxed the curly locks that normally bounced up on her shoulders. Kitty was in her early forties, but she didn't look a day over thirty-nine. And she definitely didn't look old enough to be the mother of a teenage daughter. And she sure didn't act like a mother, either.

I scowled, realizing that this wasn't the opening of a frightening dream. It was indeed a fairy tale. I was Little

Red Riding Hood. And she was the Big Bad Wolf. *Two days later, she finally decides to show her face to blow my house down.*

"When the cat's away, the mice will play," she said in a singsong voice. "Or in this case my sweet, sweet Spencer will. So, tell me. Does this magazine article have anything to do with why you're sleeping 'til noon? Or could it be the two million hits on YouTube that have worn you out? Oh, wait. Perhaps I should be the one tired from *Hustler* magazine, *Playboy*, and *XXX Girls* calling me nonstop to see if you're eighteen. Yeah, that's it. I should be the one exhausted."

I blinked as she pulled back the drapes, inviting a stream of bright light into my room. *How rude!* "Because," I said, trying to adjust my eyes to the flood of rays, "that's what I always do on Saturdays. But you wouldn't know that."

"Oh, really? Well it seems here..." she said, opening the teen magazine. "That along with sleeping 'til noon, you've been on your knees in bathrooms, sleeping with your friend's boyfriend. That's what I do know. Have you no discretion? How crude."

I sat up in bed, folded my arms across my chest. "*How crude?* You have a lot of nerve, Mother. Besides, I get it from you. 'Cause while your husband's away Miss Kitty-Kitty likes to play in her little litter box with the new boy-toy she keeps locked away at her New York City penthouse suite."

She chuckled, then clapped. "Touché, I'm impressed. But you have a ways to go before you'll ever be me."

I scowled again. "Don't drown yourself in that entire ego of yours. I don't ever wanna be you."

"Oh, my delusional darling Spencer. You're already me. The difference is I know to keep my dirt well-hidden. Now stop sulking, and come give Mother a hug." She leaned in to hug me. The signature aroma of the Clive Christian perfume she religiously wore engulfed me. My body stiffened. "I've missed you," she said.

"Oh, really? Was that before or after boy-toy number one? Or boy-toy number two? Or maybe boy-toy number seven? Oh, no, of course not. It must've been before Daddy ran off to dance with Buddah." I clasped my hands together. "Oh, no. Maybe that's not it either. Maybe it was when I only knew how to speak French."

She let out an exasperated sigh. "Oh, Spencer, not this again. How many times do we have to keep going down this road? I am not going to apologize for things that can't be undone. And I'm definitely not going to be made to feel guilty about it. I don't live my life with any regrets. And neither should you. So stop trying to berate me and be grateful that I'm here."

Be grateful? Was she serious? For what, the fact that she called me three times a week to check in on me instead of being home to parent me? If this was where Kitty really wanted to be, she'd pack up her TV show and move it out here instead of staying in New York. But this is not where she wanted to be. No. Kitty wanted to be on stage, seen as anything other than a mother. But no...that's not true. She wanted to be regarded as a great mother; a woman who put family before all else. Well, guess what? She failed!

"Yeah, you're here all right. Two days too late. Why didn't you come home when I got into that accident?"

"Oh, Spencer, just stop it. You were still alive. There was no need for me to come home."

So I have to be in a box before she comes home. I gasped. "I can't believe you just said that. So had someone from Potter's Field called you—"

"Oh, Spencer, you wouldn't be at Potter's Field. Stop exaggerating. You're being so sensitive. You're alive, and that's all that matters."

I climbed out of bed, sliding my feet into my slippers. My feet sank into the plush carpet. "So what do you want, Mother, an Emmy for finally finding your way back home? But you're right, the road is closed. And I'm done traveling it. So welcome home."

I walked into my bathroom and shut the door, leaving behind a trail of resentment. There was a part of me that felt like crying, but I wasn't even sure if I cared enough to. I'd shed enough tears over her already.

Thirty minutes later, I was showered and dressed in pink loungewear, sitting downstairs at the breakfast nook, eating a fruit salad with cottage cheese when Kitty walked into the room. I crossed my ankles.

"I do hope you behave yourself. And, umm...you're special...and umm...your body is a treasure..." She glanced over at Vera, tapping her fingers on the lava countertop. "Vera, what's the other part of what you used to say? That was so cute."

Vera looked at me, then over at my mother and said, "It's...you are beautiful and I love you."

"Oh, yeah, that's right. That was so sweet. Umm, what else? Oh, yeah...do well in school because I am spending a lot of money for you to be at Hollywood High. Although, now that I think of it, I'm still saving several thousands of

dollars a year since you managed to find a way to get yourself tossed out of boarding school. Do me a favor. Don't
go macing people again. It's so urban. Oh, and call your
father. He's finally leaving Asia and heading back to South
Africa. Now he wants to be out there in the jungles. That
man goes from one extreme to the next."

I rolled my eyes and continued eating, pretending
she'd already disappeared.

"Oh, and two more things. No more videos, please,
please, please. The attorney fees are killing me. Oh, yeah,
and remember...discretion is key. So please exercise
good judgment. I have a network to run, I can't babysit
you. And I don't need any further embarrassment. You're
a mature woman. And I expect you to conduct yourself as
such." She looked back at Vera. "Vera, please look after
her. And make sure she doesn't get herself into any more
trouble."

She walked over and gave me a hug and a kiss on the
side of my head. "I'll see you sometime next week. If that
changes, I'll call you. Love you."

"Safe travels," I replied snidely over my shoulder as the
phone rang and the Wolf huffed and puffed her way out
the door.

Vera walked over to me with the cordless in her hand.
"It's for you?"

"Hello?"

"Speeeeeeeeeeeeeeeeeeeencer," Heather blared in my
ear. "Girl, I haven't heard from you in two. Whole. Days.
What has been going on? Have you heard from the Skank
Squad?"

I frowned. "Ummm, Heather why are you yelling in my
ear? I'm not deaf. And no, I haven't heard from them hood

roaches. I'm not speaking to them. After what they did to me, I don't care if I ever talk to them again. Those hoes are trash."

"And why did I know you would say that, boo?" All of a sudden she broke out in song. *"Don't speak to the hoes again...don't speak to the hoes again...don't speak to the hoes again..."* I imagined her throwing her arms up in the air, stepping from side to side dressed in some kind of outlandish Wu-Wu costume. I shuddered at the thought. Heather popped her lips in my ear. "Girl, now stop. Don't be like that. You know we have to be the bigger person. We both know how stupid Rich is. And London is stupid and weak."

I nodded. "Yeah, with her big Amazon self. I can't stand her."

"I can't stand her, either. But you remember what happened Labor Day weekend when we were all down at South Beach and those girls tried to attack us. London jumped in and fought those girls with us. And we had only known her for like a month."

"Well, I'll send her a thank you card. But, I'm done. They jumped me in the ditch when I was trapped in my car. Punched me all upside my head. That's not what friends do."

"And friends don't sleep with each others' boyfriends, either. That was real messy what you did, Spencer. And you know it." Heather paused, then started singing again. *"Aaaaah...messy...beep, beep...Messy...Messy...get it, get it...crunked up...messy..."*

"Uh, what the heck are you doing, Heather? Why do you keep singing off key like that? I really think you need to stick to acting because your singing is horrible. I'm saying one thing and you're turning it into a song. I don't wanna hear that."

"I'm just making a point that what you did was wrong."

"Rich didn't even want him. So what's the big deal?"

"The big deal is he was her boyfriend whether she wanted him or not."

"Well, exactly, he *was*—operative word—her boyfriend. He dumped her."

"How do you know that?"

"Because he told me."

"And Joey told you he wasn't homeless, but he was. *Liar, liar, liar... the roof's on fire... Aaah Wu-Wu...* okay, okay let me bring it back. The point is—"

"No, the point is that no one was supposed to know. I don't know how anyone found out about it. Who would take a video of us? There was no one else in that bathroom except for me and..."

"That no-good mofo," Heather snapped.

"Corey?" Spencer paused. "Oh...no...You think...?"

"Think what?"

"Think he videotaped us?" Before I could answer, she said, "That's exactly what he did. He videotaped me... Then leaked it to the press...He's the one who broke up our friendship."

"And now the Pampered Princesses have been dragged through the press as has-beens."

I frowned, feeling my pressure shoot to my eyeballs. "Wait a minute, now. I'm no has-been. My last name is Ellington."

"Exactly. Now we need to make this right before we get back to school on Monday and find another crew sitting at our table, trying to claim our throne."

I clenched my teeth. "I will. Mace. Them. Down. And, Heather, you know I will."

Silence.

She continued, "So what do we do now? We can't let Corey get away with ruining our friendship like this!"

"No we can't!"

"And when I stop speaking to them scallywags it has to be because that's what I want to do. Not because some no-good Nutty-Buddy took advantage of me and tried to set me up. Why would he do that?"

"I don't know why he did it. But that's not important. What's important is the four of us getting back together again. And that's why I was calling you. We need an immediate girls' intervention—today. Right away. This is an emergency like never before. We're all over the Internet with the wrong headlines."

I sighed. "And I got two million hits on YouTube."

Heather huffed in my ear, like she was annoyed with me. "Spencer, bring it back. That makes it worse."

"Not really. At least I know that out of the two million people who saw me, four hundred and fifty-seven of them clicked the 'Like' button. But you're right, Heather. Even though I don't want to, we need to make up. I'm willing to meet, but I am *not* calling them."

"No worries, boo. I got this."

23

Heather

I hung up the phone with Spencer and fell straight back on my bed, causing my pillows to spill onto the floor. If I could have high-fived myself I would have. I had to say I was quite impressed with my work. I'd torn those Humpty Dumpties down and now all the media kings and gossiping horses couldn't put them back together again. I had to do it. "Ahh, Wu-Wu's in the house!" I dusted my shoulders and popped my invisible collar.

"Heather!" Camille shouted from her bedroom. "I have a headache, what are you doing in there? Shut up! Enough of the Wu-Wu!" She slammed her bedroom door and all I could do was fall out laughing all over again.

"Ahh, Wu-Wu's in the house!"

I reached over on my nightstand for my cell phone. I knew I needed to be rehearsing my lines for my upcoming taping, but this was much more important.

I dialed Rich's number and she picked up on the first ring. "You're so silly, Knox," she laughed.

Knox? Oh, really?

She continued, "I need to get this. Hello?"

I popped my lips. "Hey, Rich?"

"Who is this?" Rich said as if her lips were curled in disgust.

"Who is this? This is Heather. Now don't act as if you didn't see my name pop up on your screen."

"No, actually I didn't see your name pop up on my screen. I never made a habit of saving your number. And what do you want? Last I checked you were team Spencer."

I laughed. This was juicy...so, so juicy. *Humpty Dumpty had a great fall.* "Rich, I'm only calling you out of concern—"

"Concern? For what? Why am I even on your mind? Outside of school and our little daily lunch date, I shouldn't even be a thought—"

"Actually you're not a thought and this is so much bigger than you. The truth of the matter is this is about the clique and the way the media is portraying us. Have you not seen the blogs, or entertainment news? Have you even been on Twitter today? The number one hashtag is 'Pampered princesses gone wild.' And when you click on it, do you know whose face pops up?"

"Whose?"

"Yours!"

"What?"

"And it's not a good picture! You had on no shoes, your mascara looked like war marks, and those little shiny bracelets on your wrists were not platinum. And what were they? Handcuffs. Squeezed extra tight, making your hands look like they belonged to the Pillsbury Doughgirl."

"Excuse you?"

"You heard me. Oh and the headline above that pic was RICH MONTGOMERY IS JAILED AND EATING HERSELF TO DEATH. And wait, wait, I just remembered there's another that read CHUBBY LIL RICH MONTGOMERY CAN'T KEEP A MAN."

"Oh hell no!"

"Oh hell yes, girlfriend."

"Clutching pearls!"

"And your big friend, London. The headline with her picture reads: NEW YORK AMAZON TAKES DOWN L.A! Oh and before I forget freaky little Spencer has two million hits on YouTube!"

"What!"

"Yes, she's an overnight sensation. Teen porn star in the making! And I just got off the phone with Spencer and she is a mess over it. Distraught!"

"Good for her!" she said sarcastically.

"No this is good for none of us!"

"None of us? What does this have to do with you? How are you affected by this? Like really?"

"Excuse me, do you really know who I am? I have a reputation to protect. I have over three hundred thousand followers on Twitter I have to keep, endorsements, and I cannot be seen in the papers, the Internet, or anywhere with the three of you bouncing off the walls like you're crazy. I can't have my name next to the headline of: THUGS IN CHANEL, PEELING FACES OFF! Now you want to know what this has to do with me? Well it seems that your reputation has me looking guilty of something I never even did. So I need your rep to be cleaned up because being associated with you all is bad for my image and my career. Now we either fix this together or I simply put all the blame on you three and let the chips fall where they may!"

"You wouldn't do that!"

"Are you willing to roll the dice?"

Silence.

"Hello, hello?" I said and a few seconds later I heard a click and it was Rich screaming into the phone, "London! London! SOS! Get your jewels, get your glamour on, we have been destroyed!"

I tried to keep my composure by biting down on my bottom lip and trying not to laugh. I felt like I was seconds away from peeing in my pants. I jumped up and started to do a dance.

"Heather!" Camille shouted. But I ignored her, this was feeling too damn good. There was no way I was going to let Camille blow this high. This kind of high you couldn't even buy.

"London," Rich continued to scream, "I have Heather on the line, too!"

"Heather?" London said confused. "What kinda games. Rich, I don't do—"

"Girl, listen, I know you don't do Heather—"

I interjected, "And Heather doesn't do you."

"Look, I know you didn't call me to argue." London said. "Because I'm busy—"

"Shut up, London, and listen!" Rich screamed. "Heather didn't call you. I called you. Heather called me!"

"Why is Heather calling you? Did I miss something? You're doing Heather now?"

"I'ma say this again," Rich said sounding as if her teeth were clenched. "Shut. Up. We have been annihilated! Dragged like dogs in the media!"

"What!" London screamed. "Dragged. I can't possibly be in the paper again. I've been locked in my room for two days trying to convince my father that I have seen the error of my ways. I cannot be back in the headlines. This is not happening to me! I should've stayed in New York!"

"You're right you should've stayed in New York! Because of you I have been to jail and now the headlines have turned on—"

"You're the one who calls the headlines. You have the media on speed dial! You're the one who sent the video of Spencer macing Heather to your publicist, who in turn sent it all over the world!"

Oh...my...God...Rich did that? That sneaky witch!

"I resent that, London!" Rich spat. "You're the one who pressed send. You're the one who attacked Co-Co Ming and got me all messed up in this mess! And now I have to find a way to get out of it!"

"Rich—!"

"Would you two be quiet!" I yelled. "And listen!"

"Wait a minute," Rich said. "Who just said that?"

"It's me. Heather!" I said. "Obviously you two rabid animals have forgotten I was on the phone!"

"Well, you can get off the phone, because London and I can handle this and we don't need you in our business."

"We sure don't!" London spat.

"You may think you don't need me. But you do, because I have this all recorded."

London gasped and Rich snapped. "You...dirty...!"

"I may be dirty but you are the dirtiest of them all. So thank you for all the juicy details because now I will release this call and only the gossiping gods will know what the headlines will read next." *Click.*

Humpty Dumpty had a great fall.... I fell back against the bed and roared with laughter.

"Heather!" Camille screamed and banged on the wall. "If I have to come down there it will be a problem. I told you that I have a headache! Now shut up!"

Before I could laugh again and torture Camille's headache even more my phone rang. A smile lit up my face as Rich's number appeared on my screen.

Not even the media kings or the gossiping horses could put them back together again.

Gotcha.

"Hello?" I said innocently.

"Heather?" Rich called out to me.

"Who is this?"

"Oh now you wanna act as if you don't know who this is. I don't have time for your games."

"And me, either," London said pissed. "Now get to the point, Rich."

"I don't even believe I'm about to ask you this, Heather," Rich said.

"And what would that be?" I asked.

"What do we need to do to fix this?"

"Spencer's at six o'clock and don't be late."

Click!

I jumped up off the bed and screamed at the top of my lungs, "Who shot ya!"

"HEATHER!"

24

London

The minute I disconnected the call with Rich, I started hyperventilating. That whole conversation had me rendered speechless. I felt paralyzed.

This little light of mine...
I'm gonna let it shine...

"Baby, baby...you all right?" my Boobie asked, rubbing my back, and feeling my head.

No I'm not all right. I'm about to be put out on the streets.

I broke out in a sweat. The only thing I could see was Daddy kicking in my bedroom door like a madman, taking back all of my designer handbags, shoes, and jewels and tossing the rest of my things out on the lawn. If everything Rich had said was true, I needed to grab my passport and flee the country, pronto. Like right now. And join one of those indigenous tribes over in the South Pacific. My life, as I had known it, was about to be over.

"Baby, baby, baby," he said again. "What's going on? What happened? You look like you're about to pass out. You need some water? Talk to me. Tell me what's the matter?"

I slowly turned my head, and stared at his nakedness. "I need you to leave."

He frowned. "What? Leave? Why? Who was that you were on the phone with?"

"Unless you want to go with me, you need to disappear now."

He looked at me confused. "Where you going? I thought we were gonna lay around in bed all day and chill."

"Change of plans," I said, jumping up from the bed, wrapping a sheet around my naked body. "I need to start packing my bags—"

"Yo, hold up. What are you talking about? Pack your bags to go where? You need to calm down because you're not making any sense right now, for real. You're scaring me."

"Well, you need to be scared. 'Cause if Turner Phillips catches you up in here, we are both going to be tagged and bagged."

"What? You're talking crazy now. Tagged and bagged? Can you calm down for one minute and explain to me what the hell you are talking about?"

"Calm down? Calm down?!" I screamed, racing into my walk-in closet and frantically pulling clothes out of my island dresser. "Are you serious? I can't calm down. My life is about to end. I don't know what you're going to do, but I gotta get out of here before my father gets his hands on me and kills me. You can stay if you want. But I won't be coming back to claim your body. So you need to get up. Get dressed. And get out!"

He followed behind me. "Look, baby. Calm down, and tell me who was that on the phone and what happened? 'Cause you are really buggin' hard."

I stopped for a moment, taking a deep breath. "That was Rich. I'm all over the Internet." He looked at me, waiting for me to elaborate.

"And?"

I recapped the whole conversation, pausing every so often to stuff more clothes and jewels into another travel bag. I screamed, "I got to get out of here! Hollywood is the worst thing that ever happened to me!"

He walked over and grabbed me. "That's not true. Hollywood brought you back to me."

"Yeah, and now it's about to tear us apart. I gotta run now while I still have both my legs. I am so dead when my father gets wind of all this."

"Wow," he said, rubbing his chin. "This is crazy. Slow down. You know what? I'm going with you. I'm not losing you to anything or anyone, ever again. We're gonna bounce outta here together."

I jumped in his arms and kissed him. "Oh for real, boo. I love you so much."

He looked me in the eyes. "Wait. They really said that: NEW YORK AMAZON TAKES DOWN L.A.?"

"Yeah, they did. It's horrible."

He burst out laughing. "Yo, that's hilarious. They got you soundin' like a real gangster-type chick."

I frowned, pushing him away from me. "Oh, you think this is funny? My life is a joke to you?"

"Nah, you already know what it is. I'm sayin'...I know you upset about being plastered all over the Internet, but baby...it's not that serious. Sounds like you're making it out to be more than what it is. But if it makes you feel better, you should definitely get up with your girl and go handle ya scandal."

I punched him in the arm. "This is so not funny. I hate you."

"No you don't. You know you love me."

I rolled my eyes.

He cracked up again. "C'mon, baby. It is funny. You know you're not an amazon. So what if that's what they called you. They're just jealous of my baby. Let the media say what they want. You know they're a buncha haters, anyway. Besides, all press is good press."

I pulled in a deep breath. "Well, tell my daddy that."

He pulled me into his arms, and said, "Right now I'm your daddy."

I sucked my teeth. "Boy, you're delusional. You'll never be my daddy."

He smirked. "Yeah, a'ight. But I will always be your man." He slapped me on the behind. "Now go get showered. I'll be here when you get back."

"I'ma beat her, I'ma beat her, I'ma beat. Her. Boom. Boom," Rich chanted over and over as we walked up the circular driveway of Spencer's home.

I pulled her by the arm. "No, you're not. If you go up in that girl's house and get to busting it up all crazy, you are on your own. I don't need any more media attention. I don't need any more cameras flashing in my face. As a matter of fact I'm getting ready to change my whole identity."

Rich looked at me, putting her hand up to her mouth. "Clutching pearls. Are you getting ready to go into the Witness Protection Program or something? Do you think they'll have room for me?"

"Girl, what are you talking about? I'm getting far away from you. You have brought me down with all of your media shenanigans. I can't deal with you anymore. I'm tired. I'm done. It's over. Now we're going to go in here, we're gonna handle these two hoes. You're gonna act right. You're gonna keep your hands to yourself...."

"Hold up. You don't tell me what to do. I'm a lady."

"You're not a damn lady!" I screamed in her face. "You're a barbarian. A media whore! A thug in Chanel! I'm sick of you!"

"Whaaaat?! How dare you! And you're an amazon!" Rich yelled back. "But they shoulda called you King Kong!" She started beating her chest. "You monster!"

The next thing I knew I had swung my handbag upside Rich's head. And we started fighting, rolling around on the grass, and down the hill, punching and slapping each other. Ripping and clawing at each other's faces and clothes.

I rolled on top of her and yelled, "Let me explain the rules to you!"

She rolled up on me. "You don't explain nothing to me!"

I rolled back on top of her. "You will learn how to act."

She flipped me over and jumped back on top of me. "You don't tell me what to do, King Kong. You gotta problem, London! You're nothing but trouble! And I'm not gonna tolerate it!"

"Get it off of me!" Before either one of us could do anything else we had rolled all the way down the hill and into the enormous man-made pond. We both screamed at the same time as we hit the water. I flung my arms around wildly trying to gather my bearings, jumping up. I didn't see Rich anywhere. All I saw were large goldfish swimming around my feet. "Rich!" I screamed. "Rich, where are you, girl? Oh God, no. You're not a barbarian. I'm sorry for calling you that. You have a little thug in you, but you're not barbarian. Rich! I didn't know."

I walked aimlessly through the water calling out for Rich. I was in a state of panic. Then out of nowhere I heard her sputtering, "London! Over here! London!"

I ran over to her. We hugged tightly. "Girl, I thought you had drowned." I looked at her. And she looked at me. We both screamed at what we looked like. Our clothes were ruined. Our hair was wet, soppy mops. Rich had a lily pad stuck on the side of her head. I felt something flopping around in my bra and screamed. Trying to get it out, I tore open my blouse and yanked up my bra. And a fish popped out. My boobies bounced and shook as I hopped up and down.

Rich and I ran out of the water, screaming and hanging on to each other for dear life. "I'm so sorry, London."

"I'm sorry too, Rich."

"We have let them two subpar hoes tear us down to the dogs. We're both better than that. Better than they'll ever be."

"I know, girl, you're right," I said as I tucked my breasts back in my bra and tried to fix my blouse. All the buttons were ripped off. I reached over and removed leaves from Rich's hair. "No more. No more."

Rich and I held hands as she said, "From this moment on, it's you and me against the world, London. Not even the headlines, nor those two dollar trollops can keep us apart. Because for all we know they could be setting us up."

I had to agree with her. "Mmmhmm. They're jealous. Spencer slept with your man and now she wants to do high tea. Yeah, I smell a setup."

Rich put a hand up on her hip and rolled her neck. She was the spitting image of her mother. "Well, I tell you what. The first one who even looks like they wanna buck, we're gonna leap up on 'em, body rock 'em and drop 'em."

"And there you have it," I said, high-fiving her. "That's how we'll do it. All while keeping it calm and keeping it cute."

25

Spencer

"They're here," I said as the doorbell chimed, yelling for Heather up the dual staircases that flowed elaborately down to the first floor of my home. A few seconds later, she came cascading down the right side of one of the staircases, holding on to the wrought-iron railing as if she were prime-time royalty.

"Wu-Wu loves you, boo," she said, waving and blowing kisses and smiling wide with each step. She stopped, placed a hand up over her heart. "I've waited all my life for this moment. I'd like to thank the Academy."

"Heather, will you snap out of it!"

She giggled. "Oh, right-right. Let me bring it back. I almost got caught up in a new sitcom I have in my head."

I sucked my teeth. "Well you need to save that. Now is not the time to be thinking about Web sites. Right now I need you on deck here."

The doorbell chimed again.

"Oh, and trust me. This is right where I want to be,"

Heather said as she walked over to me. She flashed me a toothy smile, then followed behind me to the door. "Now let's get this show on the road."

I opened the door and Heather and I both gasped.

"Ohmysweetluckycharms...I do believe my eyes deceive me," I said breathlessly. "They look like two wild boars. I'm thinking I may need my spear," I whispered to Heather, who was in such shock that her bottom lip drooped.

Maybe they think its Halloween? But whether they do or not, there's no way I can let them in my house. "Excuse me but you two—"

"Are here." Rich slammed her hand on her hip. And I couldn't help but stare at the green leaves stuck in her teeth.

"That's right, we're here," London said, as water dripped from her tangled hair and down her scratched face. They both looked like they'd been wrestling wild sheep, no...I mean, deer. No. Not deer...hungry mountain lions. They were tore-up-to-the-door down! "And," London continued, "we're not in any mood for your tomfoolery!"

I frowned, mostly because looking at these two tore my stomach up. "I think you're at the wrong house. Tom Foolery's estate was foreclosed on about three months ago."

"Whatever," London huffed as she pushed her way through the door and into my home's three-story foyer. All I could think about is how she and Rich looked as if they were melting all...on...my...floor. London carried on, "The point is that what you did was whorish...."

Wait, what did she say?

"Straight skeezer," Rich stated.

Are they talking about me?

"Sluttish," London added.

"Real STD-like," Rich continued.

I know they are not talking about me....

"And you and your overused coochie, Spencer," London snapped, "are a train wreck headed straight to skid row!"

Screetch! These two wild hawks are talking about me!

"And you're lucky," Rich interjected, letting her handbag drop down into the crook of her arm, "that I'm being a lady about it instead of boom-bop-droppin' it upside your head for you being a nasty, lowdown, dirty, trifling skank. Because had I gone with my first instinct I would've bashed your head in and that would've been the real reason that London and I did hard time!"

"We were only there for a few hours, Rich," London said.

"London," Rich said, shaking her head. "Now, you and I both know that you were seconds away from being some muscular woman's wife!"

I gasped.

Rich continued, "What you did to me was downright rat-certified!"

"For what I did to *you*?!" I screeched. "What about what the two of you did to *me?* Both of you attacked me for no reason!"

"Bzzz," London interrupted. "Wrong answer. We didn't attack you for no reason, we attacked you because of your mouth!"

My eyes bucked. "Whaaat? Wait a minute—"

London pointed a dirt-caked finger at me. "No. You wait a minute, Miss Drop Down and Get Your Bobble On. We didn't come way over here to argue with you..."

"We came in peace," Rich butted in, waving her arms and flinging water all over the marble floor. "Something we didn't have to do. Therefore, we don't have any time for your drama, your rants, or your trickery. We've had enough. So you will speak to us like ladies. And—"

London jumped in and snapped her fingers. "Keep it calm. Keep it cute."

Rich tilted her matted and tangled head. "Or there will be a problem." She looked over to Heather. "Or two." Then these two freak-nasty-beetle-juice boogers high-fived each other, then slammed their hands up on their hips for emphasis.

I blinked.

Heather blinked. "Who let the hood out?" Heather asked. "I mean really, I could've sworn the po-po and racial profiling shut y'all down." She dropped down and popped back up. "Is this supposed to be a part of your initiation?"

"Excuse you?" Rich snarled.

"You heard me," Heather went on. "You two came up in here like y'all have left Hollywood to run the skreets now. Seriously, are we supposed to be scurrrrrrred, homie?" Heather exaggerated her voice as she did a two-step, then a Michael Jackson moonwalk.

Rich popped her lips and rolled her neck. "Listen here, little crackhead baby."

"No, you listen here!" I snapped back, pointing a finger at Rich. "Because now you're going too far! Heather hasn't done crack up in here. Crack is whack! The only thing she's done is tequila. Now get out of my house, you swamp creature, and take your clucker-doodle-do with you. I don't allow Section Eight to run through here! And

I don't need either one of you leaving your wet, nasty feathers all up in my house. Now out!" I pointed toward the door. "Before I call the police and have both of you tossed out on your funk-buckets." I walked over to the door and swung it open. "OUT!"

London and Rich both folded their arms and said, "We're not leaving."

I blinked again.

"Psst, please I wish I would." Rich popped her huge lips.

I tilted my head, then glanced over at Heather. She shrugged. "Drop it, boo. Give 'em what they came here for."

I walked over to the marble-topped console, pulling open a drawer. "Oh, you little Miss Potato Heads think I'm playing, huh?" I pulled out a fresh can of Mace, shaking it. "I'll show you." I walked back over to them. "Now, what was that you two pigeons were saying? You said you weren't gonna do what...?"

London and Rich started backing up toward the door.

Heather laughed. "No. Don't leave. Y'all bad; real gutter-gangster with it. Real Long Beach, real Watts with it. But let it be known. The next slore who runs her mouth"—she pointed her fingers at Rich and London like two loaded guns—"will get dropped."

"Now tick-tock, tick-tock," I said, holding the can of Mace in the direction of their faces. "I'm about to spin your clocks."

They both put their hands up in the air. "You know what," Rich said, easing back. "I'll tell you what. We'll just slide quietly on out the door. We see you wanna get it crunked and we don't do drama. We didn't come here for that. So we'll come back at another time when you're feeling better."

"No, you were the one busting up in here tryna get it stunk!" I said. "Didn't your mommas tell you never bring lip gloss to a gunfight?"

Heather fired an imaginary shot up in the air. "*Pow, Pow*! 'Cause we got guns blazing over here. Now how you wanna do this?"

Rich huffed as they stood in the doorway. "Heather, get over yourself! You're the one who told London and me to meet you over here because Spencer was distraught over what she did to me!"

"And what about what you did to me?!" I screamed.

"I didn't do anything to you!" Rich screamed. "You're crazy, Spencer! You should be begging my forgiveness, not getting all nasty and pulling out weapons and whatnot on us. Obviously, the two of you didn't call us over here to deal with how we're being dragged in the media. You called us over here to set me and London up!"

"Set you up? You two barged up in my house," I snapped, lowering the can. "Like both of you wanted to set it off."

Rich flicked her hand at me. "It's not even my style to set anything off! That's all you, trampy-boo! 'Cause obviously you like to set it off wherever there's a bathroom!"

"Oh no you didn't call me a tramp, you troll doll! *Lady and the Tramp* may have been a great movie but I'm no dog!" I waved my finger.

"And I'm no troll doll, you are a drop-to-her-knees whore! How could you sleep with my boyfriend, you freak?!"

"He wasn't your boyfriend! And I know it and you know it, matter of fact the whole world knows all your chubby behind can keep is a plate of food. You definitely can't keep a boo! So don't worry about me and what I did with my man, Corey, worry about the waistline you lost last week! For the next month all you need to eat is yogurt."

I could tell that messed her up.

"You little—" Rich said.

"Stop it!" Heather screamed. "Would both of you shut the hell up! Enough!"

"You don't tell me to shut up!" Rich said.

"I just did!" Heather yelled. "So you better shut your trap, or else!" She looked at me and I shook my can of Mace. Heather continued, "I swear you all are soooo selfish! Here you all created this damn mess, and then you rotten hoes drag me all up in it!"

"I'm not rotten!" Rich insisted.

"Would you shut up!" Heather screamed. "Because none of this had anything to do with me. Nevertheless, in every paper, every article, there I am standing right in the middle of your foolishness. I'm the star here! I'm the one who has the most to lose. Not you, but Wu-Wu!"

"Tell 'em, Heather!" I said, giving her a sympathetic look, then looking back at these two smutty maniacs. "Unlike you two silver spoon beasts Heather can't afford to lose it 'cause like you told me last year in homeroom, Rich, she is really one step away from trailer park trash. So she really does need her money."

"Ohmy, clutching pearls," Rich said, placing a hand up to her neck.

"Oh, Rich. Stop. You're the one that said Heather was living down in the projects so stop acting surprised. And you're right, they are doing hard time. It's a crime! They can barely keep up with that eight-thousand-dollar-a-month rent as it is, or keep their other bills paid. It's a mess. So, Heather's right. She does have a lot to lose. It's bad enough she said her drunken mother is nothing but a Hollywood nobody. Norma Marie—"

"Norma Marie?!" Rich and London both shrieked.

"Clutching pearls, diamonds, and momma's favorite emerald ring," Rich added.

Poor Heather was standing there looking like someone had wrapped her in a white sheet. That's how pale her face had gotten. All she did was blink.

"Heather, it's okay," I continued, walking over to her and rubbing her back. "I know it must be hard to live with a drunkard who sits around groveling about how she's still Oscar-worthy. I don't want you to lose everything because of us." I shot a look over at Rich and London. "We can all look at Norma...I mean, Camille, and see what it's like to be blackballed. Is that what y'all are trying to do? Have Heather out on the streets moving into a shelter? The last thing she needs is a bunch of untamed animals rolling through here like this is a zoo. This is not Disneyland, or a safari, this is Heather's life. And right now it is a tragedy!"

"This is *not* about me!" Heather snapped. "This is about you three wretches. Now let's get back to why we're really here, and get to the business of being friends so we can clean up all the nasty things the media is saying about all of you."

Rich and London folded their arms, staring me down.

I grunted. "Well all right, I'll be the first to forgive. Even though I know one of you sent that video of me in the bathroom, and I have all these new followers on Twitter now, I'm not trying to be a porn star. Who knew I would

break a YouTube world record. I didn't expect to be offered covers of magazines and have to do a press release
telling the world that no one was peeing on me and that
the boy in the bathroom was Corey and not R. Kelly. I
never expected any of that but still I'm willing to be the
bigger person and move on."

Rich scowled. "Well, you can forgive all you want. But,
I'm not willing to get past you sleeping with my boyfriend.
Why did you do that?"

I frowned back at her. "First of all, I didn't sleep with
him. He was standing up. And I was down on my knees.
So let's get that straight. And second of all, I didn't think
he was still your boyfriend. You said you didn't want him!
And he never once claimed you!"

Rich huffed, "Really, Spencer? I told you that I didn't
want him six months ago. I changed my mind an hour
after I told you that! Duh!"

"Well, you should've told me that!"

"I didn't have to tell you anything!"

"Then how did you expect me to know that you two
were still together? Seriously, he never talked to you in
school. And when he did he was always playing you like a
dust mop."

"That was me and Corey's business, trick, not yours!
Hmph, maybe I like the silent treatment! Maybe it turns
me on! And anyway that's beside the point. It still didn't
give you the right to put your hands, mouth, or anything
else on him. You had absolutely no business messing with
him." She shook her hair, spraying water on me. "What
you did to me, Spencer, was despicable. I know we don't
always get along, but you and I have been friends the
longest. And you crossed the damn line."

I folded my arms. "Yeah, and you crossed the river when you jumped the rowboat and got all London on me. Ever since Queen Kong…"

"Um, don't do it, boo," London snapped, opening and closing her fist. "Please don't tempt me. Now, I've been quiet this entire time, so back up. Back. All. The. Way. Up!"

I rolled my eyes. "…I mean, London. Ever since she showed up swinging from the rooftops, everything changed between us. What we shared. And you're right, Rich. We don't always get along. But it was never like this. You've turned into Richzilla. And I don't like it one bit."

"So what does that have to do with you sleeping with Corey?" she asked. "You were still dead wrong for doing that."

"And where I come from you don't do that," London said, eyeing me. "Your friends' boyfriends—past and present—are always off limits. You've violated all the rules in the girlfriends' handbook. And that's not written in small print."

"And neither is kicking each others' backs in," Heather added, narrowing her eyes at me. "And that's not written in small print either!"

I rolled my eyes up in the air. "Oh, Heather, simmer your tea, boo. I've never kicked anyone's back in. The only thing I've ever done was maced you." I looked back over at Rich and said, "You're right. What I did to you was wrong. I shouldn't have done you like that."

Rich glared at me. "Is that your half-assed way of apologizing to me?"

"Rich," I huffed. "Now you're going too dang far. I'm not the one with deflated booty cheeks." I cut my eyes over at Heather on the sly.

"I saw that, ho," she snapped. "So are you going to apologize to Rich or not?"

"Yes," I said, walking over to Rich, grabbing her crusty hand. "I'm truly sorry for what I did. I won't ever do that to you again."

"Now don't you have something to say to her, Rich?" Heather asked, eyeing her.

She rolled her eyes up in her head. "Yeah, I accept your apology."

Heather put a hand up on her rubberized hip, compliments of bootypadcentral. "Even though this ho tried to drag me. From where I'm standing, you still owe her an apology, too."

"I owe her what?" Rich asked. "Oh, girl, please. I don't do that."

"Mmmmph. That's the problem," Heather said. "It's always what you don't do. So what's your suggestion, Rich, since *you* don't do that? How should we resolve this? Do nothing and part here as enemies? Or try to come together."

London huffed, "Let's hurry up and get this over with. I need to get out of these wet clothes and my feet are aching from standing in these heels. But for once, I have to agree with Heather—scary, I know. But whatever! Bottom line, how do we end this? I can't be messed up in the media again because I can't have any more negative headlines. The next article written about me needs to be worshipping and praising me otherwise *all* three of you will be visiting me in a casket."

Hotholywildfires... what kind of sick games is London into? I'm not visiting her in a casket. Mmmph, she's crazier than I thought.

I frowned. But kept my mouth shut.

"I got it," Rich said, unfolding her arms and never offering an apology. "How about we throw a Making Up party to show the world that the Pampered Princesses still got it?!"

"A party?!"

"Over the top!" Rich beamed.

"That's a great idea!" I said, smiling.

"Bam! This is bigger than no-good boyfriends." Heather popped it, dropped it, and snapped her fingers.

"Yeah, because up until a few minutes ago we'd all lost sight of who we really were," London reminded us.

Rich snapped her fingers. "Yeah, because I am Rich Montgomery. And we are..."

"The Pampered Princesses!" the four of us yelled, snapping our fingers.

"Still doing it, baby," Heather said, doing a two-step.

"Still hot like fire," London chimed in.

"And I'm *not* tryna have a Kim Kardashian meltdown," Rich said. "I'm tryna reign supreme forever. I have fans. People adore me. Little girls tryna be me. So there's no way in hell we're gonna let the likes of Corey or any other boy come in between us." Rich looked at me. "You know, Spencer. I realize that Corey might have taken advantage of you being real special. But you know what? We're gonna move past this. And we're gonna show the world that *we* are about our business. That nothing can stop us!"

"Oh Rich!" I said. "You finally realize that I am special! And that party was such a great idea!"

"That's right! *Meeeeeeeeow*, snap-snap!" Rich said.

"Snap-snap," we all said in unison, laughing.

"Now let me call my publicist," Rich said, excitedly swiping strands of wet hair from out of her face, and pulling out her cell. "We need to get ready for the press release. I can see the headlines now." She waved her arms in the air. "PAMPERED PRINCESSES GOT THE BOOM-BOP ON LOCK! Claire!" Rich yelled into her cell phone. "SOS! I need a press conference scheduled pronto! Snap-snap baby! The Pampered Princesses are throwing the royal party of the century!"

"Umm, Rich." I tried to call for her attention.

She held her index finger up. "Wait a minute," she mouthed. "Okay, Claire. I'm at Spencer's, have them outside and waiting for us in an hour." She disconnected her call and smiled at us. "It's all set and ready to go!" She shook her hair. "Now tell me, how do I look?"

"Ummmm, boo," Heather said, pointing at London and Rich. "Wu-Wu loves you, baby. But, uh...I don't know what the hell y'all were doing before you got here but both of you might wanna hurry and shower before the cameras arrive."

"Why?" Rich popped her lips.

"Because," I said, walking over to her and London. "You two look as if you've been to war."

"Oh God!" Rich screamed. "I need to use your shower!"

"You sure do," I said. "The one in the pool house. I don't allow aliens to bathe in here. No offense."

26

London

Iknew I was beautiful. I knew I had a banging body. And I knew every voluptuous curve that went along with it in the way I knew Chanel, Dior, Louis Vuitton, YSL, Cavalli, and Versace. But a girl could only look for comfort and confirmation in a mirror for so long before it became too damn depressing. Before she wanted to take a hammer and smash her reflection into pieces, causing shards of glass and insecurities to scatter about her stiletto-clad feet.

My God, London. At the rate you're going, you'll never make it on the runway. You'll only be good enough to bounce and shake for rap videos....

Taking a deep breath, I untied my robe, allowing it to slide off my shoulders and gather around my ankles. I turned my naked body from side to side, checking out my profile in the mirror. I loved my melon-sized breasts. I loved my flat stomach. I loved the way my long, milk chocolate legs were sculpted. And most of all, I loved, loved, loved my big, juicy booty. Still...

For the love of God, London, why did you have to ruin your body...you just had to go and screw up everything I've worked so hard for....

"If I don't have a problem with how I look, then why should you?" I said to my reflection.

Your body, beauty, and youth are your tickets to fame and fortune. You lose them and you'll have nothing. No one in the industry wants a fat, ugly, old-looking girl on their runway....

"I'm not fat, ugly, or old-looking," I replied back at the mirror image before me.

Well, you're definitely not ugly. And you're far from old-looking, yet. Thank God you have my genes. But, fat... mmmph. You're well on your way. I blame your father's genes for that...I should have married more carefully.

I shook the voice from my head, then snatched my robe up and put it back on. "I'd be so glad when I don't have to deal with this anymore," I thought aloud as I walked back into my bedroom suite. I walked into the adjoining sitting area and picked up my favorite Swarovski butterfly sitting on the end table. I held it up to the morning light that bum-rushed its way into the room, taking in the way the light danced through the crystal in my hand. I admired the distinctive beauty in each color.

I, too, am a butterfly!

Mmmph, I wish I could spread my wings and flutter my way out of here!

Wait. Did you know Native American legend has it that whispering a wish to a butterfly, then releasing it to carry it to the heavens, will make the wish come true? I learned that in one of my advanced literature classes. But I didn't know how true that myth was since I'd been wishing to butterflies since the eighth grade. And nothing remarkably close to anything I had ever wished for had happened yet. Still, I believed—or at least I wanted to like hell—in miracles.

I stared at the beautiful sculpture one last time, then closed my eyes and made another wish. I was sure, as I had done many times before, to be very specific about what I wanted, hoped for. And like with all the other times, I promised myself that I wouldn't share my wishes with anyone else until after they had come true. I had read somewhere while traveling the Slovenian coast with my parents that talking about a wish in progress could disrupt its energy and break the spell. So my lips were sealed! With everything else I had been risking, I couldn't take chances on jinxing myself.

"Oh, there you are, sweetheart," my mother's voice said, slicing into my moment, robbing me of peace and solitude. "Good morning."

Now I was extra annoyed that so far one of my many wishes still hadn't been granted. "Good morning," I mumbled, turning to face her. "When did you get home?"

"A little after two in the morning. My flight got delayed. I thought they were going to cancel it."

I wish they had!

I looked her over. No matter how hard I wanted to downplay how beautiful she was, I couldn't. Her looks alone quieted the noisiest rooms and mesmerized onlookers. And it's what lured Daddy and had him chasing her for almost three years before she gave in to his advances. Well, not to mention my grandmother, Jacqueline Obi, guarded her precious jewel with her life until Mother turned eighteen. Then she allowed Daddy to date her. A year later, he married her. By that time my mother had already been well-established in the modeling industry and was the most sought after model.

I smiled. She had her shoulder-length hair pulled back into a chignon, her face lightly dusted, her lips freshly coated.

Always runway ready...

Head up...back straight...one foot in front of the other...bounce with it...own the catwalk...

"I'm glad you're back safe."

I kept my eye on her as she glided across the carpet toward me wearing a gorgeous pearl silk kimono over a matching spaghetti-strapped nightgown that had slits on the sides, showing glimpses of her beautiful legs as she moved about the room. It almost reminded me of a wedding gown. Around her neck she wore a Van Cleef & Arpels ruby and diamond butterfly necklace. I gasped at its beauty, secretly coveting the exquisite piece. And in her diamond-embellished hands, she held her morning supplies: a scale, a leather-bound logbook, her 18-karat Tibaldi Spartacus rollerball pen, and a measuring tape.

She kissed me on the cheeks, then gave me a one-armed hug. "I've missed you."

I smiled, inhaling the hyacinth, orchard, and amber scent of her fragrance. The smell reminded me of springtime in Paris. Still, as much as I wanted to reciprocate her sentiments, I couldn't. But the truth is I did miss her. I just didn't miss the constant monitoring of my weight, or her incessant—almost compulsive—measuring of my body fat. I wanted a mother who didn't obsess over caloric intake or cringe every time I wanted to eat a bag of Doritos, or bite into a candy bar, or sink my teeth into a double-fudge chocolate cake. I wanted a mother who didn't care if I gained ten pounds or only lost two.

"Okay, let's weigh in," she said, sitting the scale down in front of me. "God only knows what kind of poisons you've contaminated your body with while I've been gone. I'm sure we'll have to do a complete detox. Diet is everything in this industry, London."

Easy for her to say. There were two types of models. The ones who were born naturally thin and had exceptionally high metabolism, allowing them to eat any-and-every-thing they wanted and never gain a pound. Then there were the ones who starved themselves and chain-smoked. Jade Phillips had the frame and metabolism to be effortlessly thin.

I rolled my eyes. "I know, Mother. 'You are what you eat,'" I repeated before she could remind me for the two hundred billionth time. She'd rather see me eat radishes, alfalfa sprouts, and the whites of a hard-boiled egg, than to indulge in any of my guilty-pleasure foods.

"Exactly," she said, smiling at me. She kissed me on the cheek again. "And the sooner you start to live by that motto, dear, the sooner you can get all this god-awful weight off and we can get you back on the runway and onto the cover of all the fashion magazines where you belong. *Sei bella mia cara, Londra*," she added in Italian, telling me how beautiful I was. "You were born to be in front of a camera. The lights, the *haute couture*...oh, London, my darling, the fashion world is yours for the taking. You can be bigger than Tyra Banks ever was. You can be greater than any of the legends in the industry, including myself, have ever been. But I need you to lose this weight and listen to me."

I stared at my mother and felt a pang in my chest. Guilt was a terrible thing. I knew that she loved me; knew it without question. And I knew she thought I was beautiful. Still, I wished when she looked at me that her eyes would light up the way they did every time she spoke about me being on the runway, modeling for one of the international fashion houses. Or anytime she reminisced about when I was a reigning print-ad beauty. Before puberty, and everything else that came along with it, changed my life.

I felt sick to my stomach and hoped like hell the laxative-induced bowel movements I had early this morning were enough to flush out the four pounds I had gained in her absence and keep her mouth shut.

She blinked back what looked like sadness, then clapped her hands. "Okay, up on the scale." I held my breath, dropping my robe and stepping on the digital scale.

I dropped my head. "Chin up, London. Don't worry about what's going on down at your feet. The scale never lies." I held my breath. "Okay, step off."

Maybe if I hold my breath long enough I'll pass out. Hit my head on my way down, and never open my eyes again.

No luck!

I watched as she opened the smooth leather binder, removed the cap off her pen, then scribbled in her ledger. I imagined her one day writing a tell-all book about the ups and downs and highs and lows of my stubborn weight. I envisioned it being titled something like: *The Wondrous Weight Gain of My Fatso Daughter.*

I shuddered as she eyed me. "You've lost two and three-quarter pounds. Still not enough to crack open the champagne. I don't understand for the life of me why you aren't losing more. You should have shed at least fifteen pounds by now."

OMG, she's delusional if she thinks I'll ever walk around looking like a damn string bean. Not. Apparently she had overlooked the memo that guys loved girls with swerves and curves.

"The only saving grace is that you're still young. But if we don't get this weight off in the next year, I might need to look into having your stomach stapled."

I gasped. "Mother, I'm not getting my stomach stapled. That's going a bit far."

"Come," she said, waving me over to her. I glanced down at my feet. *130 pounds.* "Well," she continued, wrapping the measuring tape around my waist, "desperate times call for drastic measures." Next she wrapped it around my hips. She grunted her dismay. "We're going to need to do something, fast. All I can see is you becoming like your grandmother and aunts on your father's side with them double-D and E-cup breasts, big-ole dimpled behinds, and those ham-hock ankles. We've already had one setback, we don't need another."

She eyed me, suspiciously. I shifted my gaze from hers.

"From what I've heard from your father and seen on the blogs you have managed to, once again, get caught up with the wrong crowd. I can only imagine what else you've been up to while I've been gone."

Damn, another wish not fulfilled! The first chance I got I was going to have to get on my knees and have a good, stern talking-to to the butterfly gods. This was ridiculous. *Can I get at least one of my wishes, please!*

She logged my measurements in the book. *If I ever get my hands on that damn thing, I'm gonna burn it!* "Oh, I bet you thought I wasn't going to say anything since your father had already addressed you on it. Do I have to bring you back to Paris with me?"

I sighed.

I wanted, needed, to believe that all wishes do come true. *No wish is impossible.*

Then why the hell is she still standing here?

"You're working your way up to becoming a common criminal before I can get you back on the runway. Is that what you want?"

"No."

"Then you must be hoping to land yourself some kind of reality-TV show, a spin-off of that god-awful show *Good Girls Gone Hood*. Is that it?"

I shook my head. Arguing with her was pointless, and sooooo not worth my energy; especially since I needed to focus on what I was going to wear to school today.

"No."

She narrowed her brown eyes until they were slits. "London, I'm warning you. Please don't have your father and me ship you to an all-girls boarding school. You know we'll do it. Is that what you want?"

I bit my tongue. But inside I was screaming, "I'm not going any-damn-where. And I'm gonna eat whatever-the-hell I want! And there's nothing you can say or do to stop me. So kiss my naturally plump fatty!" But, being the rational child that I am, I settled for, "No, Mother."

"Your father and I gave you a choice to either move to London to attend school, or come out here—against our better judgment. But we let you decide. And you promised, swore to us, that you wouldn't get into any trouble. Please don't make us regret it. I do not want a repeat of what happened in New York. Do you understand me?" I nodded. "We've already pushed the release of your trust fund once. The next time it'll be pushed back until your twenty-first birthday. Please don't force my hand because the next time, it's going to be pushed back until you're forty. And we'll be shutting down your allowance and frivolous shopping sprees."

I felt my knees buckle. *OMG! She wouldn't dare!*

Uh, yes she would!

"How's Anderson?" she asked, changing the subject while gauging my reaction. "You *have* been spending time with him, *haven't* you?"

I nodded. "Kind of." She raised a brow. "Well, we did spend time at this club out in Santa Monica a few weeks ago." Okay, okay... it was a lie. But so what? Well, wait... it wasn't totally a lie. I mean, after all we *did* spend time together at the club—fighting, that is. Still, we were together. "And I spent the whole day with him yesterday." Now that was unfortunately the truth. And the only reason I remotely considered it is because Daddy—before he left for New York with Rich's dad yesterday—demanded I spend time with Anderson and threatened to cut off my allowance for another two weeks if I didn't. So there you have it. Begrudgingly, I went. The thought of not having access to money is enough motivation needed to get my mind right. For the moment, until I could figure out a better plan of action.

Anyway, Anderson picked me up here around three-thirty—two hours before my Boo finally snuck up out of here—in a stretch Rolls-Royce Phantom.

He was dressed in a tailored suit and wore an ascot! To sum it up, Anderson was a cornball. There was no other way to say it. He was *swaaaaaaaagless*! I'm talking dud.com! He had no rhythm, no personality, and no damn business trying to be with a fabulous girl like me. Yet, everything about him spelled money. And it reeked from his dark chocolate skin. He was well-bred, well-educated, and well-dressed—yeah, as a banker, accountant, or the CEO of a Fortune 500 company. But for an eighteen-year old, Anderson dressed like somebody's grandfather. All he needed was a cigar, a pocket watch, and a pair of suspenders to add to his ensemble.

He kissed me on the cheek as I climbed into the cabin and sat across from him.

"You look beautiful," he said, smiling.

"Of course I do," I said with more edge than I had intended.

He dismissed me with the flick of his hand. "Well, I'm glad you finally came to your senses, London. Your behavior has been atrocious lately. You've acted like a common trollop long enough. It's about time you come back to reality and play your position—as *my* girl."

I blinked, then frowned. *WTF?!* "Screw you, C-Smoove, the wannabe-wankster. You're lucky I even allow you to breathe the same air as me. I don't have—"

He picked up the car phone. "Stop the car," he said into the receiver. The driver pulled over on the side of the I-10 freeway. Anderson reached over and opened the door. "Get out."

I blinked. "Wh-what? You're joking, right?"

"Do you see me smiling, *home skillet?* Since you like it

hood, Miss Thug in Chanel. Let me chop it up for you. Since you've been out here, you've partied like a rock star, sexed—God knows who—like a porn star, and done everything else, *except* what you've been directed to do."

My mouth flew open. "You wait one damn—"

"Shut your trap. I'm talking. As a matter of fact, why are you still sitting here? Didn't I tell you to get out?"

I felt like he had just backhanded me. My cheeks burned. I folded my arms defiantly across my chest. "Who the hell do you think you are? You can't throw me out on the side of the road like this. Wait until I get my father on the phone. He will have your head!"

He snarled at me. "Oh shut up. The only head he's gonna have is yours, *Amazon*. In the meantime, I'll tell you who I am since you can't seem to remember. I'm the one who's going to keep your spoiled, ostentatious, disrespectful, hot-in-the-tail behind from having your inheritance snatched away from you and you ending up as some waitress at some greasy-spoon diner somewhere; that's who the hell I am. And the sooner you recognize it, the better. Now. Get. Out. Before I make that phone call to your father my damn self and tell him how you had your little gangster Boo up in his house for the last two-and-a-half days, sexing him up."

I immediately felt the color from my face drain. *How in the hell did he know that? "Whaaaaaaaat?!* You don't know what you're talking about, *C-Smoove, Anderson*, or whatever the hell your stage name is."

He smirked. "Oh, I know exactly what I'm talking about. And I know all I need to know. And the one thing I do *know* is you don't want your father to find out just how slutty you've been. So, what's it gonna be, *ma-ma?* The road to poverty and despair? Or the freeway to the rich and fabulous?"

I tried to assess the situation at hand but quickly realized Anderson had me cornered and trapped. There was no escaping him. So I did the only smart thing to do. I reached over and slammed the door, fuming.

"Good. Now I'm going to tell you what I expect. I expect you to spend at least two days out of the week with me—any more time than that will make me sick. You disgust me...."

I blinked.

"...Out in public, you *will* hold my hand, kiss me on the lips, rub my back and *act* like you're in love. And you *will* smile for the cameras, since we both know how much you enjoy being in the spotlight...."

"I'm not doing that!"

He raised a brow, pulling out a Mac laptop. He started clicking keys. "Oh, so you think I'm bluffing, don't you?" He clicked onto something, then handed the computer to me.

Ohmygodohmygodohmygod!!!!

I clutched my chest and started hyperventilating. "Wh-where...h-how...did you get this?"

He snatched the laptop from out of my hands. "Don't worry about all that. Just know I have my eye on you when you least expect it."

"You've been spying on me. H-h-how...dare you! You have no right invading my privacy like this!"

"No. I have every right. I'm protecting my investment. That's what I've been doing. And this right here is my insurance policy that you will do what has been agreed upon." He twirled his hand dramatically in the air. "Now, you were saying?"

I turned and looked out the window. Wondering how much it would cost to hire someone to snuff him out. If I wasn't so afraid of spending my life behind bars I'd put a hit out on him for sure. He finished running down his laundry list of things I was expected to do. Then he had the audacity to say, "I'm the best thing that will ever happen to you. And don't have me have to remind you again."

Needless to say, the rest of our ride to wherever we were headed was deadpan silent. I felt like I was riding in a hearse, instead of a plush limo, en route to my own funeral.

We ended up at a private landing field where Anderson whisked me off in one of his family's helicopters. From there, we flew over Beverly Hills and past the Hollywood Bowl to Universal Studios. The pilot flew so close to the Hollywood Sign that I could almost reach out and touch it. Then he swooped down a hundred and fifty feet above the shoreline, so that I could see the beautiful beach cities before flying us over the Santa Monica Pier. If I wasn't so pissed at him, I would have actually enjoyed myself. Whatever! The tour ended with the pilot hovering over the rear deck of Anderson's family's hundred-and-fifty-foot, three-level yacht, *Buff Daddy*.

Yuck!

"Anderson is such a gentleman," my mother said, smiling approvingly as I recapped the horrific experience, leaving out the details I knew she wouldn't care about. "He's a real thoughtful young man."

And a bore!

"He'll make a fine husband."

I'm not marrying that, that...pompous idiot!

Anyway, we landed on the helipad. And when the doors opened, Anderson took me by the hand and helped me out, acting as if he hadn't talked all reckless and nasty to me hours earlier. He waited for the chopper to go airborne again before grabbing my hand and pulling me.

I flinched.

"I have something for you," he said, leading me down to the main level of the beautiful boat. Still, the name was ugly. He told me to have a seat in the living room. Then, a few minutes later, he reappeared holding a gift box from Cartier. Inside was a breathtaking Trinity-draped diamond necklace. Had this been someone else, who shall be nameless, I would have jumped in his lap, kissed him passionately, then made sweet love to him up on the deck beneath the stars. But I was there stuck with cornball.com.

My mother continued smiling.

"Anderson isn't who I want," I blurted out.

My mother's facial expression, body language, and tone changed. And the temperature in the room had dropped by twenty degrees. "You will learn to love him. Now that's enough."

27

Heather

Relax... You got this...

R"Lights. Camera. Action! Take two! You're on!"

I stood behind the prop's makeshift door, awaiting my cue to enter the set's '50s-style vintage kitchen. I leaned from one foot to the next and did my best to focus and envision my lines the exact way they were in the script.

But I couldn't.

All my mind's eye could see was a blur.

I had to wing it and pray that this time the director would be happy with my ad-libs.

Think... Think... Think... come on, Wu-Wu. My eyes shifted from the director to the stagehands, the cameramen, to Spencer—who I'd invited to watch me tape the first episode of the season.

I had to get this right.

I had to.

"Where's Wu-Wu? I hope she's up and ready for school!"

That was my cue.

Focus...focus...focus...

"Ahh, Wu-Wu's in the house!" I said, extremely high-pitched and animated. I shook my coils and flopped down in the kitchen chair, next to my television father, who resembled George Lopez.

I quickly eyed my director. He grimaced but he didn't stop tape.

"Good morning, Wu-Wu!" my television mother said, smiling, as the rosy cheeks on her porcelain face glowed. "How's my little Snuckums-Snuckums-Wukums doing this wonderful morning?"

The laugh track boomed through the set and immediately I had a migraine. I could've sworn that it was louder this time than it was two takes ago. Not to mention that *that Snuckums-Snuckums-Wukums* line may have been classic and killed the TV audience with laughter, but the last thing I found it to be was funny.

It actually worked my last nerve.

Seriously.

But whatever, I forced a stupid smile on my face and did all I could to push Heather back and allow Wu-Wu to rock the forefront.

Wu-Wu was losing.

I looked at Jani Rossi, the actress who played my TV mother, and I knew by the look on her face that I'd paused too long, so I hurried and spat my line...what I could remember of it. "Your Snuckums-Snuckums-Wukums is soooo bummed, Mom."

I looked at my director, and the slight grin on his face said that I'd gotten my line right.

Thank God...okay, I can do this. Now feed the dog the bacon. Ugh, I hated that dog. But I did what the episode called for and reached for a piece of bacon and then slyly fed it to the dog—a humongous chestnut brown and white St. Bernard—who barked like crazy—the exact way he was supposed to.

His owner beamed from across the room.

"Wu-Wu Tanner," José, my television father, said, pulling my attention back onto the set. "You know better than to feed Bird bacon. You know bacon gives him gas." Bird looked up at us and whimpered and there went that stupid laugh track again.

My head's going to explode!

I swallowed, sat up in my chair, and said, "Awl, Dad, leave Bird alone. He's got bigger problems than bacon. He's a St. Bernard named Bird." I pointed toward the floor where Bird lay lazily.

"I happen to like the name Bird," Jani said, sitting a stack of pancakes on the table. She kissed me on my cheek, smiled, and fluffed my curls. "Now tell Mother why my little Pinky-Poo's all bummed out?"

I folded my arms and pouted. "Because Robert didn't call me at all last night!" My eyes watered. "And I don't know what to do!"

"Robert? Who's Robert?" José interjected, ruffling his newspaper and peering around the side of it. "That must be a nickname for Roberta."

It took everything in me not to scream at that damn laugh track! Ugggggggg! And this St. Bernard was licking my legs. Slobbering on my sandals. If he wasn't so big and I knew I could get away with it, I'd kick him.

You need a Black Beauty . . .

No I don't . . .

Yes you do . . .

"You're a junkie!" Camille's voice invaded my thoughts.

I'm not a junkie!

"You're nothing!"

I'm Wu-Wu!

"I made you. I'm the real star!"

"Cut!" the director yelled, jumping up from his chair. "What the hell are you doing, Heather?"

"Huh?" I blinked, and looked around at my television parents, who stared back at me in confusion. I shot them a fake smile.

Before I could say anything the director yelled, "Have you gone insane! What is wrong with you? This is the third time we've had to redo this take!" He violently clapped his hands together. "We're wasting time and time is money!" He clapped his hands again. "Now take it from the top for the fourth time!" He rolled his eyes and huffed his way back into his chair.

I need a Black Beauty.

No I don't. I can do this. Okay…okay…I got this… here goes. It was like déjà vu as I stood at the makeshift door, waited for my cue, skipped across the set, said my lines, fed this overgrown dog a piece of bacon, and just as my television dad said, "I know that's a nickname for Roberta"…I drew a blank. A complete and utter blank and just as I saw my director turn beet red I said, "Umm, I have diarrhea."

Where in the hell did that come from…?

"CUT!" The director jumped from his seat, purposefully knocked it to the floor, and kicked it out of his way. In the midst of him throwing a two-year-old's tantrum he shook the script in the air and sailed it toward the set. The ceiling looked to be raining paper, scaring the dog. "What the hell is wrong with you!" he screamed at me. "Are you an idiot?! You have screwed up four takes in a row!" He held up four fingers. "FOUR TAKES! I don't know what your problem is, Heather. But I need Wu-Wu! Wu-Wu Tanner. Do you have any idea where in the hell she is? You know what, maybe, maybe we need to take five. Take ten. Matter of fact maybe we need to take twenty while you go and get Wu-Wu and let her know that if she doesn't resume her place on the show, she will be unemployed!" He stormed off the set, speaking in angry tongues.

I felt like a Navy knot had made its way into my throat and was threatening to strangle me at any moment.

My eyes welled and Jani patted my hand. "It'll be okay," she said. "It happens to the best of us. Go to your dressing room, relax, and we'll see you in twenty."

I looked over at José and he smiled. "Don't sweat it, kiddo. Things happen. Like Jani said, go back to your dressing room and maybe meditate. It'll come to you."

I looked over at Spencer, who looked just as embarrassed as I was. My full eyes were about to overflow at any moment.

"You're nothing…!"

Maybe you're right….

I jumped from my seat and ran straight to my dressing room. Never once looking back. I quickly slammed the door and locked it behind me.

I'm nothing…nothing…nothing…can't even get my lines straight…

I felt like I was about to hyperventilate. "What the hell is wrong with me?" I screamed, knocking everything off of the glass vanity's counter with one swing of an arm. The make-up, perfume, barrettes, and copies of the script swished to the floor. The broken bottles of perfume quickly saturated the script, causing the words to disappear from the paper the same way they'd disappeared from my head.

I can't do anything!

I'm nothing!

I ruin everything!

I grabbed a handful of costumes and yanked down my wardrobe. I tossed all the clothes to the floor and sweat gathered on my forehead, drenching my face.

Why can't you get yourself together, Heather!

"*Because you're a junkie!*" Camille's voice raced into my head. The walls were closing in on me and the ceiling looked like it would fall on my head at any moment. My silk-walled dressing room had gone from a customized space to a place that I no longer wanted to be in.

I don't think I can breathe.

I can't breathe....

Get it together.

"*I will replace you!*" the director's voice echoed in my head.

"*I made you! I'm the real star!*" Camille's voice taunted me.

"Get out of my head!" I screamed as tears fell from my eyes.

Knock...Knock...

I jumped. Wiped my eyes and yelled, "What!"

"Heather, it's Spencer."

"I'll be out soon, Spencer." The last thing I needed was for her to see me like this....

"Let me in," she said. "I wanted to talk to you."

I took a deep breath and wiped my eyes. I thought

about telling her to go away. Of all the days to invite her here...

"Heather, open up."

I sighed as I cracked the door open enough for Spencer to slide into the dressing room. I quickly locked it behind her.

Spencer leaned back against the door and eyed the room slowly, soaking up every inch of my self-made hurricane. "Umm, Heather, is this what has you so upset? That they didn't send housekeeping? I don't blame you because I'd be mad, too. You're a star and obviously by your director's hissy fit the show can't go on without you. So they really, really need to clean your dressing room."

This girl had no idea. For a moment I wondered what it must be like to be Spencer, to not have a care or a clue in the world....

"And umm, Heather, what is a Snuckum-Snuckum-Wukums and a Pinky-Poo? Those names are just so, so... stupid. And why did they add that hideous laugh track? For a moment I thought a bunch of hyenas had escaped from the San Diego Zoo. Dear Jesus, it tore my nerves to pieces."

I wiped my eyes and snapped. "Spencer, really, who cares!"

"I care. I don't want them calling you that. And I don't want to hear that stupid laugh track." She paused. Walked over to me and squinted, "Are you crying, Heather?"

"No," I said, with my eyes full and threatening to spill a river of tears any second. "I'm overdosing on Visine."

"Really?"

I quickly turned away and did everything I could not to break down. "Just give me a minute, Spencer."

"No, Heather," she said. "I can't leave you here upset like this. And I'm really concerned about you overdosing on Visine."

"Spencer, I was being sarcastic. I'm not overdosing on Visine."

"Then what is it? Are you upset with that nasty director of yours? If you need me to I will mace him down to his smiley-face booty shorts. I will bring him to his flour-caked knees and you know it. Just say the word 'Mace' and I'll cuss him out in French and give him a burning sensation to scream about! Trust me, that'll be the last time he gets it crackadank with you! And if you want, that St. Bernard can get it, too!"

"I don't want to mace the director or that nasty dog!" Tears spilled from my eyes without my permission. "I just want to get out of here!" I grabbed my purse and walked toward the door.

"Heather, wait!" Spencer ran and blocked the door.

"Move, Spencer!"

"Just wait!"

"I'm tired of waiting!" I flung my arms in the air. "What the hell am I waiting for? To mess up again? This is over, Spencer! I'm done! Finished. And I really don't give a damn what happens next! I'm tired and I've had enough."

"Just relax, Heather. You only tripped over a few lines and they were stupid anyway."

"It's not about the lines! It's about everything!" My head pounded, my hands trembled, and my stomach boiled. I hated this feeling!

I hated that every time I took a break and didn't snort Black Beauty for a day that I crashed. Sank to the bottom of hell. Couldn't think straight. Couldn't eat. Couldn't focus. All I could think about was Black Beauty.

It was never supposed to be like this. Black Beauty was only supposed to relieve my stress and put me in the mood to party.

Not make me sick if I didn't have a hit.

Not interfere with my job.

Not become my out-of-control personal assistant.

I felt like…like…I was caught up in a torturous love affair and I didn't want this sick and twisted pervert anymore.

It couldn't keep me happy and I was tired of chasing the same dream. The dream that I would feel like I did the first time Black Beauty gave me an orgasmic high.

Like I was floating on air.

Like everything that was wrong was suddenly right. And I didn't care that Camille was a drunk, who I just wanted so badly to love me. And it didn't matter that I didn't have a dad. I was Superwoman. I could walk on water if I wanted to.

But when the high left I was back to being a wreck. Out of control.

Instantly paranoid and haunted by the nagging monkey who loved to whisper in my ear about how messed up I truly was. "I have to go, Spencer!"

"You can't run out like this!" She grabbed my arm.

I snatched it away. "Get off of me! Now move!"

"What the hell is wrong with you?" Spencer screamed with tears racing to her eyes. "You're going crazy! You're scaring me! Would you stop it? Just stop it, stop running. Tell me what's wrong, Heather! Please. Let me help you!"

As if I was placed on pause I stopped, looked at Spencer and said, "You can't help me."

"Try me."

Tears soaked my cheeks. And no matter how hard I tried to stand up, my legs became brittle branches and I fell onto Spencer's arms. "Oh, Heather," she said. "No matter what's wrong, it's going to be okay." She rubbed my back. "Nothing is this bad."

"I'm just a mess. I have messed up my life."

"No you haven't. And you're not a mess, you're smart. You're pretty. You're talented. You have people who look up to you."

"Then they must be pretty low down, because I am knee deep in it."

"Heather, stop saying those things about yourself, they're not true. You have fans who love you!"

"They don't love me! They don't even know me! All they know is what the paper writes about me or the life they imagine me to have. But they don't know me. They know Wu-Wu. They love Wu-Wu, but they don't know a thing about Heather!"

"What don't they know?"

"They don't know how tired I am. How it's soooo much pressure."

"Let the pressure go."

"I wish it was that easy."

"It can be."

"But it's not. It's like everywhere I turn everybody's looking at me. Like I'm a mirror and everyone gets to stand still, judge my life, and give me their opinion! I'm tired of that! Sometimes I just want to throw my hands in the air and say to hell with it! Just throw everything away!"

"Heather, you can't throw everything away. Because if you do then who will I walk the red carpet with?"

"You have Rich and London."

"Now you know those two angry ostriches make my nose run! I'm trying to get to the Oscars. The only place Shaneeka and Laquita will ever be are the BET Awards with two gangsta rappers on their arms."

Despite what I felt I couldn't help but chuckle. "Spencer, it's just *soooo* much. And I don't have anybody."

"You have me." She wiped my tears. "And you know what?"

"What?"

"I look up to you."

What did she say? "You do what? Are you serious?"

"Cross my heart." She gave a slight giggle. "I love The Wu-Wu Tanner Show." She rolled her eyes in delight.

"Really? Or are you just saying that?"

"No, I really watch your show faithfully."

"You do?" I said surprised.

"Yes! I know every episode," she said excitedly. "I even have the first season on DVD."

"Really?"

"Yes. And you know what my favorite episode was?"

"What?"

"It was the episode where Wu-Wu wanted to perform at a talent show, but didn't think she could do it. But Wu-Wu's parents encouraged her and told her that she could do anything she put her mind to; and they told her that they loved her and would be there to support her. So, she had nothing to worry about. After that, she took a chance and when Wu-Wu stepped up on that stage and belted out that *sooooong...*" Spencer snapped her fingers. "That was when I knew you were special, girlfriend! That's when I knew you had it! And that had nothing to do with you being Wu-Wu Tanner. That had everything to do with you being the beautiful and talented Heather Cummings! The amazing actress and beautiful songbird!

"And do you wanna know what else, girlfriend, my heart fluttered with so much pride and joy that I knew you. You were in *my* crew. And that bearilla Rich would never admit this, but she came to school bragging about you to everyone."

"Rich?" I asked, shocked.

"Yes, Rich! The original jealous dream killer. That was the only day I didn't feel like smacking her face."

I chuckled. "You really don't like her, do you?"

"Can't stand her! And if I ever get her in a dark closet I would tear her up!"

I laughed and wiped tears. "Yeah, beat her and her diamonds down into the ground."

"Karate-kick her straight to Jesus! And that London—" Spencer squinted her eyes and rubbed her hands together. "Oh, London, I'd take her by the nape of her thick neck and mollywhop her up and down Hollywood Boulevard."

"Smear all the New York out of her!"

"Yup. And even though we made up with them and everything, that night when they left my house I still ordered a super-sized can of Mace and marked it 'Whup-azz'!'"

I laughed and the next thing I knew Spencer and I were cracking up. We laughed so hard that we fell against the walls and slid to the floor. "See, Heather," Spencer said, as we tried to collect ourselves. "Things aren't so bad after all."

"Maybe not." I shrugged, unsure.

"There's no maybe. It's not that bad. And you can do this, Heather!"

I looked at Spencer, whose eyes were filling with tears. "I just want you to believe in yourself the way I believe in you," she said.

I wiped her tears and said, "I believe it."

We hugged tightly and at that very moment I felt closer to her than I'd ever felt to anyone.

"Now come on." Spencer rose from the floor and extended me her hand. "Let's get it together, because if that director yells at you like that again, I will be all over him. As a matter of fact I'm going to speak to him now and then I'll be dealing with somebody in housekeeping. This dressing room is an absolute wreck!"

I wiped my eyes and hugged her again. "Thank you, Spencer."

"Don't thank me. You just get Wu-Wu together."

"I will," I said as Spencer gave me a high five and walked out of my dressing room. She closed the door behind her and I looked at myself in the mirror.

This is the last time...

No more after this...Just enough to get my Wu-Wu back.

I freshened up. And ten minutes later, I felt like I'd had a makeover. I strutted back on the set, my Wu-Wu was in full effect, and by the time the take was finished I'd murdered each and every one of my lines. "Now that's what I'm talking about!" the director yelled. "Now that's the Wu-Wu everybody loves!"

We wrapped up, I introduced Spencer to the cast, and then we said our good-byes to everyone.

I felt like a brand-new person as Spencer and I walked out of the studio and to the parking lot. My curls bounced as I pulled my shoulders back, held my head up high, and did a two-step with my oversized bag in the crook of my arm. "Ahh, Wu-Wu's in the house!" I said.

"Without a doubt!" Spencer said as we walked toward her truck.

She clicked her doors open and I said, "Thank you for coming. I couldn't have made it through this without you."

"That's what friends are for. And besides I wouldn't have missed this for anything!" She smiled and slid into her Range Rover. She started her engine, pressed on the gas, and revved it a little too hard, scaring a few people in the parking lot, including me.

I jumped back and as Spencer backed out of her parking space I noticed that she never looked behind her.

Jesus!

Crash! Bash! Boom!

"Oh no! Why would somebody park directly behind me!" she screamed out the window, looking toward the studio van she'd just about cracked in half. "Ohmy-begeezus!" she yelled. "That's a big dent. And is that the front bumper on the ground? You know what, Heather, since you owe me one, do me a favor, pick that up and write a note for me. Tell them to put some tape on that and I'll be back and we can work out the damages later."

All I could do was laugh. Gotta love Spencer. I waved bye and a few seconds later my driver pulled up beside me and opened the door. I slid into the backseat and just as I lay back and thought about my day my cell phone rang.

I answered, "Wassup, Co-Co Pops!"

"Hey Wu-Wu," he said, sounding somber.

"What's wrong?"

"Oh nothing," he attempted to assure me. "I just want you to know that I'm going to give you my gold necklace with the single pearl on it."

"Why?"

"Because it's special to me and I want you to have it."

"You love that necklace though, Co-Co."

"I know and I love you. I'm glad that we became friends."

"I'm glad, too, Co-Co but why are you sounding like that? Is everything okay? Is something wrong?"

"No. Nothing's wrong. Nothing that I can't make right."

"What are you talking about, Co-Co?"

"I love you, Wu-Wu."

"I love you, too. Are you sure you're okay?"

"Yes, I'm fine. I love you and talk to you later." He hung up.

I love you...? I'll talk to you later...? That sounds nothing like the party boy dressed in pink that I know....

"I'm going to give you my gold necklace with the pearl on it," I repeated in my head.

I hate that necklace, but he loves it...said he would never part from it...

I lay back against the backseat and as the driver pulled onto the highway I said, "Lawrence, take me to Co-Co Ming's."

28

Spencer

Oh poor, poor Heather. It's so terrible how they treat her over there at that studio. I made a right turn onto Ventura Boulevard, heading toward the Hollywood Freeway. *And that Mr. Fatso director of hers with that tacky-looking nose job really pissed in my sugar jar the way he yelled and screamed at her like that. It's no wonder her Raggedy-Ann-looking self was so shaken. I'm so, so glad I was there to keep her from falling apart.*

I sped down the Boulevard. *Sweethairyballsoffire... this sun is blinding,* I thought, flipping down the sun visor, then searching the car for the extra pair of shades I kept inside the truck. "Now I know they're in here somewhere." I leaned over and searched inside the glove compartment as I approached an intersection.

Boom!

Ohsweetjeezus... what in the hell is wrong with these dang, crazy drivers? I laid down on the horn, letting my window down. "What in the hell are you doing?" I yelled out. "Can't you see I'm trying to go?" I continued pressing down on the horn.

"Ohfortheloveofhigheelsandhandbags...who would park a limo right in the middle of the road? I don't know why these idiots have to try me today!" I put my truck in park, then swung open my door and got out. I was ready to flip somebody's light switch for causing this mess.

A tall, dark-skinned man wearing a black suit with a white shirt and black tie got out of the car the same as I hopped out of my truck ready to set it off. "Ma'am, are you all right?"

I frowned. "What do you mean, am I all right? Of course I'm not all right, you're blocking traffic and I have somewhere to be. Well, not really. But, that's beside the point. What if I did? Now what in the hell are you doing? Why would you stop in the middle of the road at a green light like that?"

"Ma'am, the light was red."

I frowned. "Red? That light was green, as in *drive*. Not as in *stop* in the center of the road. And tear up the front of my truck. Do you need your eyes checked, or them cataracts removed?"

"Ma'am, you ran into the back of us."

I huffed, "Well what in the heck you expect me to do, you dumb bunny. Don't get snotty with me. You were in the wrong. You lucky I don't get back in my truck and run you down."

"Ma'am, are you threatening me?"

"I'm not threatening. I'm informing you. You just insulted me. Usually I'd just run up on you. But I'm being nice today and giving you a warning. Any other day you'd already be on the ground rolling and burning."

"Ma'am..."

"And another thing, sir, I don't do the back and forth. You better shut your mouth. And let me see your credentials. I wanna know where you got your license from. Toys "R" Us? And did you rent them from the Matchbox aisle?" He stared at me with his old-looking self. "You need to be on that blue citizen bus that comes through here every Tuesday. What are you, about forty-five? You too dang old to be on the road, anyway, with your non-driving self. You need to hang your license up and stay off the road, buster."

"Ma'am, I was just thinking the same thing about you. Can I see *your* credentials?"

"*My* credentials? What are you trying to say?"

My mouth flew open. I'm only sixteen. I can't show him my credentials. I'm not even supposed to have a real license until next year. Thank God I had a connection down at the Motor Vehicles who forged the birth date on my paperwork. But I can't tell the police that. I'd be thrown up against a wall, patted down, and strip-searched. And that big burly woman Rich and London left behind might still be there waiting for me, especially since I'm prettier. I can't have that.

I gave him a flick of the wrist. "You know what, you're dismissed. You're fired. I'm not dealing with you." I stormed off toward the side of the limo and banged on the window. It slowly rolled down. "I need to talk to you. Are you aware that your driver is..." I paused, taking him in.

Ohmy...

"My driver is what?"

"Umm, harassing me. That's what he's doing. And I won't stand for it."

"Harassing you?" he asked, raising an eyebrow. "How?"

"By talking real slick and nasty to me. And I've been nothing but nice to him while he stood there and cursed me out, talking to me any ole kind of way. Now you need to do something about him. He needs to be reprimanded for his rudeness."

He chuckled.

Ooooh, he's so cute!

"I beg your pardon. This isn't funny. Now I see why your driver is so rude and obnoxious. He's driving around the King of Rudeness. But I won't have it. That's exactly why I fired him. So you're going to need to find yourself another driver."

"Enough."

"Enough?"

"Yeah, enough. Be quiet."

"Be quiet? I don't know who you think—"

"Shut. Up."

"Shut up?"

"Yeah, shut. Up. You've spent five minutes making a big production about something that's not all that serious. Are you hurt?"

"No."

"Do I look hurt?"

I huffed, impatiently, "Well. No. Not that I can tell."

"Then that's all that matters, beautiful. Now shut them pretty lips up and listen."

My mouth opened to say something else, then quickly shut. I don't know if I complied because he told me to shut up. Or if it was because I needed a moment to observe just how fine he was. He had skin the color of cocoa with dark chocolate eyes that almost looked black. My mouth started watering.

"Now go back to your car, get in, and pull over to the side of road."

"Wait a minute now. What are trying to do? Get me in a back alley somewhere? This is not that kind of party. You've got the wrong one."

He shook his head, rolling the window up in my face. I heard him say to his driver, "Call the police. I'm not getting anywhere with this girl."

I felt my knees buckle. I knocked on the window again. Flashed him a sparkling white smile, then said, "Look. I didn't say I wasn't going to pull over. I just want to make sure that I don't end up in the backwoods somewhere tied to a rock."

He gave me a confused look.

"Because in all the horror movies the black girls die first. I just want to make sure it's not going down like that. But I'm going to walk back over to my truck, get in and pull over. It's all good, right?"

He stared me down as if everything I said sounded ridiculous or something. "Listen. I don't know what movies you're talking about. But this isn't one of those scenes. All you're doing is driving up the street to get out of the middle of the road."

Lord, please don't let this fine man be a serial killer. And if he does kidnap me, please let it be somewhere safe and clean. Like a remote island, where I can still relax.

"Well? Are you going to keep blocking traffic, or are you going to move?"

"Yeah. I'll move. But I'm going to snap a picture of your

license plate and send it to my girls just in case you try some monkey business and I end up missing."

"Trust me, beautiful. You have nothing to worry about."

"*Trust* you? I don't know you. I mean you're cute and all—nice and chocolate. And them eyes of yours sparkle like black diamond dust but that doesn't mean I can trust you. So you go first."

He grinned, amused. "No, I already had you following me. That's why we're in this mess. You drive in front of me. And I'll follow *you*. You've done enough for one day."

I blinked. "I don't appreciate what you just said to me, but before I go off on you, I'm going to let it go. And do what you said because I don't want problems, okay. Just don't block me in. I don't want to cause any more damage ramming out of here. But I will."

I flipped my hair, turned on my heels, and walked back over to my truck, adding an extra shake to my fries, hoping like heck he had his eyes zoomed in all over my juicy Whooper.

I pulled around him, drove through the light, then pulled over. His driver pulled the limo up in front of me. The passenger door opened. And the minute Mr. Chocolate Drop stepped out of his car I immediately knew I needed to freshen my lips with another coat of lip gloss. He was so fine that my mouth watered.

He was a hot, steamy cup of cocoa that I wanted to sip and savor. I wanted him. And I was going to leave there with two things accomplished. No cops. And his phone number. *Hello, Sex Kitten.*

I sized him up, from the bottom to the top. I spotted a pair of leather Louis Vuitton loafers stuffed with big, long feet. The kind of feet that made me unbutton two more buttons on my blouse. Whew, it was getting hot and I had to let the steam out.

I continued my journey up his dress pants and admired how well they hung on his frame. I eyed the black Ferragamo belt that held his pants up on his thick waist. My naughty thoughts had me wondering what kind of underwear he had on. Boxers, or boxer briefs? And what he'd look like without any on. I imagined his pants dropping around his ankles and his buckle hitting the floor. I swallowed.

Come to Mama, baby...

He watched me, watching him as he made his way over to my truck. Yes, I was checking him out. Please. Guys did it to girls all the time. His head was up and he walked like he owned the streets. He took charge like he was a man on a mission. Not like that dumb bucket Corey who didn't know who or what he wanted. And not like Joey who walked around confused and lost, carrying a cardboard box because he couldn't get his science project right. Oh, no. This cocoa-dipped hottie glided over to me like he was a man who knew what he wanted. And he knew exactly how to get it. Oooh, he had it. And he brought the grown woman out of me. A moment Kitty would be proud of. *Rrrrrrrrrooowwwrrr!*

I rolled my window down, batted my eyes, eased out of the truck, then leaned up against the hood.

He walked up in my space. "I'm not gonna stand here all day playing games with you. Now, how are we going to handle this? 'Cause your driver is fired. Oh, he's sooooo fired. My truck needs to be fixed. And I need to know who's going to handle it. And I don't do roadside mechanics."

"Well, do you do dates?" he asked, eyeing me.

"*Whaaaaaat?* Dates? I never dated a mechanic." I paused. *Wait. A. Minute. Dates? Escorts go out on dates. Oh, he thinks I'm a prostitute!* "Oh you done tore your drawers down. And here I thought you were some fine prey I needed to pounce on. But all you are is roadkill. You think I'm some woman of the night. Goes to show how much you know, Mr. Sandman. Women of the night don't come out in the daytime. I'm not gonna stand for you calling me names." I put a finger up. "You wait right there. I got something for you. You don't know about me."

I marched back over to the passenger side of the truck, swung open the door, and grabbed my handbag. And as I yanked it open and searched for my can of get-right, he spoke over my shoulder. "Spencer, what are you doing?"

"I'm getting ready to teach you real good. I'ma mace you down."

He laughed. "I was asking you for a date with me."

"Oh, now you want a personal escort. I don't do that, either."

He continued laughing and boldly put his hand up on my waist and pulled me in front of him, causing me to drop my can of Mace. Now I was defenseless, on my way to a remote island. "Listen. I was asking *you* out on a date with *me* because I think you're beautiful. The truck is only scratched. And there's only a dent in my bumper. It's not that big of a deal."

"But your driver—your ex-driver, who I fired, remember?—was going to call the police on me like I had cracked your precious car in half."

"Enough with the car already. How about, seven o'clock...you and me? I'll have a driver come get you."

"And where do you think you're going to be taking me?"

He grinned. "It's a surprise."

"Now wait a minute. This surprise won't have anything to do with corners, blindfolds, or ropes, will it?"

He chuckled again. "No."

"Is it a remote island?"

He sighed. "Spencer. Just be ready. My driver will be waiting in front of your house at seven."

I blinked. "Wait a minute. How do you know my name?"

He grinned. "I got it off the cover of *Diva Girlz Weekly*, on page seventeen. Everyone knows you."

"Well, how do you know where I live? Are you a stalker? 'Cause I don't do stalkers. They're crazy. And here you want me to go off with you to some surprise. I don't think so."

"I'm not a stalker. I'm not a kidnapper. I'm not a murderer. And I'm not a pimp. I know where you live because I do. I'm simply interested in taking out a beautiful young woman. Now, give me a yes or no answer. No extras."

"No."

He looked at me. "All right, no problem."

He dropped his hands from my waist and turned to walk away. Just as he opened his door, I yelled out, "I can't do seven o'clock. How about seven-thirty?"

He smiled. "Seven-thirty it is. By the way, don't you think you should ask me for my name?"

"Ooops, I got so wrapped up in you being a pimp or kidnapper that I had simply forgotten." I tilted my head, toyed with the end of a curl. "What's your name?"

"Anderson," he said, slipping into his car, disappearing into the City of Angels.

29

Heather

My Dear Father:
I am who I am not because I wanted to shame any-
one; I just wanted to be myself. I know this is not what
you wanted for me but I didn't choose this. And I didn't
choose this pain, but I am choosing to end it. You no
longer have to wonder why God has cursed you with
me. And you no longer have to carry the shame of
having a son who you feel is not normal. I'm sorry
that you couldn't love me.

> *Your son,*
> *Yi-Ying*
> *aka Co-Co*

Co-Co lay on his bed dead. At least I thought he was dead when I'd walked into his house and into his room. I'd knocked and knocked until my raps turned into pounds and somehow the door simply opened—it was unlocked. I walked in and my heart sank to the floor. No matter how much I shook him or how loud I screamed he didn't wake up. There was no response. My tears wet his face as I pressed my forehead against his and called his name over and over and over again. Trying to make sense out of why he would do this to himself.

"Co-Co, please wake up!" I whispered against his lips. "Please."

My mind kept telling me that this wasn't real. This was a dream. That once I clicked my heels we would be in the middle of a rave, waving our hands in the air.

But this wasn't a dream. This was real.

I picked up the phone and called 9-1-1.

"9-1-1. What's your emergency?"

"He's dead," I said, practically in a whisper.

"Ma'am, can you repeat that?"

"I think he killed himself!" I screamed, hysterical, feeling as if I was going out of my mind.

"Ma'am, please stay as calm as you can. I can't understand a word you said, please tell me your location?"

"3610 Crescent Lane, Baldwin Hills!"

"Ma'am, just stay with me. Someone's on their way."

"Please hurry!"

"Is he bleeding?"

"No. He took a bottle of pills."

"Are you sure he's dead? Is there a pulse, please check to see if there's a pulse."

I reached for Co-Co's wrist and pressed my index finger into it. There was a faint pulse. "He's alive!" I screamed. "Please hurry!"

I don't remember when the EMT workers came into the house and into Co-Co's room. I just knew they were there, checking his vitals. There was no color in his face and his eyes sank deep into his high cheeks.

I knew the police were asking me questions. The same questions over and over again...but I couldn't answer them. All I could see was Co-Co. All I could see was my friend being rushed out on the stretcher, and I didn't understand why.

He had a mother. He had a father. He had life. He was life. And his smile, and laughter, and his snap-back-get-it-together-boo attitude made me believe that he could be who he wanted to be...and I envied that freedom only to find out that it was an illusion.

Now I didn't know what was real.

I took a step toward the door, my head started to spin, and suddenly I felt as if I were having an out of body experience and everything disappeared....

I didn't know what Co-Co's parents were saying. They were speaking in Chinese. All I knew is that whatever they were talking about was heated. Co-Co's mother sobbed. She had a fistful of wet tissue and his father sat as if he were unimpressed by the mother's emotions, as security asked them to quiet down.

I felt lost in the back of the room. The waiting was killing me. The not knowing was sending me over the edge. I wanted to beg someone—anyone—to promise me that Co-Co would stabilize and that the last time he was revived, it worked and he would stay alive. He already died twice and each time pieces of me died with him.

I didn't know how much he meant to me. He was much more than a fan club president. My love for him went beyond the parties, the Skittles, or the bags of Adderall we shared. He was my friend, my brother, and I loved him. I just wanted him to live. I just prayed that for once God heard me and gave me a chance to tell Co-Co that if we could make it through this, we could make it through anything. . . .

I just couldn't take sitting here anymore so I got up from my chair and as Co-Co's mother sobbed into her tissues I turned to his father and asked, "Mr. Ming, have you heard anything about Co-Co?"

His face turned to stone and he gave me an ice-cold stare. He clenched his teeth. "I don't know anyone by the name of Co-Co."

I swallowed. My heart hit the bottom of my stomach. For the life of me I couldn't remember Co-Co's real name. I hadn't called him that in years, and then it came to me. "Mr. Ming, is Ying okay?"

"*Yi*-Ying is not okay. He's sick." And he quickly turned his back on me.

"Mr. and Mrs. Ming," the doctor called as he walked over and tapped Mr. Ming on the arm. "He's conscious now and you can go in to see him."

My heart felt lighter. "Doctor," I said. "Can you please let him know that his friend Heather is here to see him?"

The doctor nodded and then he led the way to Co-Co's room as his parents followed behind.

For the next twenty minutes I paced the waiting room area. Hoping that his parents would hurry so that I could get to see Co-Co's face. I desperately needed to erase the image of him lying lifeless on his bed.

I chewed my inner cheek. I'd lost my patience and was barely holding on.

You need a Black Beauty....

No I don't....

I did all I could to shake the thoughts from my head. Unable to keep waiting I eased toward Co-Co's room. His father spoke to him in Chinese and I heard Co-Co cry, "Where am I supposed to go? I can't help who I am."

I wished I could understand what his father said. All I knew is that his tone was cold as he spoke. A few seconds later he turned toward the door, looked through me, and left the room. His wife cried as she followed closely behind him.

I walked slowly toward Co-Co, who lay in his hospital bed with his head turned toward the window. I grabbed his hand and he slowly turned his head toward me. I gave him a faint smile and said, "I'm so happy to see you're alive."

"I'm not."

"Don't say that. You have so much to live for."

"I don't have anything to live for. I couldn't even kill myself right. Why am I still here? My father thinks I'm a queer. He can't accept me for who I am. My mother has no voice. I'm not allowed back in my home. The guy who I thought loved me and accepted me for who I am has abandoned me. He won't return my calls. He doesn't want to be seen with me in public, because he wants to pretend that he's straight. No one wants to accept me. So no, Heather, you're wrong. I have nothing to live for."

"Co-Co..." I squeezed his hand and sat on the edge of his bed. Tears crept down my face. I felt like his words were slicing me. His words were my reality. I never thought they were his. I was unloved. Nobody wanted me. People only loved who they wanted me to be. I thought everybody loved Co-Co just as he was. "Why didn't you tell me?"

"Tell you what, Heather? That I'm gay? That my father thinks I'm a queer who chooses to like boys? A father who doesn't want to accept that I was born this way and I'm tired of hiding it."

"Then don't hide it. I love you and accept you the way that you are."

"So what about my father?"

"Then it's his loss. All I know is that you have to love yourself."

Co-Co's eyes welled with tears and he turned his head away from me and toward the window. I got up and crawled into bed with him. I draped my arm over his shoulder and kissed him on the side of his forehead. "Don't worry, Co-Co, no matter what we're in this together."

30

London

I knew he had no business being here again—beneath the covers, lying next to me, locked behind the double doors of my suite. But, he was. And I *knew* that I was playing with a loaded gun that could, and would, go off in my manicured hand if I didn't handle it with care. But, I was still toying with it. Still willing to spin the chamber and put the barrel to my head.

I glanced over at my secret weapon as he slept. He looked so peaceful. As if he didn't have a care in the world. And maybe he didn't. I had all the worries.

My mind flashed back to the first time we shared a kiss. It was two weeks after we'd met at the fashion show and exchanged numbers. He'd asked me out. And, although I knew he was someone who my parents would have never approved of, I snuck out to meet him, anyway. Nervous that someone would spot us; that my parents would find out and ground me for the rest of my life. But he didn't care who saw us, where we were, or what would happen if we got caught. He simply pulled me into his arms and kissed me right in the middle of The Top of the Rock Observation Deck at Rockefeller Center. His lips were soft. And I could taste the watermelon Jolly Rancher he'd had in his mouth. He was the first boy I had ever kissed with an open mouth and with a lot of tongue. I kissed him back. Tongued him as if I had been tonguing boys all of my life. And it was something in those sweet, warm kisses that told me he was the one; that we were meant to be together. And there were no coincidences. I was thirteen. He was sixteen. Now, fast-forward three years later and so much had happened between us. Yet, so much had remained the same. We were forever connected. My parents still would never approve of him. And I was still sneaking around with him, defying my parents at every turn. All in the name of love.

"Why you up?" he mumbled, lifting his head up from his pillow.

"I couldn't sleep."

He reached out for me, pulling me into his arms. "I got something for that."

I fell into his embrace, closed my eyes, and tried like hell to steady my racing thoughts and beating heart. "I love you like crazy, girl," he whispered in my ear as he started nibbling on my earlobe. A rush of desire immediately coursed through me. I needed this boy like I needed air. He was essential to my existence. And I had become dependent on him for survival. He was everything.

His hands roamed my body. I could feel his excitement rising as he pressed up against me.

You will learn to love him....

I don't want a repeat of what happened in New York....

"Justice, we need to talk."

"What, *now?*"

"Yes, now."

"C'mon, baby. Can't you see I'm in the middle of trying to rock you back to sleep? We can talk after."

I broke free from his embrace, sitting up in bed and flicking on the lamp on the nightstand.

"I was, uh, thinking that maybe...um, we should come up with another plan."

He quickly sat up in the bed. "Another plan? Like what?"

I took a deep breath, to calm my nerves, and then continued. "Like, maybe you could go, um, independent."

"Independent?"

"Yeah, baby, there are a lot of independent labels out there. And a lot of their artists are doing really, really well."

"Oh, really?" he asked, bewildered. "Is that why she hasn't called me back?"

"Whaaat? What are you talking about? Who hasn't called you back?"

"Rich."

"I introduced you. It's not my fault she hasn't called you back. I did my part. She's barely even calling me."

He huffed, "Yeah, right. You half introduced us. Nothing like what we planned. You're a liar."

My mouth dropped open. I couldn't believe he had called me a liar.

"And now you want me to go to independent because your jealousy sabotaged everything for me."

"Justice, what are you talking about? You think it's that easy to hook you up with my friend? That's my friend. How do you think I feel about that?"

"Your friend? Oh, now she's your friend. Now you running to parties and plastered all up in the newspaper with her, and she's your friend. Before you couldn't stand her, remember that? Fat, bougie, worked your nerves. Now all of a sudden y'all sisters."

"Yeah, in the beginning I did say all that because I didn't know her like that. But I don't feel like that now."

"So, it's back to how you feel again. Everything's always about you. This ain't about you. That's the problem. You just don't want me to do better than you."

"That's not true," I said, defensively. My lips quivered. "I love you so much. I'd do anything for you."

He screwed his face up. "Yo, you must be on crack! Talkin' about some independent. I haven't been puttin' in all this time with you to be hustlin' out of the trunk of my whip. I coulda stayed in New York for that. What the hell I look like? I'm mad talented. And I damn sure didn't have to be laying up here with you if you weren't gonna follow through. Got me sweatin' you. Got me caged in your room, like I'm some animal."

He scowled at me. "Independent? I don't need you to tell me to be independent. What, you wanna be my manager? I need you to handle your damn business like we discussed. I need you to be a grown woman to support me the way you're supposed to. Stand by your man. That's what a grown woman does. And I'm supposed to be ya man. I asked you to marry me. And this is what you do. Everybody else comes before me. Justice ain't nothing. Is that what you believe, London? Miss Hollywood. Miss All Up in the Press. Got me sitting around here lookin' like a clown. I ain't diggin' that."

I gulped hard. At that moment, I regretted ever bringing any of this up to him. But there was nothing I could do to change what had already been said. "Baby...you know I love you."

"You don't love me," he scoffed. "You love ya damn self. You too effen selfish to love anyone other than ya'-self."

I winced. "That's not true. I love you and I believe in you."

"Yeah, right," he snorted. "Like I'm supposed to believe anything that comes outta ya mouth now. You standin' here talkin' real sideways. I put my life on hold for you. And now you wanna play games, after all we've been through together."

The way Justice glared at me with contempt made me feel like I had opened a hornet's nest and stuck my head inside. The stinging of his words was killing me. "Justice, please, baby. You have to believe—"

"What? That you've gone out and found Jesus and now you have a conscience? Is that what ya want me to believe?"

"No, that I love you." I reached for his hand, but he jerked it away from me.

"Tell that to someone who really cares," he spat. "Let me know what you gonna do, London. You gonna get ya mind right? Or are you still gonna be hung up? 'Cause now you wanna be friends with some damn media ho."

I was torn by emotions. Love. Hurt. Fear. Disgust. And the fear of losing my man was the most intense. Right there on the spot, I wanted to vomit, or run into his arms and hold him tightly, or fall to my knees and plead for mercy.

"I'm not playin' with you, London. I've already wasted too many years effen around with ya. I'm tryna make moves and you tryna play games. I ain't got time for that. I need a grown woman. I don't need no lil girl and her games. Save that for ya billionaire 'cause I'm a real dude. So you're either with me, or against me. What's it gonna be?"

My knees were weak as he went on. "Everything's what's best for London. First I thought it was ya parents. But now I realize it's you. You're the problem here. Not them."

His words slapped me across the face. I blinked back the burning sensation, trying to absorb the meaning behind everything he was saying to me. I struggled to wrap my mind around what had just happened between us. He had turned on me, and I didn't understand why.

I put a hand up. "Wait a minute, wait a minute. You're going too far. I'm trying to put things in motion, but it's not that simple."

He grunted. "Yeah, I guess it wouldn't be that simple if all you're doing is BS-ing me."

"I resent that. That's not what I'm doing. That's so unfair of you to say that."

"London, quit the theatrics. What I resent is the fact that you're stylin' 'n profilin' like everything's everything while I'm playin' the background. That's not how this was supposed to go down. All this was your idea from the rip. You're the one who said you'd do whatever it took. You were supposed to play house with the billionaire and put me on. But from where I'm standing, you the only one bubblin' up. What, you wanna be with him? Is that what this is really all about?"

"Ohmygod, nooooo," I said incredulously. "I can't believe you'd ask me something like that. You know he's not who I want to be with."

"Yeah, whatever. I can't tell. You said you were going to come out here and hold me down. Now you're standin' here hittin' me with the okey-doke like I'm supposed to be good with that."

"I did say that. And I meant it."

"Then why you standin' here now, tryna throw salt all up in the mix? You must think I'm some crab-type dude, like I'm supposed to keep scraping at the bottom of the barrel waitin' on you. Like I should just be some broke-down nothing. How long before you look at me and laugh? I wanna come up, too. Don't you think I wanna shine, too? But you wanna keep me up in here like I'm ya sex slave. But check this. I'm not ya damn daddy, I ain't gonna keep givin' you what you want. It's time you start givin' me what I want. Starting now. So, what's it gonna be?"

The tears built up in my eyes, matching the hurt and disappointment that were already eating away at my heart. "What are you saying? What do you want?"

"I didn't stutter. Right now, I wanna be away from you."

"So you're breaking up with me?"

"You figure it out since you so busy figuring out everything else except for how you gonna stick to the plan."

I felt like he had hit me over the head with a brick, then hit me in the chest with it. He had knocked the air out of me. I gasped. Here I was risking everything for him. And the only thing he'd done for me was leave an imprint on my sheet. And now he was standing here telling me that I was making a fool out of him. That I was jealous of him. When all I've ever done was love him.

I couldn't help it if Rich wasn't calling him back. And, no, I didn't feel bad about it. Still, I had upheld my part of the plan. I did what I was supposed to do.

I wanted to beg and cry at his feet, for him to forgive me for what he said I'd done, even though I wasn't sure if I had really done it. But at this moment it wasn't about love. I loved the hell out of him. This was about pride. And if nothing else, I had pride. I fought back the tears.

"You know what, Justice? You're right."

"Right about what?"

"About everything you just said. Now get your things and get out."

He looked at me in disbelief. "What?"

"You heard me. I love you and all. But, uh, I'm good."

I said this, but knew I didn't really mean it. But he played me so hard, cursed me, and had taken my heart and pissed on it, then threw it in my face.

He snorted. "Oh, you good. You follow me all the way out here to L.A. to be with me, but you good. London, please. But, yeah, I'ma leave. That's probably the best idea you've come up with yet, Miss Independent. But I tell you what. I'ma show you what being independent is all about."

He grabbed his bags, threw up the two-finger peace sign, swung open the bedroom doors, and walked out.

I wanted to break down. But I was scared because he had boldly walked out of my bedroom and stomped down the front staircase instead of using the butler's stairs that led directly to back of the house, where I had diverted the security cameras. Now I knew anyone watching the security monitors would see him. I raced down the stairs after him.

"Justice, wait. Please," I whispered, hoping no one was in earshot.

He kept walking.

I grabbed him by the arm. "Please, let's talk about this."

He yanked his arm away from me and continued his cocky stride toward the front door. He treated me as if I were some two-dollar trick with stained teeth and bad breath. I stopped in my tracks.

Our housekeeper, Genevieve, popped out from nowhere just as Justice walked past her, not caring who saw him, or what would happen to me if my parents caught him. I was terrified. I watched as my man opened the door and walked out, never looking back.

"What is all that noise out there?" I heard and almost fainted. *Ohmygod, Daddy's here.* I felt the floor open up and suck me in. I could hear him walking down the hall headed toward the foyer. I jumped.

Genevieve pursed her lips, raising her bushy brows. For the first time in a long time, I felt like I was sinking into a deep, dark hole. And this time I wouldn't be able to get my way out of it. "Genevieve, please don't say anything," I said, no, begged, putting my hands up as if I were praying to her.

She eyed me. "I won't. But you know better." Her tone sounded as if she were trying to scold me. But right now I needed her on my side, so checking her wasn't in my best interest at that moment.

I lowered my head. "I know. Please."

I held my breath.

"Mr. Phillips, sir," she said, swiftly walking toward the direction of my father's footsteps. "Sorry for disturbing you, sir. It won't happen again."

"Is everything all right?"

"Yes, sir. Everything's fine. Would you like me to bring you a light snack or something?" Daddy told her that wouldn't be necessary, then headed back down the hall and back into his study.

I exhaled.

"He's not good for you, Miss London," Genevieve said the moment she returned. "That boy means you no good. He's nothing but trouble."

I frowned. See, now she was crossing boundaries. Her job was to dust, mop, wax, and clean up behind me. Not dole out opinions, or any damn unsolicited advice. "He's not trouble. And I didn't ask you for counsel on the matter. I just asked you not to say anything."

I narrowed my eyes for emphasis.

"My lips are sealed, Miss London."

"Good."

I took a deep breath, breaking my stare from her long enough to glance back at the door, hoping like hell that Justice would miraculously come to his senses and walk back through that door, scoop me up in his arms, and tell me this was all a bad dream. That he hadn't meant any of those cruel things he said to me.

He never came back.

I raced back to my room, horrified. My man had just cursed me out. My daddy was home. Genevieve saw. And only God knew who else. I could only hope that the surveillance cameras hadn't been recording. In a state of panic, I started crying, and ended up in the bathroom, crouched down on the floor between the bidet and toilet. Glad no one was around to hear me boo-hooing like a two-year-old, but I couldn't hold it in any longer. I was overwhelmed. I knew Justice loved me. And I knew he wanted to secure his future, and mine, so that we could be together, *forever*, like we'd promised one another. But everything had changed. Not because I wanted it to. Not because I didn't want to follow through. But because I had allowed someone else to come into my space, besides Justice. I allowed Rich to become my best friend and I knew—in the end—someone was going to end up getting hurt.

I felt desperate and crazed.

Everything in me ached. I needed to see Justice. Needed to hear his voice. Needed to feel his touch. I picked up my cell and called him. Fifteen minutes later, I sent him a text. Then I sent another and another, each one more desperate than the one before, begging him to please call me. But, two hours and thirty-seven text messages later, he still hadn't called.

And I was alone.

31

Rich

A month later

"**R**ich, wake up…"
I opened my eyes slowly and for a moment I couldn't place where I was.

I felt awful.

I'd been sick for about three weeks. Throwing up in the morning, at lunchtime, and again at eight o'clock in the evening—on the hour—without fail. I barely ate, had nightly bouts with the chills, and for about a week straight I thought for sure that I had a stomach virus.

Until I checked the calendar and realized I was close to two weeks late.

I knew then this wasn't a stomach virus and this was nothing that antibiotics would cure.

I was pregnant.

And the double lines on my EPT test confirmed it.

Problem was, I didn't know what to do about it…or if I wanted to do anything about it.…

This situation was not new to me. The last one ended

on the doctor's table with my feet in cold stirrups and me counting backward until I drifted into a forced sleep, and woke up with my mother instructing me that this had never happened; I didn't know if I wanted to relive that.

"Rich, come on baby, you got to get up."

"I just need another hour of sleep."

"Babe, you don't have another hour. We overslept."

"Overslept?" My eyes popped open and I sat straight up in Knox's full bed. "What time is it?" I asked in a panic. My eyes scanned the room and landed on the clock; 9:30 A.M.

My heart dropped to my stomach and my mouth started to water. I was delirious, nervous, scared as hell, and about to throw up at any minute.

"Rich," Knox said as he stroked my back. "You a'ight?"

You need to tell him.

"I don't want no babies... We need to use condoms..."

"What if I was pregnant...?"

"I'd be pissed off. Neither one of us are ready for any kids. I'm eighteen and you're only sixteen. No haps. I got too much to do, which is why we'll be using condoms from now on..."

Too late...

I shook my thoughts, doing all I could to erase the conversation that Knox and I had last night before we made love. This time with a condom. If only he knew it made no difference.

I flew from the bed and into the bathroom. Before I could close the door I was bent over the toilet throwing up my guts into the water.

"Are you all right?" Knox came to the door, dressed in loose basketball shorts.

"Yeah, I'm fine. Just the pizza from last night didn't

agree with me." I stood up and washed my mouth out over the sink. I glanced at his reflection in the mirror and saw that he was studying me. We clashed gazes. "You sure you a'ight?" he asked.

I shifted my eyes, scared that he was reading my mind and was uncovering my dirt. "I just gotta get out of here." I rushed past him and back into his bedroom. "I am in so much trouble!" I panicked, snatching my clothes off of the chair next to Knox's bed. "This is crazy, how did I over-sleep?" I bit my lip as my heart thundered. I couldn't help but think about my parents' morning routine:

Up by six.

Breakfast together by six thirty.

Daddy calling my name by seven to say, "Have a good day, baby girl."

And by eight my mother knocking on my door telling me it was time to wake up and get ready for school.

"OMG! Of all days, this is the day I had to oversleep, this would be the one that my mother convinced my father to have Drake perform and we give out invitations to the Pampered Princesses party!"

"What party?" Knox asked, looking at me like I was crazy.

"It's nothing," I said, tossing my clothes on like a whirl-wind.

"What do you mean it's nothin'? A party is more than nothin'."

I stopped for a moment, turned around, and looked at him. He had to be crazy. "Are you serious right now? Really? I don't have time for you questioning me about a party!" I slipped my heels on.

"No, you don't ever have time. The only time you have

dar in about eights months you'll be a daddy. So you put your condoms back in the drawer because you're two weeks and two days too damn late!"

I stormed out and slammed the door behind me.

I pulled up in the driveway and according to my cell-phone I had ten missed calls: seven from Logan, one from Daddy, and two from London.

I had to find a way to get in and out of here quickly and the only way to do that was through the servants' entrance and tiptoe up the back staircase to my room. I eased in through the French doors and did all I could not to make eye contact with the house manager. The last thing I needed was her opinion.

The kitchen was clear and I was practically home free until I stepped onto the staircase and there was Logan—not smiling—waiting for me.

"Where. Have. You. Been?"

I hesitated. "Umm, Ma, I was at London's and she—"

"No you weren't."

What is he doing here? I swallowed. Hard. That was my father. He looked at me coldly. "Your mother asked you a question. And don't lie again. Because you weren't at London's."

"Yes, I was, you can call London right now."

"Really," Daddy said. "Do you really think I would call your cell mate and ask her if you spent the night with her, knowing that she would lie for you? How about this. I called Turner and he told me that you weren't there. Now, who do you think I'll believe, my lawyer or my lyin' daughter?"

I felt like I was about to pass out at any moment. I

could feel my stomach bubbling and I knew that I was seconds away from throwing up again. "I need to go to the bathroom."

"Go on," my mother said. "And while you're in there, take that pregnancy test that I left on the counter. Because you are about two weeks and two days late. And the last time this happened I didn't know what the problem was. But this time I do. Now do you still have to go to the bathroom or do you have some explaining to do?"

"Run this by me again?" my father said as he turned to my mother. "The last she was what?"

My mother looked toward me. "Tell him, Rich. And you better not lie. Or you will be down the rest of those stairs and the last service we had will be for free."

Tears poured down my face.

"Don't cry," my mother said. "Little girls cry. Grown women own their behavior. Now square your shoulders, stand up right, and tell your father what happened this summer when we were in the Hamptons. And made the mistake to believe that you were responsible enough to be here alone. Tell him how you had your legs all up, spread wide. How you were far from Daddy's little girl. You had a different kind of daddy. You laid up here where your father pays the bills and the only two who are supposed to be getting action is us. Not you. But explain to your father. Better yet, tell me if I left anything out. And you still haven't said where you've been." She walked down two steps closer to me. "Now speak."

I grabbed the rail as I took a step backward and almost lost my balance. My heart felt as if it were jumping out of my chest.

"Logan," my father interjected. "Forget all this talking.

Rich, get up these stairs and take that pregnancy test. And Logan, you stand in there with her. And it better be negative or it will be a problem."

I looked at my father with a river of tears falling from my eyes. "There's no need to take the test."

My mother lifted her hand in the air and as it landed across my face she said, "Just as I thought."

32

Heather

Cell phone goin' off in my hand!
Poppin' Beauties, sippin' yak!
Keak Da Sneak on deck.
Skittles at the door.
More than enough yak in the back.
Privileged kids snortin' and gettin' their thizzle on.
So how you wanna act? Wu-Wu straight killin' the
    track.
I'm holdin' it down.
I don't think they know.
That's my word!
I'm reppin' for the mofos who know how to act!
My definition of hyphie is leaving your pills at the
    door, sniffin' lines, and tossin' back. Wu-Wu in
    the building and I'm feelin' fine. And I'm blowin'
    minds. R.I.P. to the phonies!

I shot up a peace sign and the crowd went wild. My
extra-large gold bamboo earrings swung from side to side
as I directed the crowd which way to move. My bangles

clacked in the air and my extension ponytail, which hung past the small of my back, swung from side to side. My whole presence was laid. My neon pink micro mini clung to my booty pads, making the back of me look like pow! I put every chick in here to shame. I wore a neon green sequin bra top that made my Betty Boops pop. I grabbed Co-Co's head and smeared his face into my cleavage. "Eat it up! Who loves you, baby!"

The crowd had lost control.

And they expected me to be at Hollywood High with those drab hoes, posing for the camera and talking about Gucci. But Gucci didn't have a thing on this!

I released Co-Co's head from my bosom and he broke out and kicked up a split in his tight white leather booty shorts and black thigh-high six-inch boots. Bare chested and nipples pierced. He was doin' it and doin' it well.

The D.J. had the music on full blast and I was rocking the mic in the center of my backyard on a makeshift stage. Camille was passed out drunk. And the treat that I slipped her in her drink made sure she stayed that way.

I didn't give a damn about no phony Pampered Princesses-Hollywood High party. I don't think they heard. That I was in my zone and yeah I took their white party idea and turned it into my own. But so what.

I hosted an impromptu Skittles party with white tents all around, white linen tables filled with flowing fountains of liquor, and an assortment of colorful pills at your fingertips: Oxycodone, Ritalin, Tylenol with codeine, Adderall, and a list of others. At least a hundred and fifty teens brought their medicine cabinets with them.

I supplied the place, the booze, the D.J., and the freestylin'.

Who had time for a Hollywood High party? This was where the real party jumped. "Who shotcha, baby!" I spat into the mic, dropped down low, popped back up, and as I waved my arms in the air I realized that there was Spencer. Her eyes popped out like a deer caught in head-lights, mouth hung open, and anti-high blower written across her face.

What. The. Hell. Is. She. Doing. Here…? I turned the mic off and as Co-Co continued to dance across the stage, entertaining the crowd, I stepped off the stage and walked over to Spencer.

"What is this! Ohmysweetholyghost. I need some oil up in here. What are you doing? Why is hell all through your backyard? I just saw the devil taking a handful of pills and shoving it down her throat!"

"What do you want, Spencer?"

"I want to know why you aren't at school? And why are all these people in your backyard? And why are all those pills at the door? Who are all these people? And why is Camille passed out on the sofa, drooling? You didn't kill her, did you? Please tell me that this is not celebrating her death. I know she wasn't the nicest but this is ridiculous. I don't know who you are but you need to go and find Heather. Because she had a party at school to attend!" Spencer slammed a hand on her hip. "And these people need to clear out of here now. And you need to get ready."

She snatched the mic from my hand, cut it back on and announced, "The party is over!"

I snatched the mic back out of her hand. This trick had lost every bit of her scattered brain. "Attention, everyone, the party is not over. It's just beginning! And it's starting with me putting this trick in her place."

"What did you just call me, Heather? Heather, I know you are not trying to shut it down. I came over here concerned and trying to get you ready for the party!"

"I don't need your concern. And I will not be going to your whack party. So I don't need you coming up in here disrupting my thug thizzle. 'Cause you're way out of line. Now either you get yourself a handful of Skittles, chase it with some yak, and get with the party. Or step off!"

"First off I don't eat Skittles!"

"You are the dumbest ho I've ever come across. Your name is wedged in between dumb and dumber. You take stupid to new heights—"

"Heather, Heather, I thought we were friends—"

"Friends? Friends? You thought? We were never friends and never will be! I don't like you. You're a sneaky, dirty, conniving little ho. Oh no, excuse me, big ho. Who loves to snatch, sneak, and run up on other people's boyfriends. Now gather your heels and walk back out the way you came in here. And since you're concerned about Camille, take her with you. 'Cause you are disrupting my get-right and disturbing my guests. Now get out of here before we all stomp you down!"

Spencer looked around and all eyes were on her. She swallowed back her tears. "Heather, I don't believe you."

"Well believe this. Y'all ready to party?" I said into the mic and headed back toward the stage.

"Yeah!" the crowd roared.

"D.J. hit me with that 'Put You on the Game' beat." I shook my head like a rock star and Co-Co continued on like he was the backup dancer and the hype man. "One time for your mind!" Co-Co yelled as I started rapping:

Let me tell you how...
I brought the Gucci clique down...
Click, click,
With the camera...behind the bathroom door
And smiling away.
Thought they could get away with the dirty tricks
and their best friend's boyfriend.
Little did they know I was recording on the other
end!
Click, click...

"Two times for your mind!" Co-Co yelled. And the crowd chanted, "Ahh, Wu-Wu's in the house!"

My rap continued:

And then I pressed send.
Brought their world right to an end.
Next thing I know Spencer got whupped down in
the ditch.
Rich found out she was tricked by the dizzy bitch.
London got caught up in the matrix.
And the Gucci clique was clearly not ready for war!
Click. Click...

"Ahh, Wu-Wu's in the house!" the crowd chanted. "Ahh, Wu-Wu's in the house!"

As I ended my rap and dropped down to do a booty pop, I searched the crowd and Spencer was nowhere to be found. I chased that ho up out of here. "Somebody hand me some Skittles!" I yelled into the crowd. "Ahh, Wu-Wu's in the house!"

33

London

I paced in my seven-inch Versace platform sandals with my cell pressed up against up my ear calling Rich for the fourth time, wondering where the hell she was. We were all supposed to meet up this morning at our lockers to go over the last-minute details before the Invitation Party kicked off this afternoon in the school's ballroom. Heather and Rich were no-shows. And Spencer, who is useless and I can't stand, had just arrived with no Heather in tow, after she left here forty-five minutes ago to go look for her.

"Rich, this is London, call me as soon as you get this. Where are you? The party starts in thirty minutes." I disconnected and called back again, leaving another message. Truth of the matter, I was livid.

Today was the day where we were to serve everyone with a taste of what the Pampered Princesses had in store for our upcoming Diamond & Stilettos Masquerade party next month. The entertainment was on lock. The ballroom was filling up. The color-coded invitations with the embossed seal were ready to be hand-delivered to five hundred carefully chosen guests. The trumpeters were positioned on both sides of the door, announcing the guests as they arrived.

The ballroom was absolutely elegant. White draped walls. Round tables smartly dressed with crisp white linen tablecloths while tall crystal vases centered in the middle of each table were filled with a bouquet of fresh calla lilies. The DJ was spinning. The stage was set. The dance floor glowed. And Drake was backstage waiting to perform. The paparazzi were swarming around with cameras on ready. And Rich was still nowhere to be found. She was somewhere else playing damn games, like always. All these students-slash-guests and only two of the other half of the so-called Pampered Princesses were here. Rich and Heather's absence simply added to the rumors: that we had fallen apart. That we were backstabbers. That we had fallen from grace. And this was not how it was supposed to be.

My cell rang and I quickly glanced at the screen hoping it was Rich. It wasn't. It was Justice. I took a deep breath, then pressed *ignore*. I hadn't heard from him in a month. He ignored my calls, ignored my texts, and simply ignored me like I was nobody. Although, seeing his name flash up on the screen lifted the burden of being disregarded. But as badly as I wanted to hear his voice, I would not allow myself to answer. Not this time. I turned the phone off.

Walked over to the mirrors lining the wall and applied a fresh coat of lipstick, then glided a coat of lip gloss over my lips to make them pop. Then I checked myself out to make sure I was still looking divalicious in my Vera Wang exclusive that wrapped around my body like a glove. I glanced at my timepiece. Fifteen minutes to show time. I had to get in the room.

As I turned from the sink to head to the ballroom, Rich burst in. She was draped in black diamonds. Her neck, ears, and wrists glistened while wearing a gorgeous black dress and a pair of royal blue and black crystal-embellished heels.

"Ohmygod, there you are. Where the hell have you been? I have been calling you..." I eyed her, taking her in. Then my expression changed. "Are you okay? What's wrong? Why are your eyes red? Are you crying?"

"No. I'm fine."

She stood at the adjoining sink beside me, unsnapping her clutch, pulling out a Chanel handkerchief and dabbing at her eyes. I studied her through the mirror, placing a hand up on her shoulder. "Rich, look at me. I'm serious. What's going on? Why are you crying?"

The tears started pouring down her face. "I-I..."

"Don't say a word yet," I said, walking over to the door and locking it, then walking back over to her. "Now, tell me. What's wrong? And please don't tell me you're crying because you ran up your credit card again."

"Girl, please, I wish."

"Well, did your parents take them?"

"I wish it was that."

I blinked. If Miss Shop-A-Holic was wishing her parents had shut down her credit cards then I knew this was some serious business. "Ohmygod, you've been banished to the mall. Is that it?"

She held her head back, wiping tears with the back of

her fingers. "Right about now, girl, I'd take the mall. But it's not that, either."

I turned her to face me, placing both of my hands on her shoulders, looking her in her wet eyes. "Rich, you're scaring me now. What is it?"

She held her head down. "I really messed up this time."

I lifted her chin, taking the handkerchief from her to dab her eyes and face. "How? What happened? I mean, I know it can't be because your father couldn't get Drake here because he's already backstage."

She shook her head. "No, that's not it."

I let out an exasperated sigh, feeling myself losing my patience. "Look, you need to tell me what the hell is going on. You come up in here four hours late. No one's heard from you. Not answering your calls and now you're standing here effen up your makeup with a bunch of tears and I have no clue as to why."

"Look, you asked me what is going on—"

"Yeah, I did. Because I'm worried. I've been calling you all damn morning and hadn't heard from you. And you're looking crazy. Now get to the point and tell me what the hell is wrong here. We have a damn party to get to. Whatever it is, it can't be that bad. Now give me your concealer." She handed me her make-up bag. I took her concealer out and dabbed her eyes with the sponge. "You're too damn beautiful to be crying like this. We don't do tears. And especially when we are draped in our jewels and fine wears." I touched up her mascara and Rich's eyes watered again. "Oh, no. Stop with the tears. This make-up is not waterproof."

"I'm pregnant," she whispered.

"What? What did you just say?"

She looked me in the eyes, fighting back what appeared to be an avalanche of tears. "I said. I'm pregnant."

"Pregnant? Ohmygod, Corey got you pregnant? You slept with Corey without a condom? Illll. Oh, you done hit rock bottom with that one. Corey?"

"No, I'm not pregnant by Corey. I only slept with him three times and we always used a condom."

"Well, I know you're not the Virgin Mary. And if Corey's not the father, then who were you out getting your creep on with because he's the only one I knew you were with. We have about five minutes of true confessions then we got to roll. So let's go. Start from the name of the baby daddy, then work your way to how the hell you let this happen, followed by what time is your appointment. And do I need to be there with. I'm waiting."

She took a deep sigh. "His name is Knox."

"Knox? Who the hell is a Knox?"

"That's not important. And there's no appointment."

I blinked. "So, what does that mean?"

She looked me in the eyes and responded, "I'm keeping it."

"Whaaaaaat? You're keeping it? A baby? Oh, now you're bugging. First of all what are you going to do with a baby? You don't even like kids. We have plans to shop and do it up. And now you're talking about keeping a baby. Remember, we're supposed to be traveling. Or did you forget? Oh, that's right, of course you did. You're pregnant. So you'd rather give up Milan in the fall, Switzerland in the winter, Paris in the spring, and wherever else we want to be in the summer to be confined between a baby's crib and the nanny's quarter, is that what you're saying? You wanna give up Chanel for Carter's, handbags for diaper bags, stilettos for some cheesy, scuffed ballet slippers and your jewels for pacifiers and drool? A mess! Have you even thought this through? A baby, Rich? Are you serious? It's one thing to be pregnant—been there, done that. And it's a whole other level to be a mother. And how are you going to boom-drop it with a damn baby up on your hip? Not the move. And definitely not a good look."

"Look, I don't need you to lecture me. I didn't ask for your advice. After the morning I've had, I don't need any more advice."

"No, you're right. What you need is to face reality because right now you're living in a fantasy. You don't spring this kind of madness on someone four minutes before a show. Now, had you come to me last night, we could have balled up and cried together and ate tubs of ice cream..."

"London! London!" Spencer disrupted our moment banging on the door. "Open this door!"

Before I walked over and unlocked the door, I glanced at Rich and said, "It's time to put your game face on. Now. And you better not let her see you sweat."

She turned back to the mirror, tugged at a few strands of her hair that had fallen out of place, then pulled out her gloss and coated her lips. She slowly turned back to me, eyes clear and lips popping, and replied, "Game time."

I unlocked the door and Spencer rushed into the bathroom. "What in the world are you..." She looked over at Rich. "Oh, there you are. It's about time you showed up."

"Have you finished digging up the rocks to find Heather?" I asked her, snidely.

She furrowed her eyebrow. "Excuse you?"

"You heard me. I said, have you gone to the junkyard

and found your damn trashy friend. She's still not here and it's three minutes before we hit the red carpet and hold court."

"Wait a minute, first of all. Let's not even talk about trashy. Would you like for me to call you a gorilla? Or fifty foot? You don't come me at like that."

"No, you wait a minute," I snapped, slamming my clutch down on the counter. "You are about to get your face cracked."

Spencer patted her clutch. "Try it. And you'll be on fire. It'll be stop, drop, and roll for your big-faced self. Now try me. And the last time I checked I wasn't on ho-patrol. When I walked in here and saw that you had found Rich, I thought that was your job." She looked over at Rich. "Now the question is where were you, somewhere having last-minute lipo to reduce your waistline?"

"Don't worry about my waistline," Rich said. "Worry about the next video you gonna make, ho. Talking about you don't check for hoes on the stroll. I don't know why not because you own it."

Spencer huffed, "Yeah, that's right. I'm a ho. I own the stroll. But at least I own it up front. And I'm not an under-cover ho, like you."

Rich walked over to Spencer, stood in her face and spoke in a low tone, clenching her teeth. "I will slap. The spit. Out of you. Today is not the day. Now if your stank friend isn't here, that is not my problem. If you're a ho, then be a ho. But you keep my name out your mouth. And when we get out there, you better act like we're the best of friends. Or we will stop, drop, and roll on the red carpet. Now freshen your gloss, and let's go."

Spencer popped her lips. "You know what. I'ma put my

knife back in my clutch, I'm gonna gloss my lips, and I am going to go out there and *pretend* to be your friend. But when the cameras stop clicking and the red carpet is rolled up, all bets are off."

Rich eyed her one last time. "Then get ready to cash in your chips." She looked over at me. "Let's go, London. It's game time."

One foot in front of the other, camera-ready, we walked out of the girls' lounge. Click, click. The three of us with our backs straight, and heads up. Hollywood's finest at its best, ready for show time as we swayed down the red carpet that had been rolled out down the hall, leading to the ballroom, stopping every so often to take pictures and answer questions.

"Hey, Rich Montgomery, what are you wearing?"a reporter for *Teen Style* magazine asked.

She flashed a bright white smile. "The dress is Gucci, the shoes are Jimmy Choo from his private collection, so don't go looking for them. The diamonds are from Chopard Jewelers. *Muah!*" Rich blew a kiss and gave a small wave toward the camera.

I had to smile at Rich. Although her stomach looked pudgy, she looked fabulous in her form-fitting dress. If only she would suck her stomach in. I couldn't give her ten stars with that stomach looking like it did. But she was every bit of eight-point-five stars. Hair, face, and jewels were all sparkling.

"Hey, London Phillips," a fashion blogger asked. "Will we ever see you on the runway again?"

I felt like she had slit me across the throat with her question, considering when I stepped on the scale this morning I had gained three pounds, throwing my mother into a hissy fit, threatening to have my jaws wired for a month. I shook the thought and pressed a smile on my face. "You never know."

"Hey Rich Montgomery, who's the new love interest you've been spotted with?"

Rich smiled sheepishly. "No comment," she said to the reporter.

"Spencer Ellington," a reporter for *Ni-Ni Girlz Glamalicious* called out. "Do you plan to stay away from Rich's new beau? Or will this one not be off limits like the other?"

"Of course she will," Rich answered, placing an arm around Spencer's shoulder, smiling for the cameras. "The last time was simply a big misunderstanding."

"Where's Heather Cummings?" another reporter asked.

Spencer whispered to Rich and me, "I got this one." She turned to the reporter, smiled and batted her eyelashes. "Heather is a little tied up right now. But I'm sure she'll make the headlines tomorrow."

Just as the trumpets sounded to announce our arrival, another reporter yelled out, "Hey, Rich, London, and Spencer, what would you like to say to your fans who are watching?"

We smiled, and said as if our lines had been rehearsed, "Welcome to Hollywood High!"

Stay tuned for the next installment of *Hollywood High*!

HOLLYWOOD HIGH

Ni-Ni Simone
Amir Abrams

ABOUT THIS GUIDE

The following questions are intended to
enhance your group's reading of
HOLLYWOOD HIGH.

Discussion Questions

1. Socialites live in an entirely different world than most. However, do you feel their problems are much different than the average teen's? If so, then how?

2. Which girl did you identify with the most and why? Whom did you identify with the least?

3. How did you feel about Heather's drug use? Do you know any teens using drugs? Have you ever tried drugs? If so, what was the outcome?

4. How much of an effect do you think Heather being a child star had on her drug use?

5. What did you think of London's mother being obsessed with London's weight? Do you know someone who has a mother like this?

6. What did you think of Justice? Do you think he loved London?

7. What did you think of Spencer's mother never being home? Do you know someone who has a mother like this?

8. What did you think of Spencer sleeping with Rich's boyfriend? Is it ever okay to date your friend's boyfriend?

9. Are the Pampered Princesses friends or frenemies?

10. If you could change anything about the story, what would it be?

Up next from *Hollywood High*'s Amir Abrams:

Crazy Love

If you saw my boo Sincere, you'd totally understand why I've dropped everything—even my besties—to be with him 24/7. After all, what girl wouldn't do whatever it takes to show her first-ever boyfriend she's all he could ever want? I *know* I'm a prize, but relationships are tough enough when you're just a high-school senior, so I've really had to up my game to keep a college freshman like Sincere interested. And if that means hacking his cell and following him everywhere, I'm down. Because I just know what we have is for always. And I'm going to prove it, no matter how far I have to go . . .

In stores in December 2012.

"Giiiiiiiiirrrrrrl, this party is fiiiiiiiyah," Zahara shouted over the beats of a Rick Ross joint. Brittani's sister, Briana, had the hookup for us since her boo of the month was one of the frat boys whose fraternity was hosting the party. So she invited us to get our party on. Brittani's sister is mad cool like that. She's always getting us into all the hot spots.

Anywaaayz, it was the weekend after Fourth of July and we were at an off-campus house party packed with mostly college heads. Mad cuties and thirsty chicks were everywhere sweating it out on the dance floor. Fraternities and sororities represented hard rocking their colors and emblems. Hot beats were blaring through the speakers as dudes danced and grinded up on chicks who were booty-popping it all up on them.

"Ooooh, I wanna dance," Zahara said, snapping her fingers and bopping her head. She did a two-step, dropped down low, then popped it back up. She danced and twirled until she got the attention she wanted. Zahara loves attention!

Anywaaayz, we had just finished our dance-through— where we dance in a line through a party all sexy-like to peep what's what and who's who before we find a spot to post up. And be cute!—when I spotted him. He was standing over in a corner with three other guys. And they were all fine, *but*... not as fine as him. I acted like I didn't see him. But the truth is. How could you *not* see him? All eyes were already on him. He was rocking a red and white Polo button-up with a pair of designer jeans and a pair of white, crispy Jordans and a red and white Yankees fitted. Tall and built with skin the color of milk-chocolate. Whew... he looked... *delicious!* Even in the dimly-lit room, I knew he was fine.

And the minute I was certain he'd seen me, I stepped, making sure to throw an extra shake in my hips as we strutted off. The minute we made it to the other side of the room, these dudes came over to where we were standing and asked each of us to dance. Zahara, Brittani, and Ameerah said yes to the dudes who asked them and bounced their booties toward the dance floor, leaving me standing there with this tall, light-skinned guy with really big teeth and gums grinning at me and licking his lips. He reminded me of a big yellow crayon.

"You sure you don't wanna dance?" he asked again, slowly looking me up and down, dragging his tongue across his lips. I blinked, blinked again, hoping I could erase him from my view. No luck. He was still there, staring down at me looking like a glow in the dark wand as he bobbed his head to the beats. Truth is I did want to dance. Just not with *him*. Not that he was busted or anything. He was just too bright and his teeth were too big for me to have to look in his face. I would either have to keep my eyes shut and zone out on the music, or keep my back to him. Lucky for me, I didn't have to do either.

This brown-skinned chick with a long black weave, wearing a skin-tight pair of jeans and a teenie-weenie shirt was on the dance floor near us, dancing all fast and nasty by herself. That caught his attention and he bounced on over to her. *Yuck*, I thought, shifting my eyes around the room to see where my girls were.

I glanced around the party and peeped Briana walking toward the stairs with her boo in tow. *Mmmph*, I thought, curling my lips up as she climbed the stairs. *Miss Hot-Box probably going upstairs to get her back blown out*. I shook the thought from my head and shifted my attention toward the dance floor, watching my girls act a fool. Every so often, I glanced over in his direction and would see a buncha birds flocked around him and he'd lean into their ears and say something to them, then they'd start smiling or giggling like real dizzy chicks before walking off. I caught him staring over in my direction a few times, trying to make eye contact with me. But I kept it fly. And, when I finally let him catch my eye, he grinned. I wanted him. Knew I had to have him. And I was going to make it my business to bag him quick, fast, and in a hurry without making myself look like a straight-up bird. Fly girls never look thirsty. They keep it cute, okay! Well, umm, that's until they reel their catch of the moment in. Then you can't be too proud to beg, or too scared to beat a trick down, to keep him.

As soon as Young Jeezy's "I Do" started playing, I started swaying to the beats, popping my hips just enough to prove a point. That I was the hottest chick in the room; that I could bag any of these boys up in there if I really wanted. A few seconds later, I heard him. And right then I knew my point was made.

"Wasssup," I heard someone say in my ear in back of me. Even over the music, the voice was mad sexy. And I knew who it was without even looking over my shoulder.

"Wasssup," I coolly said back, eyeing him real slow and sexy.

"Looks like ya boy did me a favor," he said, grinning at me.

I raised my brow. "Excuse you. He did you a favor how?"

" 'Ole boy made it easy for me not to have to tell him to step off."

"Oh, really?"

He smirked. "Yeah, really. You know you wanna be mine."

"How you know that?"

"You been wanting me to notice you from the moment you stepped through the door with your girls."

I smiled, twirling the ends of my hair. "Obviously it worked. So you wanna dance or what?"

"No doubt."

"Then follow me and take notes," I said, taking him by the hand and leading him onto the dance floor. . . .